PRAISE FOR
"The Colossus of Science Fiction"

"Arthur Clarke's own favorites among his short stories are the best from the top rank of science fiction. Within the field of science fiction the author has turned his powerful imagination loose on stories of horror, humor, detection, religion, and politics. . . . If you know Clarke's storytelling, you'll want this book; if you want to sample science fiction, start here."

—*Publishers Weekly*

"Anyone faintly familiar with the 20th century publishing phenomenon of science fiction knows that Arthur C. Clarke is a household word in this realm."

—*Library Journal*

"Science fiction readers are sure to agree that Mr. Clarke's best are among the genre's best. . . . Mr. Clarke provokes his readers to think constructively about man's future, and to be concerned for man to have one. . . ."

—*Chicago News*

"Clarke has written over a hundred short stories . . . but these are his twenty-five favorites and they combine to make fine reading. . . . The reader will find much to entertain and challenge."

—*Virginia Kirkus Service*

S0-BMR-041

More SIGNET Books by Arthur C. Clarke

The Nine Billion Names of God

The Best Short Stories of

ARTHUR C. CLARKE

A SIGNET BOOK

NEW AMERICAN LIBRARY

TIMES MIRROR

To "Mitty" (Captain E. B. Mitford)
who encouraged my initial scribblings
at Huish's Grammar School, 1930-36,
and became my first editor

 SIGNET TRADEMARK REG. U.S. PAT. OFF. AND FOREIGN COUNTRIES
REGISTERED TRADEMARK—MARCA REGISTRADA
HECHO EN CHICAGO, U.S.A.

SIGNET, SIGNET CLASSICS, MENTOR, PLUME, MERIDIAN AND NAL BOOKS *are published by The New American Library, Inc., 1633 Broadway, New York, New York 10019*

FIRST SIGNET PRINTING, JUNE, 1974

9   10   11   12   13   14   15   16

PRINTED IN THE UNITED STATES OF AMERICA

Contents

Introduction

Over the last thirty years I have written about a hundred short stories, in such varied locales as wartime RAF camps, islands on the Great Barrier Reef, New York hotels, Miami apartments, London suburbs, transatlantic liners, and Cinnamon Gardens, Colombo. They have appeared in magazines ranging from *Astounding Stories* to *Vogue,* from *Galaxy* to *Playboy,* and since 1953 have been published in the five collections: *Expedition to Earth, Reach for Tomorrow, Tales from the "White Hart," The Other Side of the Sky,* and *Tales of Ten Worlds.* In addition, these stories have appeared in various combinations with six novels in the anthologies *Across the Sea of Stars, From the Ocean, From the Stars,* and *Prelude to Mars.* This is all very satisfying, but for some time I have felt the need for a single volume containing the stories which I like best.

Every author must have his favorite stories, though he would often be hard put to give reasons for his preferences. Sometimes these may be completely illogical—or at least unliterary. A story written at a time and place associated with pleasant memories may be more highly rated, in retrospect, than a much better tale provoked by unhappiness or penury—the two greatest sponsors of art.

Whether this selection is free from such bias, I have no idea; whatever the reasons may be, these are my favorites.

Arthur C. Clarke

New York
August 1966

The Nine Billion
Names of God

The title story was written, for want of anything better to do, during a rainy weekend at the Roosevelt Hotel. Its basic arithmetic was later challenged by J. B. S. Haldane, but I managed to save the situation by alphanumeric evasions whose precise nature now escapes me.

"J. B. S." also remarked of this story, and "The Star" (q.v.): "You are one of the very few living presons who has written anything original about God. You have in fact written several mutually incompatible things. If you had stuck to one thelogical hypothesis you might have been a serious public danger." I am glad of my self-contradiction, preferring to remain a prophet with a small p.

Nevertheless, I appear to have created a durable myth: not long ago, a radio talk on the BBC referred to the opening situation of this story as actual fact. And now that IBM computers have entered the field of biblical scholarship, perhaps this theme is coming a little closer to reality.

———— ◆ ◆ ◆ ————

"This is a slightly unusual request," said Dr. Wagner, with what he hoped was commendable restraint. "As far as I know, it's the first time anyone's been asked to supply a Tibetan monastery with an Automatic Sequence Computer. I don't wish to be inquisitive, but I should hardly have thought that your—ah—establishment had much use for such a machine. Could you explain just what you intend to do with it?"

"Gladly," replied the lama, readjusting his silk robes and carefully putting away the slide rule he had been using for currency conversions. "Your Mark V Computer can carry out any routine mathematical operation involving up to ten digits. However, for our work we are interested in *letters*, not numbers. As we wish you to modify the output circuits, the machine will be printing words, not columns of figures."

"I don't quite understand. . . ."

"This is a project on which we have been working for the last three centuries—since the lamasery was founded, in fact. It is somewhat alien to your way of thought, so I hope you will listen with an open mind while I explain it."

"Naturally."

"It is really quite simple. We have been compiling a list which shall contain all the possible names of God."

"I beg your pardon?"

"We have reason to believe," continued the lama imperturbably, "that all such names can be written with not more than nine letters in an alphabet we have devised."

"And you have been doing this for three centuries?"

"Yes: we expected it would take us about fifteen thousand years to complete the task."

"Oh," Dr. Wagner looked a little dazed. "Now I see why you wanted to hire one of our machines. But exactly what is the *purpose* of this project?"

The lama hesitated for a fraction of a second, and Wagner wondered if he had offended him. If so, there was no trace of annoyance in the reply.

"Call it ritual, if you like, but it's a fundamental part of our belief. All the many names of the Supreme Being—God, Jehovah, Allah, and so on—they are only man-made labels. There is a philosophical problem of some difficulty here, which I do not propose to discuss, but somewhere among all the possible combinations of letters that can occur are what one may call the *real* names of God. By systematic permutation of letters, we have been trying to list them all."

"I see. You've been starting at AAAAAAA . . . and working up to ZZZZZZZZ. . . ."

"Exactly—though we use a special alphabet of our own. Modifying the electromatic typewriters to deal with this is, of course, trivial. A rather more interesting problem is that of devising suitable circuits to eliminate ridiculous combinations. For example, no letter must occur more than three times in succession."

"Three? Surely you mean two."

"Three is correct: I am afraid it would take too long to explain why, even if you understood our language."

"I'm sure it would," said Wagner hastily. "Go on."

"Luckily, it will be a simple matter to adapt your Automatic Sequence Computer for this work, since once it has been programed properly it will permute each letter in turn and print the result. What would have taken us fifteen thousand years it will be able to do in a hundred days."

Dr. Wagner was scarcely conscious of the faint sounds from the Manhattan streets far below. He was in a different world, a world of natural, not man-made, mountains. High up in their remote aeries these monks had been patiently at work, generation after generation, compiling their lists of meaningless words. Was there any limit to the follies of mankind? Still, he must give no hint of his inner thoughts. The customer was always right. . . .

"There's no doubt," replied the doctor, "that we can modify the Mark V to print lists of this nature. I'm much more worried about the problem of installation and maintenance. Getting out to Tibet, in these days, is not going to be easy."

"We can arrange that. The components are small enough to travel by air—that is one reason why we chose your machine. If you can get them to India, we will provide transport from there."

"And you want to hire two of our engineers?"

"Yes, for the three months that the project should occupy."

"I've no doubt that Personnel can manage that." Dr. Wagner scribbled a note on his desk pad. "There are just two other points—"

Before he could finish the sentence the lama had produced a small slip of paper.

"This is my certified credit balance at the Asiatic Bank."

"Thank you. It appears to be—ah—adequate. The second matter is so trivial that I hesitate to mention it—but it's surprising how often the obvious gets overlooked. What source of electrical energy have you?"

"A diesel generator providing fifty kilowatts at a hundred and ten volts. It was installed about five years ago and is quite reliable. It's made life at the lamasery much more comfortable, but of course it was really installed to provide power for the motors driving the prayer wheels."

"Of course," echoed Dr. Wagner. "I should have thought of that."

The view from the parapet was vertiginous, but in time one gets used to anything. After three months, George Hanley was not impressed by the two-thousand-foot swoop into the abyss or the remote checkerboard of fields in the valley below. He was leaning against the wind-smoothed stones and staring morosely at the distant mountains whose names he had never bothered to discover.

This, thought George, was the craziest thing that had ever happened to him. "Project Shangri-La," some wit back at the labs had christened it. For weeks now the Mark V had been churning out acres of sheets covered with gibberish. Patiently, inexorably, the computer had been rearranging letters in all their possible combinations, exhausting each class before going on to the next. As the sheets had emerged from the electromatic typewriters, the monks had carefully cut them up and pasted them into enormous books. In another week, heaven be praised, they would have finished. Just what obscure calculations had convinced the monks that they needn't bother to go on to words of ten, twenty, or a hundred letters, George didn't know. One of his recurring nightmares was that there would be some change of plan, and that the high lama (whom they'd naturally called Sam Jaffe, though he didn't look a bit like him) would suddenly announce that the project would be extended to approximately A.D. 2060. They were quite capable of it.

George heard the heavy wooden door slam in the wind as Chuck came out onto the parapet beside him. As usual, Chuck was smoking one of the cigars that made him so popular with the monks—who, it seemed, were quite willing to embrace all the minor and most of the major pleasures of life. That was one thing in their favor: they might be crazy, but they weren't bluenoses. Those frequent trips they took down to the village, for instance . . .

"Listen, George," said Chuck urgently. "I've learned something that means trouble."

"What's wrong? Isn't the machine behaving?" That was the worst contingency George could imagine. It might delay his return, and nothing could be more horrible. The way he felt now, even the sight of a TV commercial would seem like manna from heaven. At least it would be some link with home.

"No—it's nothing like that." Chuck settled himself on the parapet, which was unusual because normally he was scared of the drop. "I've just found what all this is about."

"What d'ya mean? I thought we knew."

"Sure—we know what the monks are trying to do. But we didn't know *why*. It's the craziest thing—"

"Tell me something new," growled George.

"—but old Sam's just come clean with me. You know the way he drops in every afternoon to watch the sheets roll out. Well, this time he seemed rather excited, or at least as near as he'll ever get to it. When I told him that we were on the last cycle he asked me, in that cute English accent of his, if I'd ever wondered what they were trying to do. I said, 'Sure' —and he told me."

"Go on: I'll buy it."

"Well, they believe that when they have listed all His names—and they reckon that there are about nine billion of them—God's purpose will be achieved. The human race will have finished what it was created to do, and there won't be any point in carrying on. Indeed, the very idea is something like blasphemy."

"Then what do they expect us to do? Commit suicide?"

"There's no need for that. When the list's completed, God steps in and simply winds things up . . . bingo!"

"Oh, I get it. When we finish our job, it will be the end of the world."

Chuck gave a nervous little laugh.

"That's just what I said to Sam. And do yout know what happened? He looked at me in a very queer way, like I'd been stupid in class, and said, 'It's nothing as trivial as *that.*'"

George thought this over for a moment.

"That's what I call taking the Wide View," he said presently. "But what d'you suppose we should do about it? I don't see that it makes the slightest difference to us. After all, we already knew that they were crazy."

"Yes—but don't you see what may happen? When the list's complete and the Last Trump doesn't blow—or whatever it is they expect—*we* may get the blame. It's our machine they've been using. I don't like the situation one little bit."

"I see," said George slowly. "You've got a point there. But this sort of thing's happened before, you know. When I was a kid down in Louisiana we had a crackpot preacher who once said the world was going to end next Sunday. Hundreds of people believed him—even sold their homes. Yet when nothing happened, they didn't turn nasty, as you'd expect. They just decided that he'd made a mistake in his calculations and went right on believing. I guess some of them still do."

"Well, this isn't Louisiana, in case you hadn't noticed. There are just two of us and hundreds of these monks. I like them, and I'll be sorry for old Sam when his lifework backfires on him. But all the same, I wish I was somewhere else."

"I've been wishing that for weeks. But there's nothing we can do until the contract's finished and the transport arrives to fly us out."

"Of course," said Chuck thoughtfully, "we could always try a bit of sabotage."

"Like hell we could! That would make things worse."

"Not the way I meant. Look at it like this. The machine will finish its run four days from now, on the present twenty-hours-a-day basis. The transport calls in a week. OK—then all we need to do is to find something that needs replacing during one of the overhaul periods—something that will hold up the works for a couple of days. We'll fix it, of course, but not too quickly. If we time matters properly, we can be down at the airfield when the last name pops out of the register. They won't be able to catch us then."

"I don't like it," said George. "It will be the first time I ever walked out on a job. Besides, it would make them suspicious. No, I'll sit tight and take what comes."

"I *still* don't like it," he said, seven days later, as the tough little mountain ponies carried them down the winding road. "And don't you think I'm running away because I'm afraid. I'm just sorry for those poor old guys up there, and I don't want to be around when they find what suckers they've been. Wonder how Sam will take it?"

"It's funny," replied Chuck, "but when I said good-by I got the idea he knew we were walking out on him—and that he didn't care because he knew the machine was running smoothly and that the job would soon be finished. After that —well, of course, for him there just isn't any After That. . . ."

George turned in his saddle and stared back up the mountain road. This was the last place from which one could get a clear view of the lamasery. The squat, angular buildings were silhouetted against the afterglow of the sunset: here and there, lights gleamed like portholes in the side of an ocean liner. Electric lights, of course, sharing the same circuit as the Mark V. How much longer would they share it? wondered George. Would the monks smash up the computer in their rage and disappointment? Or would they just sit down quietly and begin their calculations all over again?

He knew exactly what was happening up on the mountain at this very moment. The high lama and his assistants would be sitting in their silk robes, inspecting the sheets as the junior monks carried them away from the typewriters and pasted them into the great volumes. No one would be saying anything. The only sound would be the incessant patter, the never-ending rainstorm of the keys hitting the paper, for the Marv V itself was utterly silent as it flashed through its thousands of calculations a second. Three months of this, thought George, was enough to start anyone climbing up the wall.

"There she is!" called Chuck, pointing down into the valley. "Ain't she beautiful!"

She certainly was, thought George. The battered old DC3 lay at the end of the runway like a tiny silver cross. In two hours she would be bearing them away to freedom and sanity. It was a thought worth savoring like a fine liqueur. George let it roll round his mind as the pony trudged patiently down the slope.

The swift night of the high Himalayas was now almost upon them. Fortunately, the road was very good, as roads went in that region, and they were both carrying torches. There was not the slightest danger, only a certain discomfort from the bitter cold. The sky overhead was perfectly clear, and ablaze with the familiar, friendly stars. At least there would be no risk, thought George, of the pilot being unable to take off because of weather conditions. That had been his only remaining worry.

He began to sing, but gave it up after a while. This vast arena of mountains, gleaming like whitely hooded ghosts on every side, did not encourage such ebullience. Presently George glanced at his watch.

"Should be there in an hour," he called back over his shoulder to Chuck. Then he added, in an afterthought: "Wonder if the computer's finished its run. It was due about now."

Chuck didn't reply, so George swung round in his saddle. He could just see Chuck's face, a white oval turned toward the sky.

"Look," whispered Chuck, and George lifted his eyes to heaven. (There is always a last time for everything.)

Overhead, without any fuss, the stars were going out.

New York   *May 1952*

I Remember Babylon

The most sensible advice ever given to writers by the very sensible man Samuel Goldwyn, was: "If you've gotta message, use Western Union." I must confess, however, that this story does have a message; it was written, in the pre-Telstar days, with the deliberate intent of making the U.S. public think seriously about communications satellites.

Needless to say, the U.S. has since done so. Only a few years after Playboy published this cautionary tale, I was watching the launch of Early Bird by closed-circuit TV at Comsat Headquarters. And viewers bored with Madison Avenue fare may still live in hopes; for Comsat's first chairman has assured me that this story is required reading for his staff.

* * *

My name is Arthur C. Clarke, and I wish I had no connection with this whole sordid business. But as the moral—repeat, moral—integrity of the United States is involved, I must first establish my credentials. Only thus will you understand how, with the aid of the late Dr. Alfred Kinsey, I have unwittingly triggered an avalanche that may sweep away much of Western civilization.

Back in 1945, while a radar officer in the Royal Air Force, I had the only original idea of my life. Twelve years before the first Sputnik started beeping, it occurred to me that an artificial satellite would be a wonderful place for a television transmitter, since a station several thousand miles high could broadcast to half the globe. I wrote up the idea the week after Hiroshima, proposing a network of relay satellites twenty-two thousand miles above the Equator; at this height, they'd take exactly one day to complete a revolution, and so would remain fixed over the same spot on the Earth.

14

The piece appeared in the October 1945 issue of *Wireless World;* not expecting that celestial mechanics would be commercialized in my lifetime, I made no attempt to patent the idea, and doubt if I could have done so anyway. (If I'm wrong, I'd prefer not to know.) But I kept plugging it in my books, and today the idea of communications satellites is so commonplace that no one knows its origin.

I did make a plaintive attempt to put the record straight when approached by the House of Representatives Committee on Astronautics and Space Exploration; you'll find my evidence on page thirty-two of its report, *The Next Ten Years in Space*. And as you'll see in a moment, my concluding words had an irony I never appreciated at the time: "Living as I do in the Far East, I am constantly reminded of the struggle between the Western World and the USSR for the uncommitted millions of Asia. . . . When line-of-sight TV transmissions become possible from satellites directly overhead, the propaganda effect may be decisive. . . ."

I still stand by those words, but there were angles I hadn't thought of—and which, unfortunately, other people have.

It all began during one of those official receptions which are such a feature of social life in Eastern capitals. They're even more common in the West, of course, but in Colombo there's little competing entertainment. At least once a week, if you are anybody, you get an invitation to cocktails at an embassy or legation, the British Council, the U.S. Operations Mission, L'Alliance Française, or one of the countless alphabetical agencies the United Nations has begotten.

At first, being more at home beneath the Indian Ocean than in diplomatic circles, my partner and I were nobodies and were left alone. But after Mike *compèred* Dave Brubeck's tour of Ceylon, people started to take notice of us—still more so when he married one of the island's best-known beauties. So now our consumption of cocktails and canapés is limited chiefly by reluctance to abandon our comfortable sarongs for such Western absurdities as trousers, dinner jackets, and ties.

It was the first time we'd been to the Soviet Embassy, which was throwing a party for a group of Russian oceanographers who'd just come into port. Beneath the inevitable paintings of Lenin and Marx, a couple of hundred guests of all colors, religions, and languages were milling around, chatting with friends, or single-mindedly demolishing the vodka and caviar. I'd been separated from Mike and Elizabeth, but could see them at the other side of the room. Mike was doing his

"There was I at fifty fathoms" act to a fascinated audience, while Elizabeth watched him quizzically—and rather more people watched Elizabeth.

Ever since I lost an eardrum while pearl-diving on the Great Barrier Reef, I've been at a considerable disadvantage at functions of this kind; the surface noise is about twelve decibels too much for me to cope with. And this is no small handicap when being introduced to people with names like Dharmasiriwardene, Tissaveerasinghe, Goonetilleke, and Jaya-wickrema. When I'm not raiding the buffet, therefore, I usually look for a pool of relative quiet where there's a chance of following more than fifty per cent of any conversation in which I may get involved. I was standing in the acoustic shadow of a large ornamental pillar, surveying the scene in my detached or Somerset Maugham manner, when I noticed that someone was looking at me with that "Haven't we met before?" expression.

I'll describe him with some care, because there must be many people who can identify him. He was in the mid-thirties, and I guessed he was American; he had that well-scrubbed, crew-cut, man-about-Rockefeller-Center look that used to be a hallmark until the younger Russian diplomats and technical advisers started imitating it so successfully. He was about six feet in height, with shrewd brown eyes and black hair, prematurely gray at the sides. Though I was fairly certain we'd never met before, his face reminded me of someone. It took me a couple of days to work it out: remember the late John Garfield? That's who it was, as near as makes no difference.

When a stranger catches my eye at a party, my standard operating procedure goes into action automatically. If he seems a pleasant-enough person but I don't feel like intro-ductions at the moment, I give him the Neutral Scan, letting my eyes sweep past him without a flicker of recognition, yet without positive unfriendliness. If he looks like a creep, he receives the *Coup d'oeil*, which consists of a long, disbelieving stare followed by an unhurried view of the back of my neck. In extreme cases, an expression of revulsion may be switched on for a few milliseconds. The message usually gets across.

But this character seemed interesting, and I was getting bored, so I gave him the Affable Nod. A few minutes later he drifted through the crowd, and I aimed my good ear toward him.

"Hello," he said (yes, he *was* American), "my name's Gene Hartford. I'm sure we've met somewhere."

"Quite likely," I answered, "I've spent a good deal of time in the States. I'm Arthur Clarke."

Usually that produces a blank stare, but sometimes it doesn't. I could almost see the IBM cards flickering behind those hard brown eyes, and was flattered by the brevity of his access time.

"The science writer?"

"Correct."

"Well, this is fantastic." He seemed genuinely astonished. *"Now* I know where I've seen you. I was in the studio once when you were on the Dave Garroway show."

(This lead may be worth following up, though I doubt it; and I'm sure that "Gene Hartford" was phony—it was too smoothly synthetic.)

"So you're in TV?" I said. "What are you doing here—collecting material, or just on vacation?"

He gave me the frank, friendly smile of a man who has plenty to hide.

"Oh, I'm keeping my eyes open. But this really is amazing; I read your *Exploration of Space* when it came out back in, ah—"

"Nineteen-fifty-two; the Book-of-the-Month Club's never been quite the same since."

All this time I had been sizing him up, and though there was something about him I didn't like, I was unable to pin it down. In any case, I was prepared to make substantial allowances for someone who had read my books and was also in TV; Mike and I are always on the lookout for markets for our underwater movies. But that, to put it mildly, was not Hartford's line of business.

"Look," he said eagerly, "I've a big network deal cooking that will interest you—in fact, *you* helped to give me the idea."

This sounded promising, and my coefficient of cupidity jumped several points.

"I'm glad to hear it. What's the general theme?"

"I can't talk about it here, but could we meet at my hotel, around three tomorrow?"

"Let me check my diary; yes, that's OK."

There are only two hotels in Colombo patronized by Americans, and I guessed right the first time. He was at the Mount Lavinia, and though you may not know it, you've seen the place where we had our private chat. Around the middle of *Bridge over the River Kwai*, there's a brief scene at a military hospital, where Jack Hawkins meets a nurse and asks her where he can find Bill Holden. We have a soft spot for this episode, because Mike was one of the convalescent naval officers in the background. If you look smartly you'll see him on the extreme right, beard in full profile, singing Sam Spiegel's name to his sixth round of bar chits. As the picture turned out, Sam could afford it.

It was here, on this diminutive plateau high above the miles of palm-fringed beach, that Gene Hartford started to unload —and my simple hopes of financial advantage started to evaporate. What his exact motives were, if indeed he knew them himself, I'm still uncertain. Surprise at meeting me, and a twisted feeling of gratitude (which I would gladly have done without) undoubtedly played a part, and for all his air of confidence he must have been a bitter, lonely man who desperately needed approval and friendship.

He got neither from me. I have always had a sneaking sympathy for Benedict Arnold, as must anyone who knows the full facts of the case. But Arnold merely betrayed his country; no one before Hartford ever tried to seduce it.

What dissolved my dream of dollars was the news that Hartford's connection with American TV had been severed, somewhat violently, in the early fifties. It was clear that he'd been bounced out of Madison Avenue for Party-lining, and it was equally clear that his was one case where no grave injustice had been done. Though he talked with a certain controlled fury of his fight against asinine censorship, and wept for a brilliant—but unnamed—cultural series he'd started before being kicked off the air, by this time I was beginning to smell so many rats that my replies were distinctly guarded. Yet as my pecuniary interest in Mr. Hartford diminished, so my personal curiosity increased. Who *was* behind him? Surely not the BBC . . .

He got round to it at last, when he'd worked the self-pity out of his system.

"I've some news that will make you sit up," he said smugly. "The American networks are soon going to have some real competition. And it will be done just the way you predicted; the people who sent a TV transmitter to the Moon can put a much bigger one in orbit round the Earth."

"Good for them," I said cautiously. "I'm all in favor of healthy competition. When's the launching date?"

"Any moment now. The first transmitter will be parked due south of New Orleans—on the equator, of course. That puts it way out in the open Pacific; it won't be over anyone's territory, so there'll be no political complications on that score. Yet it will be sitting up there in the sky in full view of everybody from Seattle to Key West. Think of it—the only TV station the whole United States can tune in to! Yes, even Hawaii! There won't be any way of jamming it; for the first time, there'll be a clear channel into every American home. And J. Edgar's Boy Scouts can't do a thing to block it."

So that's your little racket, I thought; at least you're being frank. Long ago I learned not to argue with Marxists and Flat-Earthers, but if Hartford was telling the truth, I wanted to pump him for all he was worth.

"Before you get too enthusiastic," I said, "there are a few points you may have overlooked."

"Such as?"

"This will work both ways. Everyone knows that the Air Force, NASA, Bell Labs, I. T. & T., Hughes, and a few dozen other agencies are working on the same project. Whatever Russia does to the States in the propaganda line, she'll get back with compound interest."

Hartford grinned mirthlessly.

"Really, Clarke!" he said. (I was glad he hadn't first-named me.) "I'm a little disappointed. Surely you know that the United States is years behind in pay-load capacity! And do you imagine that the old T.3 is Russia's last word?"

It was at this moment that I began to take him very seriously. He was perfectly right. The T.3 could inject at least five times the pay load of any American missile into that critical twenty-two-thousand-mile orbit—the only one that would allow a sattellite to remain fixed above the Earth. And by the time the U.S. could match that performance, heaven knows where the Russians would be. Yes, heaven certainly *would* know. . . .

"All right," I conceded. "But why should fifty million American homes start switching channels just as soon as they can tune in to Moscow? I admire the Russians, but their entertainment is worse than their politics. After the Bolshoi, what have you? And for me, a little ballet goes a long, long way."

Once again I was treated to that peculiarly humorless smile. Hartford had been saving up his Sunday punch, and now he let me have it.

"You were the one who brought in the Russians," he said. "They're involved, sure—but only as contractors. The independent agency I'm working for is hiring their services."

"That," I remarked dryly, "must be some agency."

"It is; just about the biggest. Even though the United States tries to pretend it doesn't exist."

"Oh," I said, rather stupidly. "So *that's* your sponsor."

I'd heard those rumors that the USSR was going to launch satellites for the Chinese; now it began to look as if the rumors fell far short of the truth. But how far short, I'd still no conception.

"You are so right," continued Hartford, obviously enjoying himself, "about Russian entertainment. After the initial novelty, the Nielsen rating would drop to zero. But not with the program *I'm* planning. My job is to find material that will put everyone else out of business when it goes on the air. You think it can't be done? Finish that drink and come up to my room. I've a highbrow movie about ecclesiastical art that I'd like to show you."

Well, he wasn't crazy, though for a few minutes I wondered. I could think of few titles more carefully calculated to make the viewer reach for the channel switch than the one that flashed on the screen: ASPECTS OF THIRTEENTH-CENTURY TANTRIC SCULPTURE.

"Don't be alarmed," Hartford chuckled, above the whirr of the projector. "That title saves me having trouble with inquisitive Customs inspectors. It's perfectly accurate, but we'll change it to something with a bigger box-office appeal when the time comes."

A couple of hundred feet later, after some innocuous architectural long shots, I saw what he meant.

You may know that there are certain temples in India covered with superbly executed carvings of a kind that we in the West scarcely associate with religion. To say that they are frank is a laughable understatement; they leave nothing to the imagination—*any* imagination. Yet at the same time they are genuine works of art. And so was Hartford's movie.

It had been shot, in case you're interested, at the Temple of the Sun, Konarak. I've since looked it up; it's on the Orissa coast, about twenty-five miles northeast of Puri. The reference books are pretty mealymouthed; some apologize for the "obvious" impossibility of providing illustrations, but Percy Brown's *Indian Architecture* minces no words. The carvings, it says primly, are of "a shamelessly erotic character that have no parallel in any known building." A sweeping claim, but I can believe it after seeing that movie.

Camera work and editing were brilliant, the ancient stones coming to life beneath the roving lens. There were breathtaking time-lapse shots as the rising sun chased the shadows from bodies intertwined in ecstasy; sudden startling close-ups of scenes which at first the mind refused to recognize; softfocus studies of stone shaped by a master's hand in all the fantasies and aberrations of love; restless zooms and pans whose meaning eluded the eye until they froze into patterns of timeless desire, eternal fulfillment. The music—mostly percussion, with a thin, high thread of sound from some stringed instrument that I could not identify—perfectly fitted the tempo of the cutting. At one moment it would be languorously slow, like the opening bars of Debussy's "L'Après-midi"; then the drums would swiftly work themselves up to a frenzied, almost unendurable climax. The art of the ancient sculptors and the skill of the modern cameraman had combined across the centuries to create a poem of rapture, an orgasm on celluloid which I would defy any man to watch unmoved.

There was a long silence when the screen flooded with light and the lascivious music ebbed into exhaustion.

"My God!" I said, when I had recovered some of my composure. "Are you going to telecast *that?*"

Hartford laughed.

"Believe me," he answered, "that's nothing; it just happens to be the only reel I can carry around safely. We're prepared to defend it any day on grounds of genuine art, historic interest, religious tolerance—oh, we've thought of all the angles. But it doesn't really matter; no one can stop us. For the first time in history, any form of censorship's become utterly impossible. There's simply no way of enforcing it; the customer can get what he wants, right in his own home. Lock the door, switch on the TV set—friends and family will never know."

"Very clever," I said, "but don't you think such a diet will soon pall?"

"Of course; variety is the spice of life. We'll have plenty of conventional entertainment; let *me* worry about that. And every so often we'll have information programs—I hate that word 'propaganda'—to tell the cloistered American public what's really happening in the world. Our special features will just be the bait."

"Mind if I have some fresh air?" I said. "It's getting stuffy in here."

Hartford drew the curtains and let daylight back into the room. Below us lay that long curve of beach, with the outrigger fishing boats drawn up beneath the palms, and the little waves falling in foam at the end of their weary march from Africa. One of the loveliest sights in the world, but I couldn't focus on it now. I was still seeing those writhing stone limbs, those faces frozen with passions which the centuries could not slake.

That lickerish voice continued behind my back.

"You'd be astonished if you knew just how much material there is. Remember, we've absolutely no taboos. If you can film it, we can telecast it."

He walked over to his bureau and picked up a heavy, dog-eared volume.

"This has been my Bible," he said, "or my Sears, Roebuck, if you prefer. Without it, I'd never have sold the series to my sponsors. They're great believers in science, and they swallowed the whole thing, down to the last decimal point. Recognize it?"

I nodded; whenever I enter a room, I always monitor my host's literary tastes.

"Dr. Kinsey, I presume."

"I guess I'm the only man who's read it from cover to cover, and not just looked up his own vital statistics. You see, it's the only piece of market research in its field. Until something better comes along, we're making the most of it. It tells us what the customer wants, and we're going to supply it."

"*All* of it?"

"If the audience is big enough, yes. We won't bother about feeble-minded farm boys who get too attached to the stock. But the four main sexes will get the full treatment. That's the beauty of the movie you just saw—it appeals to them all."

"You can say that again," I muttered.

"We've had a lot of fun planning the feature I've christened 'Queer Corner.' Don't laugh—no go-ahead agency can afford to ignore *that* audience. At least ten million, if you count the ladies—bless their clogs and tweeds. If you think I'm exaggerating, look at all the male art mags on the newsstands. It was no trick, blackmailing some of the daintier musclemen to perform for us."

He saw that I was beginning to get bored; there are some kinds of single-mindedness that I find depressing. But I had done Hartford an injustice, as he hastened to prove.

"Please don't think," he said anxiously, "that sex is our only weapon. Sensation is almost as good. Ever see the job Ed Murrow did on the late sainted Joe McCarthy? That was milk and water compared with the profiles we're planning in 'Washington Confidential.'

"And there's our 'Can You Take It?" series, designed to separate the men from the milksops. We'll issue so many advance warnings that every red-blooded American will feel he has to watch the show. It will start innocently enough, on ground nicely prepared by Hemingway. You'll see some bull-fighting sequences that will really lift you out of your seat—or send you running to the bathroom—because they show all the little details you never get in those cleaned-up Hollywood movies.

"We'll follow that with some really unique material that cost us exactly nothing. Do you remember the photographic evidence the Nuremburg war trials turned up? You've never seen it, because it wasn't publishable. There were quite a few amateur photographers in the concentration camps, who made the most of opportunities they'd never get again. Some of them were hanged on the testimony of their own cameras, but their work wasn't wasted. It will lead nicely into our series 'Torture Through the Ages'—very scholarly and thorough, yet with a remarkably wide appeal. . . .

"And there are dozens of other angles, but by now you'll have the general picture. The Avenue thinks it knows all about Hidden Persuasion—believe me, it doesn't. The world's best *practical* psychologists are in the East these days. Remember Korea, and brainwashing? We've learned a lot since then. There's no need for violence any more; people enjoy being brainwashed, if you set about it the right way."

"And you," I said, "are going to brainwash the United States. Quite an order."

"Exactly—and the country will love it, despite all the screams from Congress and the churches. Not to mention the networks, of course. They'll make the biggest fuss of all, when they find they can't compete with us."

Hartford glanced at his watch, and gave a whistle of alarm.

"Time to start packing," he said. "I've got to be at that unpronounceable airport of yours by six. There's no chance, I suppose, that you can fly over to Macao and see us sometime?"

"Not a hope; but I've got a pretty good idea of the picture now. And incidentally, aren't you afraid that I'll spill the beans?"

"Why should I be? The more publicity you can give us, the

better. Although our advertising campaign doesn't go into top gear for a few months yet, I feel you've earned this advance notice. As I said, your books helped to give me the idea."

His gratitude was quite genuine, by God; it left me completely speechless.

"Nothing can stop us," he declared—and for the first time the fanaticism that lurked behind that smooth, cynical façade was not altogether under control. "History is on our side. We'll be using America's own decadence as a weapon against her, and it's a weapon for which there's no defense. The Air Force won't attempt space piracy by shooting down a satellite nowhere near American territory. The FCC can't even protest to a country that doesn't exist in the eyes of the State Department. If you've any other suggestions, I'd be most interested to hear them."

I had none then, and I have none now. Perhaps these words may give some brief warning before the first teasing advertisements appear in the trade papers, and may start stirrings of elephantine alarm among the networks. But will it make any difference? Hartford did not think so, and he may be right.

"History is on our side." I cannot get those words out of my head. Land of Lincoln and Franklin and Melville, I love you and I wish you well. But into my heart blows a cold wind from the past; for I remember Babylon.

Colombo   *October 1959*

Trouble with Time

This is my only detective story: I was all the more gratified, therefore, when "Ellery Queen" used it in one of his collections.

The problem it deals with is not, perhaps, the most serious obstacle to the colonization of Mars. But it exists—and there's not a thing anyone can do about it.

Except to avoid buying real estate at "Meridian City."

———◆◆◆———

"We don't have much crime on Mars," said Detective Inspector Rawlings, a little sadly. "In fact, that's the chief reason I'm going back to the Yard. If I stayed here much longer, I'd get completely out of practice."

We were sitting in the main observation lounge of the Phobos Spaceport, looking out across the jagged, sun-drenched crags of the tiny moon. The ferry rocket that had brought us up from Mars had left ten minutes ago, and was now beginning the long fall back to the ocher-tinted globe hanging there against the stars. In half an hour we would be boarding the liner for Earth—a world upon which most of the passengers had never set foot, but which they still called "home."

"At the same time," continued the Inspector, "now and then there's a case that makes life interesting. You're an art dealer, Mr. Maccar; I'm sure you heard about that spot of bother at Meridian City a couple of months ago."

"I don't think so," replied the plump, olive-skinned little man I'd taken for just another returning tourist. Presumably the Inspector had already checked through the passenger list; I wondered how much he knew about me, and tried to reassure myself that my conscience was—well—reasonably clear. After all, everybody took *something* out through Martian Customs—

25

"It's been rather well hushed up," said the Inspector, "but you can't keep these things quiet for long. Anyway, a jewel thief from Earth tried to steal Meridian Museum's greatest treasure—the Siren Goddess."

"But that's absurd!" I objected. "It's priceless, of course—but it's only a lump of sandstone. You couldn't sell it to anyone—you might just as well steal the Mona Lisa."

The Inspector grinned, rather mirthlessly. "*That's* happened once," he said. "Maybe the motive was the same. There are collectors who would give a fortune for such an object, even if they could only look at it themselves. Don't you agree, Mr. Maccar?"

"That's perfectly true. In my business, you meet all sorts of crazy people."

"Well, this chappie—name's Danny Weaver—had been well paid by one of them. And if it hadn't been for a piece of fantastically bad luck, he might have brought it off."

The Spaceport P.A. system apologized for a further slight delay owing to final fuel checks, and asked a number of passengers to report to Information. While we were waiting for the announcement to finish, I recalled what little I knew about the Siren Goddess. Though I'd never seen the original, like most other departing tourists I had a replica in my baggage. It bore the certificate of the Mars Bureau of Antiquities, guaranteeing that "this full-scale reproduction is an exact copy of the so-called Siren Goddess, discovered in the Mare Sirenium by the Third Expedition, A.D. 2012 (A.M. 23)."

It's quite a tiny thing to have caused so much controversy. Only eight or nine inches high—you wouldn't look at it twice if you saw it in a museum on Earth. The head of a young woman, with slightly oriental features, elongated earlobes, hair curled in tight ringlets close to the scalp, lips half parted in an expression of pleasure or surprise—that's all. But it's an enigma so baffling that it's inspired a hundred religious sects, and driven quite a few archaeologists round the bend. For a perfectly human head has no right whatsoever to be found on Mars, whose only intelligent inhabitants were crustaceans —"educated lobsters," as the newspapers are fond of calling them. The aboriginal Martians never came near to achieving space flight, and in any event their civilization died before men existed on Earth. No wonder the Goddess is the solar system's number-one mystery; I don't suppose we'll find the answer in my lifetime—if we ever do.

"Danny's plan was beautifully simple," continued the Inspector. "You know how absolutely dead a Martian city gets on Sunday, when everything closes down and the colonists stay home to watch the TV from Earth. Danny was counting on this, when he checked into the hotel in Meridian West, late Friday afternoon. He'd have Saturday for reconnoitering the Museum, an undisturbed Sunday for the job itself, and on Monday morning he'd be just another tourist leaving town. . . .

"Early Saturday he strolled through the little park and crossed over into Meridian East, where the Museum stands. In case you don't know, the city gets its name because it's exactly on longitude one hundred and eighty degrees; there's a big stone slab in the park with the prime meridian engraved on it, so that visitors can get themselves photographed standing in two hemispheres at once. Amazing what simple things amuse some people.

"Danny spent the day going over the Museum, exactly like any other tourist determined to get his money's worth. But at closing time he didn't leave; he'd holed up in one of the galleries not open to the public, where the Museum had been arranging a Late Canal Period reconstruction but had run out of money before the job could be finished. He stayed there until about midnight, just in case there were any enthusiastic researchers still in the building. Then he emerged and got to work."

"Just a minute," I interrupted. "What about the night watchman?"

The Inspector laughed.

"My dear chap! They don't have such luxuries on Mars. There weren't even any alarms, for who would bother to steal lumps of stone? True, the Goddess was sealed up neatly in a strong glass-and-metal cabinet, just in case some souvenir hunter took a fancy to her. But even if she were stolen, there was nowhere the thief could hide, and of course all outgoing traffic would be searched as soon as the statue was missed."

That was true enough. I'd been thinking in terms of Earth, forgetting that every city on Mars is a closed little world of its own beneath the force-field that protects it from the freezing near-vacuum. Beyond those electronic shields is the utterly hostile emptiness of the Martian Outback, where a man will die in seconds without protection. That makes law enforcement very easy; no wonder there's so little crime on Mars. . . .

"Danny had a beautiful set of tools, as specialized as a watchmaker's. The main item was a microsaw no bigger than a soldering iron; it had a wafer-thin blade, driven at a million cycles a second by an ultrasonic power pack. It would go through glass or metal like butter—and left a cut only about as thick as a hair. Which was very important for Danny, since he had to leave no traces of his handiwork.

"I suppose you've guessed how he intended to operate. He was going to cut through the base of the cabinet, and substitute one of those souvenir replicas for the real Goddess. It might be a couple of years before some inquisitive expert discovered the awful truth; long before then the original would have traveled back to Earth, perfectlly disguised as a copy of itself, with a genuine certificate of authenticity. Pretty neat, eh?

"It must have been a weird business, working in that darkened gallery with all those million-year-old carvings and unexplainable artifacts around him. A museum on Earth is bad enough at night, but at least it's—well—*human*. And Gallery Three, which houses the Goddess, is particularly unsettling. It's full of bas-reliefs showing quite incredible animals fighting each other; they look rather like giant beetles, and most paleontologists flatly deny that they could ever have existed. But imaginary or not, they belonged to this world, and they didn't disturb Danny as much as the Goddess, staring at him across the ages and defying him to explain her presence here. She gave him the creeps. How do I know? He told me.

"Danny set to work on that cabinet as carefully as any diamond cutter preparing to cleave a gem. It took most of the night to slice out the trap door, and it was nearly dawn when he relaxed and put down the saw. There was still a lot of work to do, but the hardest part was over. Putting the replica into the case, checking its appearance against the photos he'd thoughtfully brought with him, and covering up his traces might take most of Sunday, but that didn't worry him in the least. He had another twenty-four hours, and would positively welcome Monday's first visitors so that he could mingle with them and make his inconspicuous exit.

"It was a perfectly horrible shock to his nervous system, therefore, when the main doors were noisily unbarred at eight-thirty and the museum staff—all six of them—started to open up for the day. Danny bolted for the emergency exit, leaving everything behind—tools, Goddesses, the lot. He had another big surprise when he found himself in the street; it should have been completely deserted at this time of day, with everyone at home reading the Sunday papers. But here were the citizens of Meridian East, as large as life, heading for plant or office on what was obviously a normal working day.

"By the time poor Danny got back to his hotel, we were waiting for him. We couldn't claim much credit for deducing that only a visitor from Earth—and a very recent one at that —could have overlooked Meridian City's chief claim to fame. And I presume you know what *that* is."

"Frankly, I don't," I answered. "You can't see much of Mars in six weeks, and I never went east of the Syrtis Major."

"Well, it's absurdly simple, but we shouldn't be too hard on Danny; even the locals occasionally fall into the same trap. It's something that doesn't bother us on Earth, where we've been able to dump the problem in the Pacific Ocean. But Mars, of course, is all dry land; and that means that *somebody* has to live with the International Date Line. . . .

"Danny, you see, had worked from Meridian West. It was Sunday over there all right—and it was still Sunday when we picked him up back at the hotel. But over in Meridian East, half a mile away, it was only Saturday. That little trip across the park had made all the difference; I told you it was rotten luck."

There was a long moment of silent sympathy; then I asked, "What did he get?"

"Three years," said Inspector Rawlings.

"That doesn't seem very much."

"Mars years; that makes it almost six of ours. And a whacking fine which, by an odd coincidence, came to just the refund value of his return ticket to Earth. He isn't in jail, of course; Mars can't afford that kind of nonproductive luxury. Danny has to work for a living, under discreet surveillance. I told you that the Meridian Museum couldn't afford a night watchman. Well, it has one now. Guess who."

"All passengers prepare to board in ten minutes! Please collect your hand baggage!" ordered the loud-speakers.

As we started to move toward the air lock, I couldn't help asking one more question.

"What about the people who put Danny up to it? There must have been a lot of money behind him. Did you get them?"

"Not yet; they'd covered their tracks pretty thoroughly, and I believe Danny was telling the truth when he said he couldn't give us any leads. Still, it's not my case; as I told you, I'm going back to my old job at the Yard. But a policeman always keeps his eyes open—like an art dealer, eh, Mr. Maccar? Why, you look a bit green about the gills. Have one of my space-sickness tablets."

"No, thank you," answered Mr. Maccar, "I'm quite all right."

His tone was distinctly unfriendly; the social temperature seemed to have dropped below zero in the last few minutes. I looked at Mr. Maccar, and I looked at the Inspector. And suddenly I realized that we were going to have a very interesting trip.

New York   *February 1959*

Rescue Party

Who was to blame? For three days Alveron's thoughts had come back to that question, and still he had found no answer. A creature of a less civilized or a less sensitive race would never have let it torture his mind, and would have satisfied himself with the assurance that no one could be responsible for the working of fate. But Alveron and his kind had been lords of the Universe since the dawn of history, since that far distant age when the Time Barrier had been folded round the cosmos by the unknown powers that lay beyond the Beginning. To them had been given all knowledge—and with infinite knowledge went infinite responsibility. If there were mistakes and errors in the administration of the Galaxy, the fault lay on the heads of Alveron and his people. And this was no mere mistake; it was one of the greatest tragedies in history.

The crew still knew nothing. Even Rugon, his closest friend and the ship's deputy captain, had been told only part of the truth. But now the doomed worlds lay less than a billion miles ahead. In a few hours, they would be landing on the third planet.

Once again Alveron read the message from Base; then, with a flick of a tentacle that no human eye could have followed, he pressed the "General Attention" button. Throughout the mile-long cylinder that was the Galactic Survey Ship S9000, creatures of many races laid down their work to listen to the words of their captain.

"I know you have all been wondering," began Alveron, "why we were ordered to abandon our survey and to proceed at such an acceleration to this region of space. Some of you may realize what this acceleration means. Our ship is on its last voyage: the generators have already been running for sixty hours at Ultimate Overload. We will be very lucky if we return to Base under our own power.

"We are approaching a sun which is about to become a

nova. Detonation will occur in seven hours, with an uncertainty of one hour, leaving us a maximum of only four hours for exploration. There are ten planets in the system about to be destroyed—and there is a civilization on the third. That fact was discovered only a few days ago. It is our tragic mission to contact that doomed race and if possible to save some of its members. I know that there is little we can do in so short a time with this single ship. No other machine can possibly reach the system before detonation occurs."

There was a long pause during which there could have been no sound or movement in the whole of the mighty ship as it sped silently toward the worlds ahead. Alveron knew what his companions were thinking and he tried to answer their unspoken question.

"You will wonder how such a disaster, the greatest of which we have any record, has been allowed to occur. On one point I can reassure you. The fault does not lie with the Survey.

"As you know, with our present fleet of under twelve thousand ships, it is possible to re-examine each of the eight thousand million solar systems in the Galaxy at intervals of about a million years. Most worlds change very little in so short a time as that.

"Less than four hundred thousand years ago, the survey ship S5060 examined the planets of the system we are approaching. It found intelligence on none of them, though the third planet was teeming with animal life and two other worlds had once been inhabited. The usual report was submitted and the system is due for its next examination in six hundred thousand years.

"It now appears that in the incredibly short period since the last survey, intelligent life has appeared in the system. The first intimation of this occurred when unknown radio signals were detected on the planet Kulath in the system X29.35, Y34.76, Z27.93. Bearings were taken on them; they were coming from the system ahead.

"Kulath is two hundred light-years from here, so those radio waves had been on their way for two centuries. Thus for at least that period of time a civilization has existed on one of these worlds—a civilization that can generate electromagnetic waves and all that that implies.

"An immediate telescopic examination of the system was made and it was then found that the sun was in the unstable pre-nova stage. Detonation might occur at any moment, and indeed might have done so while the light waves were on their way to Kulath.

"There was a slight delay while the supervelocity scanners on Kulath II were focused onto the system. They showed that the explosion had not yet occurred but was only a few hours away. If Kulath had been a fraction of a light-year further from this sun, we should never have known of its civilization until it had ceased to exist.

"The Administrator of Kulath contacted Sector Base immediately, and I was ordered to proceed to the system at once. Our object is to save what members we can of the doomed race, if indeed there are any left. But we have assumed that a civilization possessing radio could have protected itself against any rise of temperature that may have already occurred.

"This ship and the two tenders will each explore a section of the planet. Commander Torkalee will take Number One, Commander Orostron Number Two. They will have just under four hours in which to explore this world. At the end of that time, they must be back in the ship. It will be leaving then, with or without them. I will give the two commanders detailed instructions in the control room immediately.

"That is all. We enter atmosphere in two hours."

On the world once known as Earth the fires were dying out: there was nothing left to burn. The great forests that had swept across the planet like a tidal wave with the passing of the cities were now no more than glowing charcoal and the smoke of their funeral pyres still stained the sky. But the last hours were still to come, for the surface rocks had not yet begun to flow. The continents were dimly visible through the haze, but their outlines meant nothing to the watchers in the approaching ship. The charts they possessed were out of date by a dozen Ice Ages and more deluges than one.

The S9000 had driven past Jupiter and seen at once that no life could exist in those half-gaseous oceans of compressed hydrocarbons, now erupting furiously under the sun's abnormal heat. Mars and the outer planets they had missed, and Alveron realized that the worlds nearer the sun than Earth would be already melting. It was more than likely, he thought sadly, that the tragedy of this unknown race was already finished. Deep in his heart, he thought it might be better so. The ship could only have carried a few hundred survivors, and the problem of selection had been haunting his mind.

Rugon, Chief of Communications and Deputy Captain, came into the control room. For the last hour he had been striving to detect radiation from Earth, but in vain.

"We're too late," he announced gloomily. "I've monitored the whole spectrum and the ether's dead except for our own stations and some two-hundred-year-old programs from Kulath. Nothing in this system is radiating any more."

He moved toward the giant vision screen with a graceful flowing motion that no mere biped could ever hope to imitate. Alveron said nothing; he had been expecting this news.

One entire wall of the control room was taken up by the screen, a great black rectangle that gave an impression of almost infinite depth. Three of Rugon's slender control tentacles, useless for heavy work but incredibly swift at all manipulation, flickered over the selector dials and the screen lit up with a thousand points of light. The star field flowed swiftly past as Rugon adjusted the controls, bringing the projector to bear upon the sun itself.

No man of Earth would have recognized the monstrous shape that filled the screen. The sun's light was white no longer: great violet-blue clouds covered half its surface and from them long streamers of flame were erupting into space. At one point an enormous prominence had reared itself out of the photosphere, far out even into the flickering veils of the corona. It was as though a tree of fire had taken root in the surface of the sun—a tree that stood half a million miles high and whose branches were rivers of flame sweeping through space at hundreds of miles a second.

"I suppose," said Rugon presently, "that you are quite satisfied about the astronomers' calculations. After all——"

"Oh, we're perfectly safe," said Alveron confidently. "I've spoken to Kulath Observatory and they have been making some additional checks through our own instruments. That uncertainty of an hour includes a private safety margin which they won't tell me in case I feel tempted to stay any longer."

He glanced at the instrument board.

"The pilot should have brought us to the atmosphere now. Switch the screen back to the planet, please. Ah, there they go!"

There was a sudden tremor underfoot and a raucous clanging of alarms, instantly stilled. Across the vision screen two slim projectiles dived toward the looming mass of Earth. For a few miles they traveled together, then they separated, one vanishing abruptly as it entered the shadow of the planet.

Slowly the huge mother ship, with its thousand times greater mass, descended after them into the raging storms that already were tearing down the deserted cities of Man.

It was night in the hemisphere over which Orostron drove his tiny command. Like Torkalee, his mission was to photograph and record, and to report progress to the mother ship. The little scout had no room for specimens or passengers. If contact was made with the inhabitants of this world, the S9000 would come at once. There would be no time for parleying. If there was any trouble the rescue would be by force and the explanations could come later.

The ruined land beneath was bathed with an eerie, flickering light, for a great auroral display was raging over half the world. But the image on the vision screen was independent of external light, and it showed clearly a waste of barren rock that seemed never to have known any form of life. Presumably this desert land must come to an end somewhere. Orostron increased his speed to the highest value he dared risk in so dense an atmosphere.

The machine fled on through the storm, and presently the desert of rock began to climb toward the sky. A great mountain range lay ahead, its peaks lost in the smoke-laden clouds. Orostorn directed the scanners toward the horizon, and on the vision screen the line of mountains seemed suddenly very close and menacing. He started to climb rapidly. It was difficult to imagine a more unpromising land in which to find civilization and he wondered if it would be wise to change course. He decided against it. Five minutes later, he had his reward.

Miles below lay a decapitated mountain, the whole of its summit sheared away by some tremendous feat of engineering. Rising out of the rock and straddling the artificial plateau was an intricate structure of metal girders, supporting masses of machinery. Orostron brought his ship to a halt and spiraled down toward the mountain.

The slight Doppler blur had now vanished, and the picture on the screen was clear-cut. The latticework was supporting some scores of great metal mirrors, pointing skyward at an angle of forty-five degrees to the horizontal. They were slightly concave, and each had some complicated mechanism at its focus. There seemed something impressive and purposeful about the great array; every mirror was aimed at precisely the same spot in the sky—or beyond.

Orostron turned to his colleagues.

"It looks like some kind of observatory to me," he said. "Have you ever seen anything like it before?"

Klarten, a multitentacled, tripedal creature from a globular cluster at the edge of the Milky Way, had a different theory.

"That's communication equipment. Those reflectors are for focusing electromagnetic beams. I've seen the same kind of installation on a hundred worlds before. It may even be the station that Kulath picked up—though that's rather unlikely, for the beams would be very narrow from mirrors that size."

"That would explain why Rugon could detect no radiation before we landed," added Hansur II, one of the twin beings from the planet Thargon.

Orostron did not agree at all.

"If that is a radio station, it must be built for interplanetary communication. Look at the way the mirrors are pointed. I don't believe that a race which has only had radio for two centuries can have crossed space. It took my people six thousand years to do it."

"We managed it in three," said Hansur II mildly, speaking a few seconds ahead of his twin. Before the inevitable argument could develop, Klarten began to wave his tentacles with excitement. While the others had been talking, he had started the automatic monitor.

"Here it is! Listen!"

He threw a switch, and the little room was filled with a raucous whining sound, continually changing in pitch but nevertheless retaining certain characteristics that were difficult to define.

The four explorers listened intently for a minute; then Orostron said, "Surely that can't be any form of speech! No creature could produce sounds as quickly as that!"

Hansur I had come to the same conclusion. "That's a television program. Don't you think so, Klarten?"

The other agreed.

"Yes, and each of those mirrors seems to be radiating a different program. I wonder where they're going? If I'm correct, one of the other planets in the system must lie along those beams. We can soon check that."

Orostron called the S9000 and reported the discovery. Both Rugon and Alveron were greatly excited, and made a quick check of the astronomical records.

The result was surprising—and disappointing. None of the other nine planets lay anywhere near the line of transmission.

The great mirrors appeared to be pointing blindly into space.

There seemed only one conclusion to be drawn, and Klarten was the first to voice it.

"They had interplanetary communication," he said. "But the station must be deserted now, and the transmitters no longer controlled. They haven't been switched off, and are just pointing where they were left."

"Well, we'll soon find out," said Orostron. "I'm going to land."

He brought the machine slowly down to the level of the great metal mirrors, and past them until it came to rest on the mountain rock. A hundred yards away, a white stone building crouched beneath the maze of steel girders. It was windowless, but there were several doors in the wall facing them.

Orostron watched his companions climb into their protective suits and wished he could follow. But someone had to stay in the machine to keep in touch with the mother ship. Those were Alveron's instructions, and they were very wise. One never knew what would happen on a world that was being explored for the first time, especially under conditions such as these.

Very cautiously, the three explorers stepped out of the air lock and adjusted the antigravity field of their suits. Then, each with the mode of locomotion peculiar to his race, the little party went toward the building, the Hansur twins leading and Klarten following close behind. His gravity control was apparently giving trouble, for he suddenly fell to the ground, rather to the amusement of his colleagues. Orostron saw them pause for a moment at the nearest door—then it opened slowly and they disappeared from sight.

So Orostron waited, with what patience he could, while the storm rose around him and the light of the aurora grew even brighter in the sky. At the agreed times he called the mother ship and received brief acknowledgments from Rugon. He wondered how Torkalee was faring, halfway round the planet, but he could not contact him through the crash and thunder of solar interference.

It did not take Klarten and the Hansurs long to discover that their theories were largely correct. The building was a radio station, and it was utterly deserted. It consisted of one tremendous room with a few small offices leading from it. In the main chamber, row after row of electrical equipment stretched into the distance; lights flickered and winked on hundreds of control panels, and a dull glow came from the elements in a great avenue of vacuum tubes.

But Klarten was not impressed. The first radio sets his race had built were now fossilized in strata a thousand million years old. Man, who had possessed electrical machines for only a few centuries, could not compete with those who had known them for half the lifetime of the Earth.

Nevertheless, the party kept their recorders running as they explored the building. There was still one problem to be solved. The deserted station was broadcasting programs, but where were they coming from? The central switchboard had been quickly located. It was designed to handle scores of programs simultaneously, but the source of those programs was lost in a maze of cables that vanished underground. Back in the S9000, Rugon was trying to analyze the broadcasts and perhaps his researches would reveal their origin. It was impossible to trace cables that might lead across continents.

The party wasted little time at the deserted station. There was nothing they could learn from it, and they were seeking life rather than scientific information. A few minutes later the little ship rose swiftly from the plateau and headed toward the plains that must lie beyond the mountains. Less than three hours were still left to them.

As the array of enigmatic mirrors dropped out of sight, Orostron was struck by a sudden thought. Was it imagination, or had they all moved through a small angle while he had been waiting, as if they were still compensating for the rotation of the Earth? He could not be sure, and he dismissed the matter as unimportant. It would only mean that the directing mechanism was still working, after a fashion.

They discovered the city fifteen minutes later. It was a great, sprawling metropolis, built around a river that had disappeared leaving an ugly scar winding its way among the great buildings and beneath bridges that looked very incongruous now.

Even from the air, the city looked deserted. But only two and a half hours were left—there was no time for further exploration. Orostron made his decision, and landed near the largest structure he could see. It seemed reasonable to suppose that some creatures would have sought shelter in the strongest buildings, where they would be safe until the very end.

The deepest caves—the heart of the planet itself—would give no protection when the final cataclysm came. Even if this race had reached the outer planets, its doom would only be delayed by the few hours it would take for the ravening wave fronts to cross the Solar System.

Orostron could not know that the city had been deserted not for a few days or weeks, but for over a century. For the culture of cities, which had outlasted so many civilizations, had been doomed at last when the helicopter brought universal transportation. Within a few generations the great masses of mankind, knowing that they could reach any part of the globe in a matter of hours, had gone back to the fields and forests for which they had always longed. The new civilization had machines and resources of which earlier ages had never dreamed, but it was essentially rural and no longer bound to the steel and concrete warrens that had dominated the centuries before. Such cities as still remained were specialized centers of research, administration, or entertainment; the others had been allowed to decay, where it was too much trouble to destroy them. The dozen or so greatest of all cities, and the ancient university towns, had scarcely changed and would have lasted for many generations to come. But the cities that had been founded on steam and iron and surface transportation had passed with the industries that had nourished them.

And so while Orostron waited in the tender, his colleagues raced through endless empty corridors and deserted halls, taking innumerable photographs but learning nothing of the creatures who had used these buildings. There were libraries, meeting places, council rooms, thousands of offices—all were empty and deep with dust. If they had not seen the radio station on its mountain eyrie, the explorers could well have believed that this world had known no life for centuries.

Through the long minutes of waiting, Orostron tried to imagine where this race could have vanished. Perhaps they had killed themselves knowing that escape was impossible; perhaps they had built great shelters in the bowels of the planet, and even now were cowering in their millions beneath his feet, waiting for the end. He began to fear that he would never know.

It was almost a relief when at last he had to give the order for the return. Soon he would know if Torkalee's party had been more fortunate. And he was anxious to get back to the mother ship, for as the minutes passed the suspense had become more and more acute. There had always been the thought in his mind: What if the astronomers of Kulath have made a mistake? He would begin to feel happy when the walls of the S9000 were around him. He would be happier still when they were out in space and this ominous sun was shrinking far astern.

As soon as his colleagues had entered the air lock, Orostron hurled his tiny machine into the sky and set the controls to home on the S9000. Then he turned to his friends.

"Well, what have you found?" he asked.

Klarten produced a large roll of canvas and spread it out on the floor.

"This is what they were like," he said quietly. "Bipeds, with only two arms. They seem to have managed well, in spite of that handicap. Only two eyes as well, unless there are others in the back. We were lucky to find this; it's about the only thing they left behind."

The ancient oil painting stared stonily back at the four creatures regarding it so intently. By the irony of fate, its complete worthlessness had saved it from oblivion. When the city had been evacuated, no one had bothered to move Alderman John Richards, 1909–1974. For a century and a half he had been gathering dust while far away from the old cities the new civilization had been rising to heights no earlier culture had ever known.

"That was almost all we found," said Klarten. "The city must have been deserted for years. I'm afraid our expedition has been a failure. If there are any living beings on this world, they've hidden themselves too well for us to find them."

His commander was forced to agree.

"It was an almost impossible task," he said. "If we'd had weeks instead of hours we might have succeeded. For all we know, they may even have built shelters under the sea. No one seems to have thought of that."

He glanced quickly at the indicators and corrected the course.

"We'll be there in five minutes. Alveron seems to be moving rather quickly. I wonder if Torkalee has found anything."

The S9000 was hanging a few miles above the seaboard of a blazing continent when Orostron homed upon it. The danger line was thirty minutes away and there was no time to lose. Skillfully, he maneuvered the little ship into its launching tube and the party stepped out of the air lock.

There was a small crowd waiting for them. That was to be expected, but Orostron could see at once that something more than curiosity had brought his friends here. Even before a word was spoken, he knew that something was wrong.

"Torkalee hasn't returned. He's lost his party and we're going to the rescue. Come along to the control room at once."

From the beginning, Torkalee had been luckier than Orostron. He had followed the zone of twilight, keeping away from the intolerable glare of the sun, until he came to the shores of an inland sea. It was a very recent sea, one of the latest of Man's works, for the land it covered had been desert less than a century before. In a few hours it would be desert again, for the water was boiling and clouds of steam were rising to the skies. But they could not veil the loveliness of the great white city that overlooked the tideless sea.

Flying machines were still parked neatly round the square in which Torkalee landed. They were disappointingly primitive, though beautifully finished, and depended on rotating airfoils for support. Nowhere was there any sign of life, but the place gave the impression that its inhabitants were not very far away. Lights were still shining from some of the windows.

Torkalee's three companions lost no time in leaving the machine. Leader of the party, by seniority of rank and race was T'sinadree, who like Alveron himself had been born on one of the ancient planets of the Central Suns. Next came Alarkane, from a race which was one of the youngest in the Universe and took a perverse pride in the fact. Last came one of the strange beings from the system of Palador. It was nameless, like all its kind, for it possessed no identity of its own, being merely a mobile but still dependent cell in the consciousness of its race. Though it and its fellows had long been scattered over the Galaxy in the exploration of countless worlds, some unknown link still bound them together as inexorably as the living cells in a human body.

When a creature of Palador spoke, the pronoun it used was always "We." There was not, nor could there ever be, any first person singular in the language of Palador.

The great doors of the splendid building baffled the explorers, though any human child would have known their secret. T'sinadree wasted no time on them but called Torkalee on his personal transmitter. Then the three hurried aside while their commander maneuvered his machine into the best position. There was a brief burst of intolerable flame; the massive steelwork flickered once at the edge of the visible spectrum and was gone. The stones were still glowing when the eager party hurried into the building, the beams of their light projectors fanning before them.

The torches were not needed. Before them lay a great hall, glowing with light from lines of tubes along the ceiling. On either side, the hall opened out into long corridors, while straight ahead a massive stairway swept majestically toward the upper floors.

For a moment T'sinadree hesitated. Then, since one way was as good as another, he led his companions down the first corridor.

The feeling that life was near had now become very strong. At any moment, it seemed, they might be confronted by the creatures of this world. If they showed hostility—and they could scarcely be blamed if they did—the paralyzers would be used at once.

The tension was very great as the party entered the first room, and only relaxed when they saw that it held nothing but machines—row after row of them, now stilled and silent. Lining the enormous room were thousands of metal filing cabinets, forming a continuous wall as far as the eye could reach. And that was all; there was no furniture, nothing but the cabinets and the mysterious machines.

Alarkane, always the quickest of the three, was already examining the cabinets. Each held many thousand sheets of tough, thin material, perforated with innumerable holes and slots. The Paladorian appropriated one of the cards and Alarkane recorded the scene together with some close-ups of the machines. Then they left. The great room, which had been one of the marvels of the world, meant nothing to them. No living eye would ever again see that wonderful battery of almost human Hollerith analyzers and the five thousand million punched cards holding all that could be recorded of each man, woman, and child on the planet.

It was clear that this building had been used very recently. With growing excitement, the explorers hurried on to the next room. This they found to be an enormous library, for millions of books lay all around them on miles and miles of shelving. Here, though the explorers could not know it, were the records of all the laws that Man had ever passed, and all the speeches that had ever been made in his council chambers.

T'sinadree was deciding his plan of action when Alarkane drew his attention to one of the racks a hundred yards away. It was half empty, unlike all the others. Around it books lay in a tumbled heap on the floor, as if knocked down by someone in frantic haste. The signs were unmistakable. Not long ago, other creatures had been this way. Faint wheel marks were clearly visible on the floor to the acute sense of Alarkane, though the others could see nothing. Alarkane could even detect footprints, but knowing nothing of the creatures that had formed them he could not say which way they led.

The sense of nearness was stronger than ever now, but it was nearness in time, not in space. Alarkane voiced the thoughts of the party.

"Those books must have been valuable, and someone has come to rescue them—rather as an afterthought, I should say. That means there must be a place of refuge, possibly not very far away. Perhaps we may be able to find some other clues that will lead us to it."

T'sinadree agreed; the Paladorian wasn't enthusiastic.

"That may be so," it said, "but the refuge may be anywhere on the planet, and we have just two hours left. Let us waste no more time if we hope to rescue these people."

The party hurried forward once more, pausing only to collect a few books that might be useful to the scientists at Base —though it was doubtful if they could ever be translated. They soon found that the great building was composed largely of small rooms, all showing signs of recent occupation. Most of them were in a neat and tidy condition, but one or two were very much the reverse. The explorers were particularly puzzled by one room—clearly an office of some kind—that appeared to have been completely wrecked. The floor was littered with papers, the furniture had been smashed, and smoke was pouring through the broken windows from the fires outside.

T'sinadree was rather alarmed.

"Surely no dangerous animal could have got into a place like this!" he exclaimed, fingering his paralyzer nervously.

Alarkane did not answer. He began to make that annoying sound which his race called "laughter." It was several minutes before he would explain what had amused him.

"I don't think any animal has done it," he said. "In fact, the explanation is very simple. Suppose *you* had been working all your life in this room, dealing with endless papers, year after year. And suddenly, you are told that you will never see it again, that your work is finished, and that you can leave it forever. More than that—no one will come after you. Everything is finished. How would you make your exit, T'sinadree?"

The other thought for a moment.

"Well, I suppose I'd just tidy things up and leave. That's what seems to have happened in all the other rooms."

Alarkane laughed again.

"I'm quite sure you would. But some individuals have a different psychology. I think I should have liked the creature that used this room."

He did not explain himself further, and his two colleagues puzzled over his words for quite a while before they gave it up.

It came as something of a shock when Torkalee gave the order to return. They had gathered a great deal of information, but had found no clue that might lead them to the missing inhabitants of this world. That problem was as baffling as ever, and now it seemed that it would never be solved. There were only forty minutes left before the S9000 would be departing.

They were halfway back to the tender when they saw the semicircular passage leading down into the depths of the building. Its architectural style was quite different from that used elsewhere, and the gently sloping floor was an irresistible attraction to creatures whose many legs had grown weary of the marble staircases which only bipeds could have built in such profusion. T'sinadree had been the worst sufferer, for he normally employed twelve legs and could use twenty when he was in a hurry, though no one had ever seen him perform this feat.

The party stopped dead and looked down the passageway with a single thought. A tunnel, leading down into the depths of Earth! At its end, they might yet find the people of this world and rescue some of them from their fate. For there was still time to call the mother ship if the need arose.

T'sinadree signaled to his commander and Torkalee brought the little machine immediately overhead. There might not be time for the party to retrace its footsteps through the maze of passages, so meticulously recorded in the Paladorian mind that there was no possibility of going astray. If speed was necessary, Torkalee could blast his way through the dozen floors above their heads. In any case, it should not take long to find what lay at the end of the passage.

It took only thirty seconds. The tunnel ended quite abruptly in a very curious cylindrical room with magnificently padded seats along the walls. There was no way out save that by which they had come, and it was several seconds before the purpose of the chamber dawned on Alarkane's mind. It was a pity, he thought, that they would never have time to use this. The thought was suddenly interrupted by a cry from T'sinadree.

Alarkane wheeled around, and saw that the entrance had closed silently behind them.

Even in that first moment of panic, Alarkane found himself thinking with some admiration: Whoever they were, they knew how to build automatic machinery!

The Paladorian was the first to speak. It waved one of its tentacles toward the seats.

"We think it would be best to be seated," it said. The multiplex mind of Palador had already analyzed the situation and knew what was coming.

They did not have long to wait before a low-pitched hum came from a grill overhead, and for the very last time in history a human, even if lifeless, voice was heard on Earth. The words were meaningless, though the trapped explorers could guess their message clearly enough.

"Choose your stations, please, and be seated."

Simultaneously, a wall panel at one end of the compartment glowed with light. On it was a simple map, consisting of a series of a dozen circles connected by a line. Each of the circles had writing alongside it, and beside the writing were two buttons of different colors.

Alarkane looked questioningly at his leader.

"Don't touch them," said T'sinadree. "If we leave the controls alone, the doors may open again."

He was wrong. The engineers who had designed the automatic subway had assumed that anyone who entered it would naturally wish to go somewhere. If they selected no intermediate station, their destination could only be the end of the line.

There was another pause while the relays and thyratrons waited for their orders. In those thirty seconds, if they had known what to do, the party could have opened the doors and left the subway. But they did not know, and the machines geared to a human psychology acted for them.

The surge of acceleration was not very great; the lavish unholstery was a luxury, not a necessity. Only an almost imperceptible vibration told of the speed at which they were traveling through the bowels of the earth, on a journey the duration of which they could not even guess. And in thirty minutes, the S9000 would be leaving the Solar System.

There was a long silence in the speeding machine. T'sinadree and Alarkane were thinking rapidly. So was the Paladorian, though in a different fashion. The conception of personal death was meaningless to it, for the destruction of a single unit meant no more to the group mind than the loss of a nail-paring to a man. But it could, though with great difficulty, appreciate the plight of individual intelligences such as Alarkane and T'sinadree, and it was anxious to help them if it could.

Alarkane had managed to contact Torkalee with his personal transmitter, though the signal was very weak and seemed to be fading quickly. Rapidly he explained the situation, and almost at once the signals became clearer. Torkalee was following the path of the machine, flying above the ground under which they were speeding to their unknown destination. That was the first indication they had of the fact that they were traveling at nearly a thousand miles an hour, and very soon after that Torkalee was able to give the still more disturbing news that they were rapidly approaching the sea. While they were beneath the land, there was a hope, though a slender one, that they might stop the machine and escape. But under the ocean—not all the brains and the machinery in the great mother ship could save them. No one could have devised a more perfect trap.

T'sinadree had been examining the wall map with great attention. Its meaning was obvious, and along the line connecting the circles a tiny spot of light was crawling. It was already halfway to the first of the stations marked.

"I'm going to press one of those buttons," said T'sinadree at last. "It won't do any harm, and we may learn something."

"I agree. Which will you try first?"

"There are only two kinds, and it won't matter if we try the wrong one first. I suppose one is to start the machine and the other is to stop it."

Alarkane was not very hopeful.

"It started without any button pressing," he said. "I think it's completely automatic and we can't control it from here at all."

T'sinadree could not agree.

"These buttons are clearly associated with the stations, and there's no point in having them unless you can use them to stop yourself. The only question is, which is the right one?"

His analysis was perfectly correct. The machine could be stopped at any intermediate station. They had only been on their way ten minutes, and if they could leave now, no harm would have been done. It was just bad luck that T'sinadree's first choice was the wrong button.

The little light on the map crawled slowly through the

illuminated circle without checking its speed. And at the same time Torkalee called from the ship overhead.

"You have just passed underneath a city and are heading out to sea. There cannot be another stop for nearly a thousand miles."

Alveron had given up all hope of finding life on this world. The S9000 had roamed over half the planet, never staying long in one place, descending ever and again in an effort to attract attention. There had been no response; Earth seemed utterly dead. If any of its inhabitants were still alive, thought Alveron, they must have hidden themselves in its depths where no help could reach them, though their doom would be nonetheless certain.

Rugon brought news of the disaster. The great ship ceased its fruitless searching and fled back through the storm to the ocean above which Torkalee's little tender was still following the track of the buried machine.

The scene was truly terrifying. Not since the days when Earth was born had there been such seas as this. Mountains of water were racing before the storm which had now reached velocities of many hundred miles an hour. Even at this distance from the mainland the air was full of flying debris—trees, fragments of houses, sheets of metal, anything that had not been anchored to the ground. No air-borne machine could have lived for a moment in such a gale. And ever and again even the roar of the wind was drowned as the vast water-mountains met head-on with a crash that seemed to shake the sky.

Fortunately, there had been no serious earthquakes yet. Far beneath the bed of the ocean, the wonderful piece of engineering which had been the World President's private vacuum-subway was still working perfectly, unaffected by the tumult and destruction above. It would continue to work until the last minute of the Earth's existence, which, if the astronomers were right, was not much more than fifteen minutes away—though precisely how much more Alveron would have given a great deal to know. It would be nearly an hour before the trapped party could reach land and even the slightest hope of rescue.

Alveron's instructions had been precise, though even without them he would never have dreamed of taking any risks with the great machine that had been entrusted to his care. Had he been human, the decision to abandon the trapped members of his crew would have been desperately hard to make. But he came of a race far more sensitive than Man, a race that so loved the things of the spirit that long ago, and with infinite reluctance, it had taken over control of the Universe since only thus could it be sure that justice was being done. Alveron would need all his superhuman gifts to carry him through the next few hours.

Meanwhile, a mile below the bed of the ocean Alarkane and T'sinadree were very busy indeed with their private communicators. Fifteen minutes is not a long time in which to wind up the affairs of a lifetime. It is, indeed, scarcely long enough to dictate more than a few of those farewell messages which at such moments are so much more important than all other matters.

All the while the Paladorian had remained silent and motionless, saying not a word. The other two, resigned to their fate and engrossed in their personal affairs, had given it no thought. They were startled when suddenly it began to address them in its peculiarly passionless voice.

"We perceive that you are making certain arrangements concerning your anticipated destruction. That will probably be unnecessary. Captain Alveron hopes to rescue us if we can stop this machine when we reach land again."

Both T'sinadree and Alarkane were too surprised to say anything for a moment. Then the latter gasped, "How do you know?"

It was a foolish question, for he remembered at once that there were several Paladorians—if one could use the phrase— in the S9000, and consequently their companion knew everything that was happening in the mother ship. So he did not wait for an answer but continued, "Alveron can't do that! He daren't take such a risk!"

"There will be no risk," said the Paladorian. "We have told him what to do. It is really very simple."

Alarkane and T'sinadree looked at their companion with something approaching awe, realizing now what must have happened. In moments of crisis, the single units comprising the Paladorian mind could link together in an organization no less close than that of any physical brain. At such moments they formed an intellect more powerful than any other in the Universe. All ordinary problems could be solved by a few hundred or thousand units. Very rarely, millions would be needed, and on two historic occasions the billions of cells of the entire Paladorian consciousness had been welded together to deal with emergencies that threatened the race. The mind of Palador was one of the greatest mental resources of the Universe; its full force was seldom required, but the knowledge that it was available was supremely comforting to other races. Alarkane wondered how many cells had co-ordinated to deal with this particular emergency. He also wondered how so trivial an incident had ever come to its attention.

To that question he was never to know the answer, though he might have guessed it had he known that the chillingly remote Paladorian mind possessed an almost human streak of vanity. Long ago, Alarkane had written a book trying to prove that eventually all intelligent races would sacrifice individual consciousness and that one day only group-minds would remain in the Universe. Palador, he had said, was the first of those ultimate intellects, and the vast, dispersed mind had not been displeased.

They had no time to ask any further questions before Alveron himself began to speak through their communicators.

"Alveron calling! We're staying on this planet until the detonation waves reach it, so we may be able to rescue you. You're heading toward a city on the coast which you'll reach in forty minute at your present speed. If you cannot stop yourselves then, we're going to blast the tunnel behind and ahead of you to cut off your power. Then we'll sink a shaft to get you out—the chief engineer says he can do it in five minutes with the main projectors. So you should be safe within an hour, unless the sun blows up before."

"And if that happens, you'll be destroyed as well! You mustn't take such a risk!"

"Don't let that worry you; we're perfectly safe. When the sun detonates, the explosion wave will take several minutes to rise to its maximum. But apart from that, we're on the night side of the planet, behind an eight-thousand-mile screen of rock. When the first warning of the explosion comes, we will accelerate out of the Solar System, keeping in the shadow of the planet. Under our maximum drive, we will reach the velocity of light before leaving the cone of shadow, and the sun cannot harm us then."

T'sinadree was still afraid to hope. Another objection came at once into his mind.

"Yes, but how will you get any warning, here on the night side of the planet?"

"Very easily," replied Alveron. "This world has a moon which is now visible from this hemisphere. We have telescopes trained on it. If it shows any sudden increase in brilliance, our main drive goes on automatically and we'll be thrown out of the system."

The logic was flawless. Alveron, cautious as ever, was taking no chances. It would be many minutes before the eight-thousand-mile shield of rock and metal could be destroyed by the fires of the exploding sun. In that time, the S9000 could have reached the safety of the velocity of light.

Alarkane pressed the second button when they were still several miles from the coast. He did not expect anything to happen then, assuming that the machine could not stop between stations. It seemed too good to be true when, a few minutes later, the machine's slight vibration died away and they came to a halt.

The doors slid silently apart. Even before they were fully open, the three had left the compartment. They were taking no more chances. Before them a long tunnel stretched into the distance, rising slowly out of sight. They were starting along it when suddenly Alveron's voice called from the communicators.

"Stay where you are! We're going to blast!"

The ground shuddered once, and far ahead there came the rumble of falling rock. Again the earth shook—and a hundred yards ahead the passageway vanished abruptly. A tremendous vertical shaft had been cut clean through it.

The party hurried forward again until they came to the end of the corridor and stood waiting on its lip. The shaft in which it ended was a full thousand feet across and descended into the earth as far as the torches could throw their beams. Overhead, the storm clouds fled beneath a moon that no man would have recognized, so luridly brilliant was its disk. And, most glorious of all sights, the S9000 floated high above, the great projectors that had drilled this enormous pit still glowing cherry red.

A dark shape detached itself from the mother ship and dropped swiftly toward the ground. Torkalee was returning to collect his friends. A little later, Alveron greeted them in the control room. He waved to the great vision screen and said quietly, "See, we were barely in time."

The continent below them was slowly settling beneath the mile-high waves that were attacking its coasts. The last that anyone was ever to see of Earth was a great plain, bathed with the silver light of the abnormally brilliant moon. Across its face the waters were pouring in a glittering flood toward a distant range of mountains. The sea had won its final victory, but its triumph would be short-lived, for soon sea and land would be no more. Even as the silent party in the control room watched the destruction below, the infinitely greater catastrophe to which this was only the prelude came swiftly upon them.

It was as though dawn had broken suddenly over this moonlit landscape. But it was not dawn: it was only the moon, shining with the brilliance of a second sun. For perhaps thirty seconds that awesome, unnatural light burned fiercely on the doomed land beneath. Then there came a sudden flashing of indicator lights across the control board. The main drive was on. For a second Alveron glanced at the indicators and checked their information. When he looked again at the screen, Earth was gone.

The magnificent, desperately overstrained generators quietly died when the S9000 was passing the orbit of Persephone. It did not matter, the sun could never harm them now, and although the ship was speeding helplessly out into the lonely night of interstellar space, it would only be a matter of days before rescue came.

There was irony in that. A day ago, they had been the rescuers, going to the aid of a race that now no longer existed. Not for the first time Alveron wondered about the world that had just perished. He tried, in vain, to picture it as it had been in its glory, the streets of its cities thronged with life. Primitive though its people had been, they might have offered much to the Universe. If only they could have made contact! Regret was useless; long before their coming, the people of this world must have buried themselves in its iron heart. And now they and their civilization would remain a mystery for the rest of time.

Alveron was glad when his thoughts were interrupted by Rugon's entrance. The Chief of Communications had been very busy ever since the take-off, trying to analyze the programs radiated by the transmitter Orostron had discovered. The problem was not a difficult one, but it demanded the construction of special equipment, and that had taken time.

"Well, what have you found?" asked Alveron.

"Quite a lot," replied his friend. "There's something mysterious here, and I don't understand it.

"It didn't take long to find how the vision transmissions were built up, and we've been able to convert them to suit our own equipment. It seems that there were cameras all over the planet, surveying points of interest. Some of them were apparently in cities, on the tops of very high buildings. The cameras were rotating continuously to give panoramic views. In the programs we've recorded there are about twenty different scenes.

"In addition, there are a number of transmissions of a different kind, neither sound nor vision. They seem to be purely scientific—possibly instrument readings or something of that sort. All these programs were going out simultaneously on different frequency bands.

"Now there must be a reason for all this. Orostron still thinks that the station simply wasn't switched off when it was deserted. But these aren't the sort of programs such a station would normally radiate at all. It was certainly used for interplanetary relaying—Klarten was quite right there. So these people must have crossed space, since none of the other planets had any life at the time of the last survey. Don't you agree?"

Alveron was following intently.

"Yes, that seems reasonable enough. But it's also certain that the beam was pointing to none of the other planets. I checked that myself."

"I know," said Rugon. "What I want to discover is why a giant interplanetary relay station is busily transmitting pictures of a world about to be destroyed—pictures that would be of immense interest to scientists and astronomers. Some one had gone to a lot of trouble to arrange all those panoramic cameras. I am convinced that those beams were going somewhere."

Alveron started up.

"Do you imagine that there might be an outer planet that hasn't been reported?" he asked. "If so, your theory's certainly wrong. The beam wasn't even pointing in the plane of the Solar System. And even if it were—just look at this."

He switched on the vision screen and adjusted the controls. Against the velvet curtain of space was hanging a blue-white sphere, apparently composed of many concentric shells of incandescent gas. Even though its immense distance made all movement invisible, it was clearly expanding at an enormous rate. At its center was a blinding point of light—the white dwarf star that the sun had now become.

"You probably don't realize just how big that sphere is," said Alveron. "Look at this."

He increased the magnification until only the center portion of the nova was visible. Close to its heart were two minute condensations, one on either side of the nucleus.

"Those are the two giant planets of the system. They have still managed to retain their existence—after a fashion. And they were several hundred million miles from the sun. The nova is still expanding—but it's already twice the size of the Solar System."

Rugon was silent for a moment.

"Perhaps you're right," he said, rather grudgingly. "You've disposed of my first theory. But you still haven't satisfied me."

He made several swift circuits of the room before speaking again. Alveron waited patiently. He knew the almost intuitive powers of his friend, who could often solve a problem when mere logic seemed insufficient.

Then, rather slowly, Rugon began to speak again.

"What do you think of this?" he said. "Suppose we've completely underestimated this people? Orostron did it once—he thought they could never have crossed space, since they'd only known radio for two centuries. Hansur II told me that. Well, Orostron was quite wrong. Perhaps we're all wrong. I've had a look at the material that Klarten brought back from the transmitter. He wasn't impressed by what he found, but it's a marvelous achievement for so short a time. There were devices in that station that belonged to civilizations thousands of years older. Alveron, can we follow that beam to see where it leads?"

Alveron said nothing for a full minute. He had been more than half expecting the question, but it was not an easy one to answer. The main generators had gone completely. There was no point in trying to repair them. But there was still power available, and while there was power, anything could be done in time. It would mean a lot of improvisation, and some difficult maneuvers, for the ship still had its enormous initial velocity. Yes, it could be done, and the activity would keep the crew from becoming further depressed, now that the reaction caused by the mission's failure had started to set in. The news that the nearest heavy repair ship could not reach them for three weeks had also caused a slump in morale.

The engineers, as usual, made a tremendous fuss. Again as usual, they did the job in half the time they had dismissed as being absolutely impossible. Very slowly, over many hours, the great ship began to discard the speed its main drive had given it in as many minutes. In a tremendous curve, millions of miles in radius, the S9000 changed its course and the star fields shifted round it.

The maneuver took three days, but at the end of that time the ship was limping along a course parallel to the beam that had once come from Earth. They were heading out into emptiness, the blazing sphere that had been the sun dwindling slowly behind them. By the standards of interstellar flight, they were almost stationary.

For hours Rugon strained over his instruments, driving his detector beams far ahead into space. There were certainly no planets within many light-years; there was no doubt of that. From time to time Alveron came to see him and always he had to give the same reply: "Nothing to report." About a fifth of the time Rugon's intuition let him down badly; he began to wonder if this was such an occasion.

Not until a week later did the needles of the mass-detectors quiver feebly at the ends of their scales. But Rugon said nothing, not even to his captain. He waited until he was sure, and he went on waiting until even the short-range scanners began to react, and to build up the first faint pictures on the vision screen. Still he waited patiently until he could interpret the images. Then, when he knew that his wildest fancy was even less than the truth, he called his colleagues in the control room.

The picture on the vision screen was the familiar one of endless star fields, sun beyond sun to the very limits of the Universe. Near the center of the screen a distant nebula made a patch of haze that was difficult for the eye to grasp.

Rugon increased the magnification. The stars flowed out of the field; the little nebula expanded until it filled the screen and then—it was a nebula no longer. A simultaneous gasp of amazement came from all the company at the sight that lay before them.

Lying across league after league of space, ranged in a vast three-dimensional array of rows and columns with the precision of a marching army, were thousands of tiny pencils of light. They were moving swiftly; the whole immense lattice holding its shape as a single unit. Even as Alveron and his comrades watched, the formation began to drift off the screen and Rugon had to recenter the controls.

After a long pause, Rugon started to speak.

"This is the race," he said softly, "that has known radio for only two centuries—the race that we believed had crept to die in the heart of its planet. I have examined those images under the highest possible magnification.

"That is the greatest fleet of which there has ever been a record. Each of those points of light represents a ship larger than our own. Of course, they are very primitive—what you see on the screen are the jets of their rockets. Yes, they dared to use rockets to bridge interstellar space! You realize what that means. It would take them centuries to reach the nearest star. The whole race must have embarked on this journey in the hope that its descendants would complete it, generations later.

"To measure the extent of their accomplishment, think of the ages it took us to conquer space, and the longer ages still before we attempted to reach the stars. Even if we were threatened with annihilation, could we have done so much in so short a time? Remember, this is the youngest civilization in the Universe. Four hundred thousand years ago it did not even exist. What will it be a million years from now?"

An hour later, Orostron left the crippled mother ship to make contact with the great fleet ahead. As the little torpedo disappeared among the stars, Alveron turned to his friend and made a remark that Rugon was often to remember in the years ahead.

"I wonder what they'll be like?" he mused. "Will they be nothing but wonderful engineers, with no art or philosophy? They're going to have such a surprise when Orostron reaches them—I expect it will be rather a blow to their pride. It's funny how all isolated races think they're the only people in the Universe. But they should be grateful to us; we're going to save them a good many hundred years of travel."

Alveron glanced at the Milky Way, lying like a veil of silver mist across the vision screen. He waved toward it with a sweep of a tentacle that embraced the whole circle of the Galaxy, from the Central Planets to the lonely suns of the Rim.

"You know," he said to Rugon, "I feel rather afraid of these people. Suppose they don't like our little Federation?" He waved once more toward the star-clouds that lay massed across the screen, glowing with the light of their countless suns.

"Something tells me they'll be very determined people," he added. "We had better be polite to them. After all, we only outnumber them about a thousand million to one."

Rugon laughed at his captain's little joke.

Twenty years afterward, the remark didn't seem funny.

Stratford-on-Avon   *March 1945*

The Curse

For three hundred years, while its fame spread across the world, the little town had stood here at the river's bend. Time and change had touched it lightly; it had heard from afar both the coming of the Armada and the fall of the Third Reich, and all Man's wars had passed it by.

Now it was gone, as though it had never been. In a moment of time the toil and treasure of centuries had been swept away. The vanished streets could still be traced as faint marks in the vitrified ground, but of the houses, nothing remained. Steel and concrete, plaster and ancient oak—it had mattered little at the end. In the moment of death they had stood together, transfixed by the glare of the detonating bomb. Then, even before they could flash into fire, the blast waves had reached them and they had ceased to be. Mile upon mile the ravening hemisphere of flame had expanded over the level farmlands, and from its heart had risen the twisting totem pole that had haunted the minds of men for so long, and to such little purpose.

The rocket had been a stray, one of the last ever to be fired. It was hard to say for what target it had been intended. Certainly not London, for London was no longer a military objective. London, indeed, was no longer anything at all. Long ago the men whose duty it was had calculated that three of the hydrogen bombs would be sufficient for that rather small target. In sending twenty, they had been perhaps a little overzealous.

This was not one of the twenty that had done their work so well. Both its destination and its origin were unknown: whether it had come across the lonely Arctic wastes or far above the waters of the Atlantic, no one could tell and there were few now who cared. Once there had been men who had known such things, who had watched from afar the flight of the great projectiles and had sent their own missiles to meet them. Often that appointment had been kept, high above the

Earth where the sky was black and sun and stars shared the heavens together. Then there had bloomed for a moment that indescribable flame, sending out into space a message that in centuries to come other eyes than Man's would see and understand.

But that had been days ago, at the beginning of the War. The defenders had long since been brushed aside, as they had known they must be. They had held on to life long enough to discharge their duty; too late, the enemy had learned his mistake. He would launch no further rockets; those still falling he had dispatched hours ago on secret trajectories that had taken them far out into space. They were returning now unguided and inert, waiting in vain for the signals that should lead them to their destinies. One by one they were falling at random upon a world which they could harm no more.

The river had already overflowed its banks; somewhere down its course the land had twisted beneath that colossal hammer-blow and the way to the sea was no longer open. Dust was still falling in a fine rain, as it would do for days as Man's cities and treasures returned to the world that had given them birth. But the sky was no longer wholly darkened, and in the west the sun was settling through banks of angry cloud.

A church had stood here by the river's edge, and though no trace of the building remained, the gravestones that the years had gathered round it still marked its place. Now the stone slabs lay in parallel rows, snapped off at their bases and pointing mutely along the line of the blast. Some were half flattened into the ground, others had been cracked and blistered by terrific heat, but many still bore the messages they had carried down the centuries in vain.

The light died in the west and the unnatural crimson faded from the sky. Yet still the graven words could be clearly read, lit by a steady, unwavering radiance, too faint to be seen by day but strong enough to banish night. The land was burning: for miles the glow of its radioactivity was reflected from the clouds. Through the glimmering landscape wound the dark ribbon of the steadily widening river, and as the waters submerged the land that deadly glow continued unchanging in the depths. In a generation, perhaps, it would have faded from sight, but a hundred years might pass before life could safely come this way again.

Timidly the waters touched the worn gravestone that for more than three hundred years had lain before the vanished altar. The church that had sheltered it so long had given it some protection at the last, and only a slight discoloration of the rock told of the fires that had passed this way. In the corpse-light of the dying land, the archaic words could still be traced as the water rose around them, breaking at last in tiny ripples across the stone. Line by line the epitaph upon which so many millions had gazed slipped beneath the conquering waters. For a little while the letters could still be faintly seen; then they were gone forever.

> Good frend for Iesvs sake forbeare,
> To digg the dvst encloased heare
>   Blest be ye man yt spares thes stones,
>   And cvrst be he yt moves my bones.

Undisturbed through all eternity the poet could sleep in safety now: in the silence and darkness above his head, the Avon was seeking its new outlet to the sea.

Stratford-on-Avon   *May 1946*

Summertime on Icarus

In 1968, Icarus will pass so close to the Earth that some hopeful scientists have predicted a collision. Should that happen, I shall delete this story from the second printing.

Unless, of course, the second printing has itself been deleted—along with everything else.

————— ◆◆ ◆ —————

When Colin Sherrard opened his eyes after the crash, he could not imagine where he was. He seemed to be lying, trapped in some kind of vehicle, on the summit of a rounded hill, which sloped steeply away in all directions. Its surface was seared and blackened, as if a great fire had swept over it. Above him was a jet-black sky, crowded with stars; one of them hung like a tiny, brilliant sun low down on the horizon.

Could it be the sun? Was he so far from Earth? No—that was impossible. Some nagging memory told him that the sun was very close—hideously close—not so distant that it had shrunk to a star. And with that thought, full consciousness returned. Sherrard knew exactly where he was, and the knowledge was so terrible that he almost fainted again.

He was nearer to the sun than any man had ever been. His damaged space-pod was lying on no hill, but on the steeply curving surface of a world only two miles in diameter. That brilliant star sinking swiftly in the west was the light of *Prometheus*, the ship that had brought him here across so many millions of miles of space. She was hanging up there among the stars, wondering why his pod had not returned like a homing pigeon to its roost. In a few minutes she would have passed from sight, dropping below the horizon in her perpetual game of hide-and-seek with the sun.

That was a game that he had lost. He was still on the night

side of the asteroid, in the cool safety of its shadow, but the
short night would be ending soon. The four-hour day of
Icarus was spinning swiftly toward that dreadful dawn, when
a sun thirty times larger than ever shone upon Earth would
blast these rocks with fire. Sherrard knew all too well why
everything around him was burned and blackened. Icarus
was still a week from perihelion but the temperature at noon
had already reached a thousand degrees Fahrenheit.

Though this was no time for humor, he suddenly remembered Captain McClellan's description of Icarus: "The hottest piece of real estate in the solar system." The truth of that
jest had been proved, only a few days before, by one of those
simple and unscientific experiments that are so much more
impressive than any number of graphs and instrument readings.

Just before daybreak, someone had propped a piece of
wood on the summit of one of the tiny hills. Sherrard had
been watching, from the safety of the night side, when the
first rays of the rising sun had touched the hilltop. When
his eyes had adjusted to the sudden detonation of light, he
saw that the wood was already beginning to blacken and
char. Had there been an atmosphere here, the stick would
have burst into flames; such was dawn, upon Icarus. . . .

Yet it had not been impossibly hot at the time of their
first landing, when they were passing the orbit of Venus
five weeks ago. *Prometheus* had overtaken the asteroid as
it was beginning its plunge toward the sun, had matched
speed with the little world and had touched down upon its
surface as lightly as a snowflake. (A snowflake on Icarus—
that was quite a thought. . . .) Then the scientists had fanned
out across the fifteen square miles of jagged nickel-iron that
covered most of the asteroid's surface, setting up their instruments and checkpoints, collecting samples and making
endless observations.

Everything had been carefully planned, years in advance,
as part of the International Astrophysical Decade. Here was a
unique opportunity for a research ship to get within a mere
seventeen million miles of the sun, protected from its fury by
a two-mile-thick shield of rock and iron. In the shadow of
Icarus, the ship could ride safely round the central fire which
warmed all the planets, and upon which the existence of all
life depended. As the Prometheus of legend had brought the
gift of fire to mankind, so the ship that bore his name would

return to Earth with other unimagined secrets from the heavens.

There had been plenty of time to set up the instruments and make the surveys before *Prometheus* had to take off and seek the permanent shade of night. Even then, it was still possible for men in the tiny self-propelled space-pods— miniature spaceships, only ten feet long—to work on the night side for an hour or so, as long as they were not overtaken by the advancing line of sunrise. That had seemed a simple-enough condition to meet, on a world where dawn marched forward at only a mile an hour; but Sherrard had failed to meet it, and the penalty was death.

He was still not quite sure what had happened. He had been replacing a seismograph transmitter at Station 145, unofficially known as Mount Everest because it was a full ninety feet above the surrounding territory. The job had been a perfectly straightforward one, even though he had to do it by remote control through the mechanical arms of his pod. Sherrard was an expert at manipulating these; he could tie knots with his metal fingers almost as quickly as with his flesh-and-bone ones. The task had taken little more than twenty minutes, and then the radioseismograph was on the air again, monitoring the tiny quakes and shudders that racked Icarus in ever-increasing numbers as the asteroid approached the sun. It was small satisfaction to know that he had now made a king-sized addition to the record.

After he had checked the signals, he had carefully replaced the sun screens around the instrument. It was hard to believe that two flimsy sheets of polished metal foil, no thicker than paper, could turn aside a flood of radiation that would melt lead or tin within seconds. But the first screen reflected more than ninety per cent of the sunlight falling upon its mirror surface and the second turned back most of the rest, so that only a harmless fraction of the heat passed through.

He had reported completion of the job, received an acknowledgment from the ship, and prepared to head for home. The brilliant floodlights hanging from *Prometheus*—without which the night side of the asteroid would have been in utter darkness—had been an unmistakable target in the sky. The ship was only two miles up, and in this feeble gravity he could have jumped that distance had he been wearing a planetary-type space suit with flexible legs, As it was, the low-powered microrockets of his pod would get him there in a leisurely five minutes.

He had aimed the pod with its gyros, set the rear jets at Strength Two, and pressed the firing button. There had been a violent explosion somewhere in the vicinity of his feet and he had soared away from Icarus—but not toward the ship. Something was horribly wrong; he was tossed to one side of the vehicle, unable to reach the controls. Only one of the jets was firing, and he was pinwheeling across the sky, spinning faster and faster under the off-balanced drive. He tried to find the cutoff, but the spin had completely disorientated aim. When he was able to locate the controls, his first reaction made matters worse—he pushed the throttle over to full, like a nervous driver stepping on the accelerator instead of the brake. It took only a second to correct the mistake and kill the jet, but by then he was spinning so rapidly that the stars were wheeling round in circles.

Everything had happened so quickly that there was no time for fear, no time even to call the ship and report what was happening. He took his hands away from the controls; to touch them now would only make matters worse. It would take two or three minutes of cautious jockeying to unravel his spin, and from the flickering glimpses of the approaching rocks it was obvious that he did not have as many seconds. Sherrard remembered a piece of advice at the front of the *Spaceman's Manual:* "When you don't know what to do, *do nothing.*" He was still doing it when Icarus fell upon him, and the stars went out.

It had been a miracle that the pod was unbroken, and that he was not breathing space. (Thirty minutes from now he might be glad to do so, when the capsule's heat insulation began to fail. . . .) There had been some damage, of course. The rear-view mirrors, just outside the dome of transparent plastic that enclosed his head, were both snapped off, so that he could no longer see what lay behind him without twisting his neck. This was a trival mishap; far more serious was the fact that his radio antennas had been torn away by the impact. He could not call the ship, and the ship could not call him. All that came over the radio was a faint crackling, probably produced inside the set itself. He was absolutely alone, cut off from the rest of the human race.

It was a desperate situation, but there was one faint ray of hope. He was not, after all, completely helpless. Even if he could not use the pod's rockets—he guessed that the starboard motor had blown back and ruptured a fuel line; something

the designers said was impossible—he was still able to move.
He had his arms.

But which way should he crawl? He had lost all sense of
location, for though he had taken off from Mount Everest,
he might now be thousands of feet away from it. There were
no recognizable landmarks in his tiny world; the rapidly
sinking star of *Prometheus* was his best guide, and if he could
keep the ship in view he would be safe. It would only be a
matter of minutes before his absence was noted, if indeed
it had not been discovered already. Yet without radio, it
might take his colleagues a long time to find him; small
though Icarus was, its fifteen square miles of fantastically
rugged no man's land could provide an effective hiding place
for a ten-foot cylinder. It might take an hour to locate him—
which meant that he would have to keep ahead of the
murderous sunrise.

He slipped his fingers into the controls that worked his
mechanical limbs. Outside the pod, in the hostile vacuum
that surrounded him, his substitute arms came to life. They
reached down, thrust against the iron surface of the asteroid,
and levered the pod from the ground. Sherrard flexed them,
and the capsule jerked forward, like some weird, two-legged
insect . . . first the right arm, then the left, then the right . . .

It was less difficult than he had feared, and for the first
time he felt his confidence return. Though his mechanical
arms had been designed for light precision work, it needed
very little pull to set the capsule moving in this weightless
environment. The gravity of Icarus was ten thousand times
weaker than Earth's: Sherrard and his space-pod weighed
less than an ounce here, and once he had set himself in
motion he floated forward with an effortless, dreamlike ease.

Yet that very effortlessness had its dangers. He had traveled
several hundred yards, and was rapidly overhauling the sinking star of the *Prometheus,* when overconfidence betrayed
him. (Strange how quickly the mind could switch from one
extreme to the other; a few minutes ago he had been steeling
himself to face death—now he was wondering if he would
be late for dinner.) Perhaps the novelty of the movement,
so unlike anything he had ever attempted before, was
responsible for the catastrophe; or perhaps he was still suffer-
ing from the aftereffects of the crash.

Like all astronauts, Sherrard had learned to orientate himself in space, and had grown accustomed to living and working when the Earthly conceptions of up and down were

meaningless. On a world such as Icarus, it was necessary to pretend that there was a real, honest-to-goodness planet "beneath" your feet, and that when you moved you were traveling over a horizontal plain. If this innocent self-deception failed, you were headed for space vertigo.

The attack came without warning, as it usually did. Quite suddenly, Icarus no longer seemed to be beneath him, the stars no longer above. The Universe tilted through a right angle; he was moving straight *up* a vertical cliff, like a mountaineer scaling a rock face, and though Sherrard's reason told him that this was pure illusion, all his senses screamed that it was true. In a moment gravity must drag him off this sheer wall, and he would drop down mile upon endless mile until he smashed into oblivion.

Worse was to come; the false vertical was still swinging like a compass needle that had lost the pole. Now he was on the *underside* of an immense rocky roof, like a fly clinging to a ceiling; in another moment it would have become a wall again—but this time he would be moving straight down it, instead of up. . . .

He had lost all control over the pod, and the clammy sweat that had begun to dew his brow warned him that he would soon lose control over his body. There was only one thing to do; he clenched his eyes tightly shut, squeezed as far back as possible into the tiny closed world of the capsule, and pretended with all his might that the Universe outside did not exist. He did not even allow the slow, gentle crunch of his second crash to interfere with his self-hypnosis.

When he again dared to look outside, he found that the pod had come to rest against a large boulder. Its mechanical arms had broken the force of the impact, but at a cost that was more than he could afford to pay. Though the capsule was virtually weightless here, it still possessed its normal five hundred pounds of inertia, and it had been moving at perhaps four miles an hour. The momentum had been too much for the metal arms to absorb; one had snapped, and the other was hopelessly bent.

When he saw what had happened, Sherrard's first reaction was not despair, but anger. He had been so certain of success when the pod had started its glide across the barren face of Icarus. And now this, all through a moment of physical weakness! But space made no allowance for human frailties or emotions, and a man who did not accept that fact had no right to be here.

At least he had gained precious time in his pursuit of the ship; he had put an extra ten minutes, if not more, between himself and dawn. Whether that ten minutes would merely prolong the agony or whether it would give his shipmates the extra time they needed to find him, he would soon know.

Where were they? Surely they had started the search by now! He strained his eyes toward the brilliant star of the ship, hoping to pick out the fainter lights of space-pods moving toward him—but nothing else was visible against the slowly turning vault of heaven.

He had better look to his own resources, slender though they were. Only a few minutes were left before the *Prometheus* and her trailing lights would sink below the edge of the asteroid and leave him in darkness. It was true that the darkness would be all too brief, but before it fell upon him he might find some shelter against the coming day. This rock into which he had crashed, for example . . .

Yes, it would give some shade, until the sun was halfway up the sky. Nothing could protect him if it passed right overhead, but it was just possible that he might be in a latitude where the sun never rose far above the horizon at this season of Icarus' four-hundred-and-nine-day year. Then he might survive the brief period of daylight; that was his only hope, if the rescuers did not find him before dawn.

There went *Prometheus* and her lights, below the edge of the world. With her going, the now-unchallenged stars blazed forth with redoubled brilliance. More glorious than any of them—so lovely that even to look upon it almost brought tears to his eyes—was the blazing beacon of Earth, with its companion moon beside it. He had been born on one, and had walked on the other; would he see either again?

Strange that until now he had given no thought to his wife and children, and to all that he loved in the life that now seemed so far away. He felt a spasm of guilt, but it passed swiftly. The ties of affection were not weakened, even across the hundred million miles of space that now sundered him from his family. At this moment, they were simply irrelevant. He was now a primitive, self-centered animal fighting for his life, and his only weapon was his brain. In this conflict, there was no place for the heart; it would merely be a hindrance, spoiling his judgment and weakening his resolution.

And then he saw something that banished all thoughts of his distant home. Reaching up above the horizon behind him, spreading across the stars like a milky mist, was a faint and ghostly cone of phosphorescence. It was the herald of the sun —the beautiful, pearly phantom of the corona, visible on Earth only during the rare moments of a total eclipse. When the corona was rising, the sun would not be far behind, to smite this little land with fury.

Sherrard made good use of the warning. Now he could judge, with some accuracy, the exact point where the sun would rise. Crawling slowly and clumsily on the broken stumps of his metal arms, he dragged the capsule round to the side of the boulder that should give the greatest shade. He had barely reached it when the sun was upon him like a beast of prey, and his tiny world exploded into light.

He raised the dark filters inside his helmet, one thickness after another, until he could endure the glare. Except where the broad shadow of the boulder lay across the asteroid, it was like looking into a furnace. Every detail of the desolate land around him was revealed by that merciless light; there were no grays, only blinding whites and impenetrable blacks. All the shadowed cracks and hollows were pools of ink, while the higher ground already seemed to be on fire, as it caught the sun. Yet it was only a minute after dawn.

Now Sherrard could understand how the scorching heat of a billion summers had turned Icarus into a cosmic cinder, baking the rocks until the last traces of gas had bubbled out of them. Why should men travel, he asked himself bitterly, across the gulf of stars at such expense and risk—merely to land on a spinning slag heap? For the same reason, he knew, that they had once struggled to reach Everest and the Poles and the far places of the Earth—for the excitement of the body that was adventure, and the more enduring excitement of the mind that was discovery. It was an answer that gave him little consolation, now that he was about to be grilled like a joint on the turning spit of Icarus.

Already he could feel the first breath of heat upon his face. The boulder against which he was lying gave him protection from direct sunlight, but the glare reflected back at him from those blazing rocks only a few yards away was striking through the transparent plastic of the dome. It would grow swiftly more intense as the sun rose higher; he had even less time than he had thought, and with the knowledge came a kind of numb resignation that was beyond fear. He would wait—if he could—until the sunrise engulfed him and the capsule's cooling unit gave up the unequal struggle; then he would crack the pod and let the air gush out into the vacuum of space.

Nothing to do but to sit and think in the minutes that were left to him before his pool of shadow contracted. He did not try to direct his thoughts, but let them wander where they willed. How strange that he should be dying now, because back in the nineteen-forties—years before he was born—a man at Palomar had spotted a streak of light on a photographic plate, and had named it so appropriately after the boy who flew too near the sun.

One day, he supposed, they would build a monument here for him on this blistered plain. What would they inscribe upon it? "Here died Colin Sherrard, astronics engineer, in the cause of Science." That would be funny, for he had never understood half the things that the scientists were trying to do.

Yet some of the excitement of their discoveries had communicated itself to him. He remembered how the geologists had scraped away the charred skin of the asteroid, and had polished the metallic surface that lay beneath. It had been covered with a curious pattern of lines and scratches, like one of the abstract paintings of the Post-Picasso Decadents. But these lines had some meanings; they wrote the history of Icarus, though only a geologist could read it. They revealed, so Sherrard had been told, that this lump of iron and rock had not always floated alone in space. At some remote time in the past, it had been under enormous pressure—and that could mean only one thing. Billions of years ago it had been part of a much larger body, perhaps a planet like Earth. For some reason that planet had blown up, and Icarus and all the thousands of other asteroids were the fragments of that cosmic explosion.

Even at this moment, as the incandescent line of sunlight came closer, this was a thought that stirred his mind. What Sherrard was lying upon was the core of a world—perhaps a world that had once known life. In a strange, irrational way it comforted him to know that his might not be the only ghost to haunt Icarus until the end of time.

The helmet was misting up; that could only mean that the cooling unit was about to fail. It had done its work well; even now, though the rocks only a few yards away must be glowing a sullen red, the heat inside the capsule was not unendurable. When failure came, it would be sudden and catastrophic.

He reached for the red lever that would rob the sun of its prey—but before he pulled it, he would look for the last time upon Earth. Cautiously, he lowered the dark filters, adjusting them so that they still cut out the glare from the rocks, but no longer blocked his view of space.

The stars were faint now, dimmed by the advancing glow of the corona. And just visible over the boulder whose shield would soon fail him was a stub of crimson flame, a crooked finger of fire jutting from the edge of the sun itself. He had only seconds left.

There was the Earth, there was the moon. Good-by to them both, and to his friends and loved ones on each of them. While he was looking at the sky, the sunlight had begun to lick the base of the capsule, and he felt the first touch of fire. In a reflex as automatic as it was useless, he drew up his legs, trying to escape the advancing wave of heat.

What was that? A brilliant flash of light, infinitely brighter than any of the stars, had suddenly exploded overhead. Miles above him, a huge mirror was sailing across the sky, reflecting the sunlight as it slowly turned through space. Such a thing was utterly impossible; he was beginning to suffer from hallucinations, and it was time he took his leave. Already the sweat was pouring from his body, and in a few seconds the capsule would be a furnace.

He waited no longer, but pulled on the Emergency Release with all his waning strength, bracing himself at the same moment to face the end.

Nothing hppened; the lever wolud not move. He tugged it again and again before he realized that it was hopelessly jammed. There was no easy way out for him, no merciful death as the air gushed from his lungs. It was then, as the true terror of his situation struck home to him, that his nerve finally broke and he began to scream like a trapped animal.

When he heard Captain McClellan's voice speaking to him, thin but clear, he knew that it must be another hallucination. Yet some last remnant of discipline and self-control checked his screaming; he clenched his teeth and listened to that familiar, commanding voice.

"Sherrard! Hold on, man! We've got a fix on you—but keep shouting!"

"Here I am!" he cried, "but hurry, for God's sake! I'm burning!"

Deep down in what was left of his rational mind he realized what had happened. Some feeble ghost of a signal was leaking through the broken stubs of his antennas, and the searchers had heard his screams—as he was hearing their voices. That meant they must be very close indeed, and the knowledge gave him sudden strength.

He stared through the steaming plastic of the dome, looking once more for that impossible mirror in the sky. There it was again—and now he realized that the baffling perspectives of space had tricked his senses. The mirror was not miles away, nor was it huge. It was almost on top of him, and it was moving fast.

He was still shouting when it slid across the face of the rising sun, and its blessed shadow fell upon him like a cool wind that had blown out of the heart of winter, over leagues of snow and ice. Now that it was so close, he recognized it at once; it was merely a large metal-foil radiation screen, no doubt hastily snatched from one of the instrument sites. In the safety of its shadow, his friends had been searching for him.

A heavy-duty, two-man capsule was hovering overhead, holding the glittering shield in one set of arms and reaching for him with the other. Even through the misty dome and the haze of heat that still sapped his senses, he recognized Captain McClellan's anxious face, looking down at him from the other pod.

So this was what birth was like, for truly he had been reborn. He was too exhausted for gratitude—that would come later—but as he rose from the burning rocks his eyes sought and found the bright star of Earth. "Here I am," he said silently. "I'm coming back."

Back to enjoy and cherish all the beauties of the world he had thought was lost forever. No—not all of them.

He would never enjoy summer again.

Colombo   *April 1960*

Dog Star

When I heard Laika's frantic barking, my first reaction was one of annoyance. I turned over in my bunk and murmured sleepily, "Shut up, you silly bitch." That dreamy interlude lasted only a fraction of a second; then consciousness returned—and, with it, fear. Fear of loneliness, and fear of madness.

For a moment I dared not open my eyes; I was afraid of what I might see. Reason told me that no dog had ever set foot upon this world, that Laika was separated from me by a quarter of a million miles of space—and, far more irrevocably, five years of time.

"You've been dreaming," I told myself angrily. "Stop being a fool—open your eyes! You won't see anything except the glow of the wall paint."

That was right, of course. The tiny cabin was empty, the door tightly closed. I was alone with my memories, overwhelmed by the transcendental sadness that often comes when some bright dream fades into drab reality. The sense of loss was so desolating that I longed to return to sleep. It was well that I failed to do so, for at that moment sleep would have been death. But I did not know this for another five seconds, and during that eternity I was back on Earth, seeking what comfort I could from the past.

No one ever discovered Laika's origin, though the Observatory staff made a few enquiries and I inserted several advertisements in the Pasadena newspapers. I found her, a lost and lonely ball of fluff, huddled by the roadside one summer evening when I was driving up to Palomar. Though I have never liked dogs, or indeed any animals, it was impossible to leave this helpless little creature to the mercy of the passing cars. With some qualms, wishing that I had a pair of gloves, I picked her up and dumped her in the baggage compartment. I was not going to hazard the upholstery of my new '92 Vik,

70

and felt that she could do little damage there. In this, I was not altogether correct.

When I had parked the car at the Monastery—the astronomers' residential quarters, where I'd be living for the next week—I inspected my find without much enthusiasm. At that stage, I had intended to hand the puppy over to the janitor; but then it whimpered and opened its eyes. There was such an expression of helpless trust in them that—well, I changed my mind.

Sometimes I regretted that decision, though never for long. I had no idea how much trouble a growing dog could cause, deliberately and otherwise. My cleaning and repair bills soared; I could never be sure of finding an unravaged pair of socks or an unchewed copy of the *Astrophysical Journal*. But eventually Laika was both house-trained and Observatory-trained: she must have been the only dog ever to be allowed inside the two-hundred-inch dome. She would lie there quietly in the shadows for hours, while I was up in the cage making adjustments, quite content if she could hear my voice from time to time. The other astronomers became equally fond of her (it was old Dr. Anderson who suggested her name), but from the beginning she was my dog, and would obey no one else. Not that she would always obey me.

She was a beautiful animal, about ninety-five per cent Alsatian. It was that missing five per cent, I imagine, that led to her being abandoned. (I still feel a surge of anger when I think of it, but since I shall never know the facts, I may be jumping to false conclusions.) Apart from two dark patches over the eyes, most of her body was a smoky gray, and her coat was soft as silk. When her ears were pricked up, she looked incredibly intelligent and alert; sometimes I would be discussing spectral types or stellar evolution with my colleagues, and it would be hard to believe that she was not following the conversation.

Even now, I cannot understand why she became so attached to me, for I have made very few friends among human beings. Yet when I returned to the Observatory after an absence, she would go almost frantic with delight, bouncing around on her hind legs and putting her paws on my shoulders—which she could reach quite easily—all the while uttering small squeaks of joy which seemed highly inappropriate from so large a dog. I hated to leave her for more than a few days at a time, and though I could not take her with me on overseas trips, she accompanied me on most of my shorter journeys. She was with me when I drove north to attend that ill-fated seminar at Berkeley.

We were staying with university acquaintances; they had been polite about it, but obviously did not look forward to having a monster in the house. However, I assured them that Laika never gave the slightest trouble, and rather reluctantly they let her sleep in the living room. "You needn't worry about burglars tonight," I said. "We don't have any in Berkeley," they answered, rather coldly.

In the middle of the night, it seemed that they were wrong. I was awakened by a hysterical, high-pitched barking from Laika which I had heard only once before—when she had first seen a cow, and did not know what on earth to make of it. Cursing, I threw off the sheets and stumbled out into the darkness of the unfamiliar house. My main thought was to silence Laika before she roused my hosts—assuming that this was not already far too late. If there had been an intruder, he would certainly have taken flight by now. Indeed, I rather hoped that he had.

For a moment I stood beside the switch at the top of the stairs, wondering whether to throw it. Then I growled, "Shut up, Laika!" and flooded the place with light.

She was scratching frantically at the door, pausing from time to time to give that hysterical yelp. "If you want out," I said angrily, "there's no need for all that fuss." I went down, shot the bolt, and she took off into the night like a rocket.

It was very calm and still, with a waning Moon struggling to pierce the San Francisco fog. I stood in the luminous haze, looking out across the water to the lights of the city, waiting for Laika to come back so that I could chastise her suitably. I was still waiting when, for the second time in the twentieth century, the San Andreas Fault woke from its sleep.

Oddly enough, I was not frightened—at first. I can remember that two thoughts passed through my mind, in the moment before I realized the danger. Surely, I told myself, the geophysicists could have given us *some* warning. And then I found myself thinking, with great surprise, "I'd no idea that earthquakes make so much noise!"

It was about then that I knew that this was no ordinary quake; what happened afterward, I would prefer to forget. The Red Cross did not take me away until quite late the next morning, because I refused to leave Laika. As I looked at the shattered house containing the bodies of my friends, I knew that I owed my life to her; but the helicopter pilots could not be expected to understand that, and I cannot blame them for thinking that I was crazy, like so many of the others they had found wandering among the fires and the debris.

After that, I do not suppose we were ever apart for more than a few hours. I have been told—and I can well believe it —that I became less and less interested in human company, without being actively unsocial or misanthropic. Between them, the stars and Laika filled all my needs. We used to go for long walks together over the mountains; it was the happiest time I have ever known. There was only one flaw; I knew, though Laika could not, how soon it must end.

We had been planning the move for more than a decade. As far back as the nineteen-sixties it was realized that Earth was no place for an astronomical observatory. Even the small pilot instruments on the Moon had far outperformed all the telescopes peering through the murk and haze of the terrestrial atmosphere. The story of Mount Wilson, Palomar, Greenwich, and the other great names was coming to an end; they would still be used for training purposes, but the research frontier must move out into space.

I had to move with it; indeed, I had already been offered the post of Deputy Director, Farside Observatory. In a few months, I could hope to solve problems I had been working on for years. Beyond the atmosphere, I would be like a blind man who had suddenly been given sight.

It was utterly impossible, of course, to take Laika with me. The only animals on the Moon were those needed for experimental purposes; it might be another generation before pets were allowed, and even then it would cost a fortune to carry them there—and to keep them alive. Providing Laika with her usual two pounds of meat a day would, I calculated, take several times my quite comfortable salary.

The choice was simple and straightforward. I could stay on Earth and abandon my career. Or I could go to the Moon— and abandon Laika.

After all, she was only a dog. In a dozen years, she would be dead, while I should be reaching the peak of my profession. No sane man would have hesitated over the matter; yet I did hesitate, and if by now you do not understand why, no further words of mine can help.

In the end, I let matters go by default. Up to the very week I was due to leave, I had still made no plans for Laika. When Dr. Anderson volunteered to look after her, I accepted numbly, with scarcely a word of thanks. The old physicist and his wife had always been fond of her, and I am afraid that they considered me indifferent and heartless—when the truth was just the opposite. We went for one more walk together over the hills; then I delivered her silently to the Andersons, and did not see her again.

Take-off was delayed almost twenty-four hours, until a major flare storm had cleared the Earth's orbit; even so, the Van Allen belts were still so active that we had to make our exit through the North Polar Gap. It was a miserable flight; apart from the usual trouble with weightlessness, we were all groggy with antiradiation drugs. The ship was already over Farside before I took much interest in the proceedings, so I missed the sight of Earth dropping below the horizon. Nor was I really sorry; I wanted no reminders, and intended to think only of the future. Yet I could not shake off that feeling of guilt; I had deserted someone who loved and trusted me, and was no better than those who had abandoned Laika when she was a puppy, beside the dusty road to Palomar.

The news that she was dead reached me a month later. There was no reason that anyone knew; the Andersons had done their best, and were very upset. She had just lost interest in living, it seemed. For a while, I think I did the same; but work is a wonderful anodyne, and my program was just getting under way. Though I never forgot Laika, in a little while the memory ceased to hurt.

Then why had it come back to haunt me, five years later, on the far side of the Moon? I was searching my mind for the reason when the metal building around me quivered as if under the impact of a heavy blow. I reacted without thinking, and was already closing the helmet of my emergency suit when the foundations slipped and the wall tore open with a short-lived scream of escaping air. Because I had automatically pressed the General Alarm button, we lost only two men, despite the fact that the tremor—the worst ever recorded on Farside—cracked all three of the Observatory's pressure domes.

It is hardly necessary for me to say that I do not believe in the supernatural; everything that happened has a perfectly rational explanation, obvious to any man with the slightest knowledge of psychology. In the second San Francisco earthquake, Laika was not the only dog to sense approaching disaster; many such cases were reported. And on Farside, my own memories must have given me that heightened awareness, when my never-sleeping subconscious detected the first faint vibrations from within the Moon.

The human mind has strange and labyrinthine ways of going about its business; it knew the signal that would most swiftly rouse me to the knowledge of danger. There is nothing more to it than that; though in a sense one could say that Laika woke me on both occasions, there is no mystery about it, no miraculous warning across the gulf that neither man nor dog can ever bridge.

Of that I am sure, if I am sure of anything. Yet sometimes I wake now, in the silence of the Moon, and wish that the dream could have lasted a few seconds longer—so that I could have looked just once more into those luminous brown eyes, brimming with an unselfish, undemanding love I have found nowhere else on this or on any other world.

Colombo   *April 1961*

Hide and Seek

We were walking back through the woods when Kingman saw the gray squirrel. Our bag was a small but varied one—three grouse, four rabbits (one, I am sorry to say, an infant in arms) and a couple of pigeons. And contrary to certain dark forecasts, both the dogs were still alive.

The squirrel saw us at the same moment. It knew that it was marked for immediate execution as a result of the damage it had done to the trees on the estate, and perhaps it had lost close relatives to Kingman's gun. In three leaps it had reached the base of the nearest tree, and vanished behind it in a flicker of gray. We saw its face once more, appearing for a moment round the edge of its shield a dozen feet from the ground; but though we waited, with guns leveled hopefully at various branches, we never saw it again.

Kingman was very thoughtful as we walked back across the lawn to the magnificent old house. He said nothing as we handed our victims to the cook—who received them without much enthusiasm—and only emerged from his reverie when we were sitting in the smoking room and he remembered his duties as a host.

"That tree-rat," he said suddenly (he always called them "tree-rats," on the grounds that people were too sentimental to shoot the dear little squirrels), "it reminded me of a very peculiar experience that happened shortly before I retired. Very shortly indeed, in fact."

"I thought it would," said Carson dryly. I gave him a glare: he'd been in the Navy and had heard Kingman's stories before, but they were still new to me.

"Of course," Kingman remarked, slightly nettled, "if you'd rather I didn't . . ."

"Do go on," I said hastily. "You've made me curious. What connection there can possibly be between a gray squirrel and the Second Jovian War I can't imagine."

Kingman seemed mollified.

"I think I'd better change some names," he said thoughtfully, "but I won't alter the places. The story begins about a million kilometers sunward of Mars. . . ."

K.15 was a military intelligence operative. It gave him considerable pain when unimaginative people called him a spy, but at the moment he had much more substantial grounds for complaint. For some days now a fast enemy cruiser had been coming up astern, and though it was flattering to have the undivided attention of such a fine ship and so many highly trained men, it was an honor that K.15 would willingly have forgone.

What made the situation doubly annoying was the fact that his friends would be meeting him off Mars in about twelve hours, aboard a ship quite capable of dealing with a mere cruiser—from which you will gather that K.15 was a person of some importance. Unfortunately, the most optimistic calculation showed that the pursuers would be within accurate gun range in six hours. In some six hours five minutes, therefore, K.15 was likely to occupy an extensive and still expanding volume of space.

There might just be time for him to land on Mars, but that would be one of the worst things he could do. It would certainly annoy the aggressively neutral Martians, and the political complications would be frightful. Moreover, if his friends *had* to come down to the planet to rescue him, it would cost them more than ten kilometers a second in fuel—most of their operational reserve.

He had only one advantage, and that a very dubious one. The commander of the cruiser might guess that he was heading for a rendezvous, but he would not know how close it was or how large was the ship that was coming to meet him. If he could keep alive for only twelve hours, he would be safe. The "if" was a somewhat considerable one.

K.15 looked moodily at his charts, wondering if it was worthwhile to burn the rest of his fuel in a final dash. But a dash to where? He would be completely helpless then, and the pursuing ship might still have enough in her tanks to catch him as he flashed outward into the empty darkness, beyond all hope of rescue—passing his friends as they came sunward at a relative speed so great that they could do nothing to save him.

With some people, the shorter the expectation of life, the more sluggish are the mental processes. They seem hypnotized by the approach of death, so resigned to their fate that they do nothing to avoid it. K.15, on the other hand, found that his mind worked better in such a desperate emergency. It began to work now as it had seldom done before.

Commander Smith—the name will do as well as any other —of the cruiser *Doradus* was not unduly surprised when K.15 began to decelerate. He had half expected the spy to land on Mars, on the principle that internment was better than annihilation, but when the plotting room brought the news that the little scout ship was heading for Phobos, he felt completely baffled. The inner moon was nothing but a jumble of rock some twenty kilometers across, and not even the economical Martians had ever found any use for it. K.15 must be pretty desperate if he thought it was going to be of any greater value to him.

The tiny scout had almost come to rest when the radar operator lost it against the mass of Phobos. During the braking maneuver, K.15 had squandered most of his lead and the *Doradus* was now only minutes away—though she was now beginning to decelerate lest she overrun him. The cruiser was scarcely three thousand kilometers from Phobos when she came to a complete halt: of K.15's ship, there was still no sign. It should be easily visible in the telescopes, but it was probably on the far side of the little moon.

It reappeared only a few minutes later, traveling under full thrust on a course directly away from the sun. It was accelerating at almost five gravities—and it had broken its radio silence. An automatic recorder was broadcasting over and over again this interesting message:

"I have landed on Phobos and am being attacked by a Z-class cruiser. Think I can hold out until you come, but hurry."

The message wasn't even in code, and it left Commander Smith a sorely puzzled man. The assumption that K.15 was still aboard the ship and that the whole thing was a ruse was just a little too naïve. But it might be a double-bluff: the message had obviously been left in plain language so that he would receive it and be duly confused. He could afford neither the time nor the fuel to chase the scout if K.15 really had landed. It was clear that reinforcements were on the way, and the sooner he left the vicinity the better. The phrase "Think I can hold out until you come" might be a piece of sheer impertinence, or it might mean that help was very near indeed.

Then K.15's ship stopped blasting. It had obviously exhausted its fuel, and was doing a little better than six kilometers a second away from the sun. K.15 *must* have landed, for his ship was now speeding helplessly out of the Solar System. Commander Smith didn't like the message it was broadcasting, and guessed that it was running into the track of an approaching warship at some indefinite distance, but there was nothing to be done about that. The *Doradus* began to move toward Phobos, anxious to waste no time.

On the face of it, Commander Smith seemed the master of the situation. His ship was armed with a dozen heavy guided missiles and two turrets of electromagnetic guns. Against him was one man in a space suit, trapped on a moon only twenty kilometers across. It was not until Commander Smith had his first good look at Phobos, from a distance of less than a hundred kilometers, that he began to realize that, after all, K.15 might have a few cards up his sleeve.

To say that Phobos has a diameter of twenty kilometers, as the astronomy books invariably do, is highly misleading. The word "diameter" implies a degree of symmetry which Phobos most certainly lacks. Like those other lumps of cosmic slag, the asteroids, it is a shapeless mass of rock floating in space with, of course, no hint of an atmosphere and not much more gravity. It turns on its axis once every seven hours thirty-nine minutes, thus keeping the same face always to Mars—which is so close that appreciably less than half the planet is visible, the poles being below the curve of the horizon. Beyond this, there is very little more to be said about Phobos.

K.15 had no time to enjoy the beauty of the crescent world filling the sky above him. He had thrown all the equipment he could carry out of the air lock, set the controls, and jumped. As the little ship went flaming out toward the stars he watched it go with feelings he did not care to analyze. He had burned his boats with a vengeance, and he could only hope that the oncoming battleship would intercept the radio message as the empty vessel went racing by into nothingness. There was also a faint possibility that the enemy cruiser might go in pursuit, but that was rather too much to hope for.

He turned to examine his new home. The only light was the ocher radianec of Mars, since the sun was below the horizon, but that was quite sufficient for his purpose and he could see very well. He stood in the center of an irregular plain about two kilometers across, surrounded by low hills over which he could leap rather easily if he wished. There was a story he remembered reading long ago about a man who had accidentally jumped off Phobos: that wasn't quite possible—though it was on Deimos—because the escape velocity was still about ten meters a second. But unless he was careful, he might easily find himself at such a height that it would take hours to fall back to the surface—and that would be fatal. For K.15's plan was a simple one: he must remain as close to the surface of Phobos as possible—*and diametrically opposite the cruiser.* The *Doradus* could then fire all her armament against the twenty kilometers of rock, and he wouldn't even feel the concussion. There were only two serious dangers, and one of these did not worry him greatly.

To the layman, knowing nothing of the finer details of astronautics, the plan would have seemed quiet suicidal. The *Doradus* was armed with the latest in ultrascientific weapons: moreover, the twenty kilometers which separated her from her prey represented less than a second's flight at maximum speed. But Commander Smith knew better, and was already feeling rather unhappy. He realized, only too well, that of all the machines of transport man has ever invented, a cruiser of space is far and away the least maneuverable. It was a simple fact that K.15 could make half a dozen circuits of his little world while her commander was persuading the *Doradus* to make even one.

There is no need to go into technical details, but those who are still unconvinced might like to consider these elementary facts. A rocket-driven spaceship can, obviously, only accelerate along its major axis—that is, "forward." Any deviation from a straight course demands a physical turning of the ship, so that the motors can blast in another direction. Everyone knows that this is done by internal gyros or tangential steering jets, but very few people know just how long this simple maneuver takes. The average cruiser, fully fueled, has a mass of two or three thousand tons, which does not make for rapid footwork. But things are even worse than this, for it isn't the mass, but the moment of inertia that matters here—and since a cruiser is a long, thin object, its moment of inertia is slightly colossal. The sad fact remains (though it is seldom mentioned by astronautical engineers) that it takes a good ten minutes to rotate a spaceship through one hundred and eighty degrees, with gyros of any reasonable size. Control jets aren't much quicker, and in any case their use is restricted because the rotation they produce is permanent and they are liable to leave the ship spinning like a slow-motion pinwheel, to the annoyance of all inside.

In the ordinary way, these disadvantages are not very grave. One has millions of kilometers and hundreds of hours in which to deal with such minor matters as a change in the ship's orientation. It is definitely against the rules to move in ten-kilometer-radius circles, and the commander of the *Doradus* felt distinctly aggrieved. K.15 wasn't playing fair.

At the same moment that resourceful individual was taking stock of the situation, which might very well have been worse. He had reached the hills in three jumps and felt less naked than he had out in the open plain. The food and equipment he had taken from the ship he had hidden where he hoped he could find it again, but since his suit could keep him alive for over a day that was the least of his worries. The small packet that was the cause of all the trouble was still with him, in one of those numerous hiding places a well-designed space suit affords.

There was an exhilarating loneliness about his mountain eyrie, even though he was not quite as lonely as he would have wished. Forever fixed in his sky, Mars was waning almost visibly as Phobos swept above the night side of the planet. He could just make out the lights of some of the Martian cities, gleaming pin points marking the junctions of the invisible canals. All else was stars and silence and a line of jagged peaks so close it seemed he could almost touch them. Of the *Doradus* there was still no sign. She was presumably carrying out a careful telescopic examination of the sun-lighted side of Phobos.

Mars was a very useful clock: when it was half full the sun would rise and, very probably, so would the *Doradus*. But she might approach from some quite unexpected quarter: she might even—and this was the one real danger—she might even have landed a search party.

This was the first possibility that had occurred to Commander Smith when he saw just what he was up against. Then he realized that the surface area of Phobos was over a thousand square kilometers and that he could not spare more than ten men from his crew to make a search of that jumbled wilderness. Also, K.15 would certainly be armed.

Considering the weapons which the *Doradus* carried, this last objection might seem singularly pointless. It was very far from being so. In the ordinary course of business, side arms and other portable weapons are as much use to a space-cruiser as are cutlasses and crossbows. The *Doradus* happened, quite by chance—and against regulations at that—to carry one automatic pistol and a hundred rounds of ammunition. Any search party would therefore consist of a group of unarmed men looking for a well-concealed and very desperate individual who could pick them off at his leisure. K.15 was breaking the rules again.

The terminator of Mars was now a perfectly straight line, and at almost the same moment the sun came up, not so much like thunder as like a salvo of atomic bombs. K.15 adjusted the filters of his visor and decided to move. It was safer to stay out of the sunlight, not only because here he was less likely to be detected in the shadow but also because his eyes would be much more sensitive there. He had only a pair of binoculars to help him, whereas the *Doradus* would carry an electronic telescope of twenty-centimeter aperture at least.

It would be best, K.15 decided, to locate the cruiser if he could. It might be a rash thing to do, but he would feel much happier when he knew exactly where she was and could watch her movements. He could then keep just below the horizon, and the glare of the rockets would give him ample warning of any impending move. Cautiously launching himself along an almost horizontal trajectory, he began the circumnavigation of his world.

The narrowing crescent of Mars sank below the horizon until only one vast horn reared itself enigmatically against the stars. K.15 began to feel worried: there was still no sign of the *Doradus*. But this was hardly surprising, for she was painted black as night and might be a good hundred kilometers away in space. He stopped, wondering if he had done the right thing after all. Then he noticed that something quite large was eclipsing the stars almost vertically overhead, and was moving swiftly even as he watched. His heart stopped for a moment: then he was himself again, analyzing the situation and trying to discover how he had made so disastrous a mistake.

It was some time before he realized that the black shadow slipping across the sky was not the cruiser at all, but something almost equally deadly. It was far smaller, and far nearer, than he had at first thought. The *Doradus* had sent her television-homing guided missiles to look for him.

This was the second danger he had feared, and there was nothing he could do about it except to remain as inconspicuous as possible. The *Doradus* now had many eyes searching for him, but these auxiliaries had very severe limitations. They had been built to look for sunlit spaceships against a background of stars, not to search for a man hiding in a dark jungle of rock. The definition of their television systems was low, and they could only see in the forward direction.

There were rather more men on the chessboard now, and the game was a little deadlier, but his was still the advantage.

The torpedo vanished into the night sky. As it was traveling on a nearly straight course in this low-gravitational field, it would soon be leaving Phobos behind, and K.15 waited for what he knew must happen. A few minutes later, he saw a brief stabbing of rocket exhausts and guessed that the projectile was swinging slowly back on its course. At almost the same moment he saw another flare far away in the opposite quarter of the sky, and wondered just how many of these infernal machines were in action. From what he knew of Z-class cruisers—which was a good deal more than he should—there were four missile-control channels, and they were probably all in use.

He was suddenly struck by an idea so brilliant that he was quite sure it couldn't possibly work. The radio on his suit was a tunable one, covering an unusually wide band, and somewhere not afar away the *Doradus* was pumping out power on everything from a thousand megacycles upward. He switched on the receiver and began to explore.

It came in quickly—the raucous whine of a pulse transmitter not far away. He was probably only picking up a subharmonic, but that was quite good enough. It D/F'ed sharply, and for the first time K.15 allowed himself to make long-range plans about the future. The *Doradus* had betrayed herself: as long as she operated her missiles, he would know exactly where she was.

He moved cautiously forward toward the transmitter. To his surprise the signal faded, then increased sharply again. This puzzled him until he realized that he must be moving through a diffraction zone. Its width might have told him something useful if he had been a good-enough physicist, but he couldn't imagine what.

The *Doradus* was hanging about five kilometers above the surface, in full sunlight. Her "nonreflecting" paint was overdue for renewal, and K.15 could see her clearly. Since he was still in darkness, and the shadow line was moving away from him, he decided that he was as safe here as anywhere. He settled down comfortably so that he could just see the cruiser and waited, feeling fairly certain that none of the guided projectiles would come so near the ship. By now, he calculated, the commander of the *Doradus* must be getting pretty mad. He was perfectly correct.

After an hour, the cruiser began to heave herself round with all the grace of a bogged hippopotamus. K.15 guessed what was happening. Commander Smith was going to have a look at the antipodes, and was preparing for the perilous fifty-kilometer journey. He watched very carefully to see the orientation the ship was adopting, and when she came to rest again was relieved to see that she was almost broadside to him. Then, with a series of jerks that could not have been very enjoyable aboard, the cruiser began to move down to the horizon. K.15 followed her at a comfortable walking pace—if one could use the phrase—reflecting that this was a feat very few people had ever performed. He was particularly careful not to overtake her on one of his kilometer-long glides, and kept a close watch for any missiles that might be coming up astern.

It took the *Doradus* nearly an hour to cover the fifty kilometers. This, as K.15 amused himself by calculating, represented considerably less than a thousandth of her normal speed. Once she found herself going off into space at a tangent, and rather than waste time turning end over end again fired off a salvo of shells to reduce speed. But she made it at last, and K.15 settled down for another vigil, wedged between two rocks where he could just see the cruiser and he was quite sure she couldn't see him. It occurred to him that by this time Commander Smith might have grave doubts as to whether he really was on Phobos at all, and he felt like firing off a signal flare to reassure him. However, he resisted the temptation.

There would be little point in describing the events of the next ten hours, since they differed in no important detail from those that had gone before. The *Doradus* made three other moves, and K.15 stalked her with the care of a big-game hunter following the spoor of some elephantine beast. Once, when she would have led him out into full sunlight, he let her fall below the horizon until he could only just pick up her signals. But most of the time he kept her just visible, usually low down behind some convenient hill.

Once a torpedo exploded some kilometers away, and K.15 guessed that some exasperated operator had seen a shadow he didn't like—or else that a technician had forgotten to switch off a proximity fuse. Otherwise nothing happened to enliven the proceedings: in fact, the whole affair was becoming rather boring. He almost welcomed the sight of an occasional guided missile drifting inquisitively overhead, for he did not believe that they could see him if he remained motionless and in reasonable cover. If he could have stayed on the part of Phobos exactly opposite the cruiser he would have been safe even from these, he realized, since the ship would have no control there in the moon's radio-shadow. But he could think of no reliable way in which he could be sure of staying in the safety zone if the cruiser moved again.

The end came very abruptly. There was a sudden blast of steering jets, and the cruiser's main drive burst forth in all its power and splendor. In seconds the *Doradus* was shrinking sunward, free at last, thankful to leave, even in defeat, this miserable lump of rock that had so annoyingly balked her of her legitimate prey. K.15 knew what had happened, and a great sense of peace and relaxation swept over him. In the radar room of the cruiser, someone had seen an echo of disconcerting amplitude approaching with altogether excessive speed. K.15 now had only to switch on his suit beacon and to wait. He could even afford the luxury of a cigarette.

"Quite an interesting story," I said, "and I see now how it ties up with that squirrel. But it does raise one or two queries in my mind."

"Indeed?" said Rupert Kingman politely.

I always like to get to the bottom of things, and I knew that my host had played a part in the Jovian War about which he very seldom spoke. I decided to risk a long shot in the dark.

"May I ask how you happen to know so much about this unorthodox military engagement? It isn't possible, is it, that *you* were K.15?"

There was an odd sort of strangling noise from Carson. Then Kingman said, quite calmly: "No, I wasn't."

He got to his feet and went off toward the gun room.

"If you'll excuse me a moment, I'm going to have another shot at that tree-rat. Maybe I'll get him this time." Then he was gone.

Carson looked at me as if to say: "This is another house you'll never be invited to again." When our host was out of earshot he remarked in a coldly cynical voice:

"You've done it. What did you have to say that for?"

"Well, it seemed a safe geuss. How else could he have known all that?"

"As a matter of fact, I believe he met K.15 after the War: they must have had an interesting conversation together. But I thought you knew that Rupert was retired from the service with only the rank of lieutenant commander. The Court of Inquiry could never see his point of view. After all, it just wasn't reasonable that the commander of the fastest ship in the Fleet couldn't catch a man in a space suit."

London   *August 1948*

Out of the Sun

If you have only lived on Earth, you have never seen the sun. Of course, we could not look at it directly, but only through dense filters that cut its rays down to endurable brilliance. It hung there forever above the low, jagged hills to the west of the Observatory, neither rising nor setting, yet moving around a small circle in the sky during the eighty-eight-day year of our little world. For it is not quite true to say that Mercury keeps the same face always turned toward the sun; it wobbles slightly on its axis, and there is a narrow twilight belt which knows such terrestrial commonplaces as dawn and sunset.

We were on the edge of the twilight zone, so that we could take advantage of the cool shadows yet could keep the sun under continuous surveillance as it hovered there above the hills. It was a full-time job for fifty astronomers and other assorted scientists; when we've kept it up for a hundred years or so, we may know something about the small star that brought life to Earth.

There wasn't a single band of solar radiation that someone at the Observatory had not made a life's study and was watching like a hawk. From the far X rays to the longest of radio waves, we had set our traps and snares; as soon as the sun thought of something new, we were ready for it. So we imagined. . . .

The sun's flaming heart beats in a slow, eleven-year rhythm, and we were near the peak of the cycle. Two of the greatest spots ever recorded—each of them large enough to swallow a hundred Earths—had drifted across the disk like great black funnels piercing deeply into the turbulent outer layers of the sun. They were black, of course, only by contrast with the brilliance all around them; even their dark, cool cores were hotter and brighter than an electric arc. We had just watched the second of them disappear around the edge of the disk, wondering if it would survive to reappear two weeks later, when something blew up on the equator.

It was not too spectacular at first, partly because it was almost exactly beneath us—at the precise center of the sun's disk—and so was merged into all the activity around it. If it had been near the edge of the sun, and thus projected against the background of space, it would have been truly awe-inspiring.

Imagine the simultaneous explosion of a million H bombs. You can't? Nor can anyone else—but that was the sort of thing we were watching climb up toward us at hundreds of miles a second, straight out of the sun's spinning equator. At first it formed a narrow jet, but it was quickly frayed around the edges by the magnetic and gravitational forces that were fighting against it. The central core kept right on, and it was soon obvious that it had escaped from the sun completely and was headed out into space—with us as its first target.

Though this had happened half a dozen times before, it was always exciting. It meant that we could capture some of the very substance of the sun as it went hurtling past in a great cloud of electrified gas. There was no danger; by the time it reached us it would be far too tenuous to do any damage, and, indeed, it would take sensitive instruments to detect it at all.

One of those instruments was the Observatory's radar, which was in continual use to map the invisible ionized layers that surround the sun for millions of miles. This was my department; as soon as there was any hope of picking up the oncoming cloud against the solar background, I aimed my giant radio mirror toward it.

It came in sharp and clear on the long-range screen—a vast, luminous island still moving outward from the sun at hundreds of miles a second. At this distance it was impossible to see its finer details, for my radar waves were taking minutes to make the round trip and to bring me back the information they were presenting on the screen. Even at its speed of not far short of a million miles an hour, it would be almost two days before the escaping prominence reached the orbit of Mercury and swept past us toward the outer planets. But neither Venus nor Earth would record its passing, for they were nowhere near its line of flight.

The hours drifted by; the sun had settled down after the immense convulsion that had shot so many millions of tons of its substance into space, never to return. The aftermath of that eruption was now a slowly twisting and turning cloud a hundred times the size of Earth, and soon it would be close enough for the short-range radar to reveal its finer structure.

Despite all the years I have been in the business, it still gives me a thrill to watch that line of light paint its picture on the screen as it spins in synchronism with the narrow beam of radio waves from the transmitter. I sometimes think of myself as a blind man exploring the space around him with a stick that may be a hundred million miles in length. For Man is truly blind to the things I study; these great clouds of ionized gas moving far out from the sun are completely invisible to the eye and even to the most sensitive of photographic plates. They are ghosts that briefly haunt the Solar System during the few hours of their existence; if they did not reflect our radar waves or disturb our magnetometers, we should never know that they were there.

The picture on the screen looked not unlike a photograph of a spiral nebula, for as the cloud slowly rotated it trailed ragged arms of gas for ten thousand miles around it. Or it might have been a terrestrial hurricane that I was watching from above as it spun through the atmosphere of Earth. The internal structure was extremely complicated, and was changing minute by minute beneath the action of forces which we have never fully understood. Rivers of fire were flowing in curious paths under what could only be the influence of electric fields; but why were they appearing from nowhere and disappearing again as if matter was being created and destroyed? And what were those gleaming nodules, larger than the Moon, that were being swept along like boulders before a flood?

Now it was less than a million miles away; it would be upon us in little more than an hour. The automatic cameras were recording every complete sweep of the radar scan, storing up evidence which was to keep us arguing for years. The magnetic disturbance riding ahead of the cloud had already reached us; indeed, there was hardly an instrument in the Observatory that was not reacting in some way to the onrushing apparition.

I switched to the short-range scanner, and the image of the cloud expanded so enormously that only its central portion was on the screen. At the same time I began to change frequency, tuning across the spectrum to differentiate among the various levels. The shorter the wave length, the farther you can penetrate into a layer of ionized gas; by this technique I hoped to get a kind of X-ray picture of the cloud's interior.

It seemed to change before my eyes as I sliced down

through the tenuous outer envelope with its trailing arms, and approached the denser core. "Denser," of course, was a purely relative word; by terrestrial standards even its most closely packed regions were still a fairly good vacuum. I had almost reached the limit of my frequency band, and could shorten the wave length no farther, when I noticed the curious, tight little echo not far from the center of the screen.

It was oval, and much more sharp-edged than the knots of gas we had watched adrift in the cloud's fiery streams. Even in that first glimpse, I knew that here was something very strange and outside all previous records of solar phenomena. I watched it for a dozen scans of the radar beam, then called my assistant away from the radio-spectrograph, with which he was analyzing the velocities of the swirling gas as it spun toward us.

"Look, Don," I asked him, "have you ever seen anything like that?"

"No," he answered after a careful examination. "What holds it together? It hasn't changed its shape for the last two minutes."

"That's what puzzles me. Whatever it is it should have started to break up by now, with all that disturbance going on around it. But it seems as stable as ever."

"How big would you say it is?"

I switched on the calibration grid and took a quick reading.

"It's about five hundred miles long, and half that in width."

"Is this the largest picture you can get?"

"I'm afraid so. We'll have to wait until it's closer before we can see what makes it tick."

Don gave a nervous little laugh.

"This is crazy," he said, "but do you know something? I feel as if I'm looking at an amoeba under a microscope."

I did not answer; for, with what I can only describe as a sensation of intellectual vertigo, exactly the same thought had entered my mind.

We forgot about the rest of the cloud, but luckily the automatic cameras kept up their work and no important observations were lost. From now on we had eyes only for that sharp-edged lens of gas that was growing minute by minute as it raced toward us. When it was no farther away than is the Moon from Earth, it began to show the first signs of its internal structure, revealing a curious mottled appearance that was never quite the same on two successive sweeps of the scanner.

By now, half the Observatory staff had joined us in the radar room, yet there was complete silence as the oncoming enigma grew swiftly across the screen. It was coming straight toward us; in a few minutes it would hit Mercury somewhere in the center of the daylight side, and that would be the end of it—whatever it was. From the moment we obtained our first really detailed view until the screen became blank again could not have been more than five minutes; for every one of us, that five minutes will haunt us all our lives.

We were looking at what seemed to be a translucent oval, its interior laced with a network of almost invisible lines. Where the lines crossed there appeared to be tiny, pulsing nodes of light; we could never be quite sure of their existence because the radar took almost a minute to paint the complete picture on the screen—and between each sweep the object moved several thousand miles. There was no doubt, however, that the network itself existed; the cameras settled any arguments about that.

So strong was the impression that we were looking at a solid object that I took a few moments off from the radar screen and hastily focused one of the optical telescopes on the sky. Of course, there was nothing to be seen—no sign of anything silhouetted against the sun's pock-marked disk. This was a case where vision failed completely and only the electrical senses of the radar were of any use. The thing that was coming toward us out of the sun was as transparent as air—and far more tenuous.

As those last moments ebbed away, I am quite sure that every one of us had reached the same conclusion—and was waiting for someone to say it first. What we were seeing was impossible, yet the evidence was there before our eyes. We were looking at life, where no life could exist. . . .

Th eruption had hurled the thing out of its normal environment, deep down in the flaming atmosphere of the sun. It was a miracle that it had survived its journey through space; already it must be dying, as the forces that controlled its huge, invisible body lost their hold over the electrified gas which was the only substance it possessed.

Today, now that I have run through those films a hundred times, the idea no longer seems so strange to me. For what is life but organized energy? Does it matter *what* form that energy takes—whether it is chemical as we know it on Earth, or purely electrical, as it seemed to be here? Only the pattern is important; the substance itself is of no significance. But at the time I did not think of this; I was conscious only of a vast and overwhelming wonder as I watched this creature of the sun live out the final moments of its existence.

Was it intelligent? Could it understand the strange doom that had befallen it? There are a thousand such questions that may never be answered. It is hard to see how a creature born in the fires of the sun itself could know anything of the external Universe, or could even sense the existence of something as unutterably cold as rigid nongaseous matter. The living island that was falling upon us from space could never have conceived, however intelligent it might be, of the world it was so swiftly approaching.

Now it filled our sky—and perhaps, in those last few seconds, it knew that something strange was ahead of it. It may have sensed the far-flung magnetic field of Mercury, or felt the tug of our little world's gravitational pull. For it had begun to change; the luminous lines that must have been what passed for its nervous system were clumping together in new patterns, and I would have given much to know their meaning. It may be that I was looking into the brain of a mindless beast in its last convulsion of fear—or of a godlike being making its peace with the Universe.

Then the radar screen was empty, wiped clean during a single scan of the beam. The creature had fallen below our horizon, and was hidden from us now by the curve of the planet. Far out in the burning dayside of Mercury, in the inferno where only a dozen men have ever ventured and fewer still come back alive, it smashed silently and invisibly against the seas of molten metal, the hills of slowly moving lava. The mere impact could have meant nothing to such an entity; what it could not endure was its first contact with the inconceivable cold of solid matter.

Yes, *cold*. It had descended upon the hottest spot in the Solar System, where the temperature never falls below seven hundred degrees Fahrenheit and sometimes approaches a thousand. And that was far, far colder to it than the antarctic winter would be to a naked man.

We did not see it die, out there in the freezing fire; it was beyond the reach of our instruments now, and none of them recorded its end. Yet every one of us knew when that moment came, and that is why we are not interested when those who have seen only the films and tapes tell us that we were watching some purely natural phenomenon.

How can one explain what we felt, in that last moment

when half our little world was enmeshed in the dissolving tendrils of that huge but immaterial brain? I can only say that it was a soundless cry of anguish, a death pang that seeped into our minds without passing through the gateways of the senses. Not one of us doubted then, or has ever doubted since, that he had witnessed the passing of a giant.

We may have been both the first and the last of all men to see so mighty a fall. Whatever *they* may be, in their unimaginable world within the sun, our paths and theirs may never cross again. It is hard to see how we can ever make contact with them, even if their intelligence matches ours.

And does it? It may be well for us if we never know the answer. Perhaps they have been living there inside the sun since the Universe was born, and have climbed to peaks of wisdom that we shall never scale. The future may be theirs, not ours; already they may be talking across the light-years to their cousins in other stars.

One day they may discover us, by whatever strange senses they possess, as we circle around their mighty, ancient home, proud of our knowledge and thinking ourselves lords of creation. They may not like what they find, for to them we should be no more than maggots, crawling upon the skins of worlds too cold to cleanse themselves from the corruption of organic life.

And then, if they have the power, they will do what they consider necessary. The sun will put forth its strength and lick the faces of its children; and thereafter the planets will go their way once more as they were in the beginning—clean and bright . . . and sterile.

Colombo   *April 1957*

The Wall of Darkness

Many and strange are the universes that drift like bubbles in the foam upon the River of Time. Some—a very few—move against or athwart its current; and fewer still are those that lie forever beyond its reach, knowing nothing of the future or the past. Shervane's tiny cosmos was not one of these: its strangeness was of a different order. It held one world only—the planet of Shervane's race—and a single star, the great sun Trilorne that brought it life and light.

Shervane knew nothing of night, for Trilorne was always high above the horizon, dipping near it only in the long months of winter. Beyond the borders of the Shadow Land, it was true, there came a season when Trilorne disappeared below the edge of the world, and a darkness fell in which nothing could live. But even then the darkness was not absolute, though there were no stars to relieve it.

Alone in its little cosmos, turning the same face always toward its solitary sun, Shervane's world was the last and the strangest jest of the Maker of the Stars.

Yet as he looked across his father's lands, the thoughts that filled Shervane's mind were those that any human child might have known. He felt awe, and curiosity, and a little fear, and above all a longing to go out into the great world before him. These things he was still too young to do, but the ancient house was on the highest ground for many miles and he could look far out over the land that would one day be his. When he turned to the north, with Trilorne shining full upon his face, he could see many miles away the long line of mountains that curved around to the right, rising higher and higher, until they disappeared behind him in the direction of the Shadow Land. One day, when he was older, he would go through those mountains along the pass that led to the great lands of the east.

On his left was the ocean, only a few miles away, and sometimes Shervane could hear the thunder of the waves as

94

they fought and tumbled on the gently sloping sands. No one knew how far the ocean reached. Ships had set out across it, sailing northward while Trilorne rose higher and higher in the sky and the heat of its rays grew ever more intense. Long before the great sun had reached the zenith, they had been forced to return. If the mythical Fire Lands did indeed exist, no man could ever hope to reach their burning shores—unless the legends were really true. Once, it was said, there had been swift metal ships that could cross the ocean despite the heat of Trilorne, and so come to the lands on the other side of the world. Now these countries could be reached only by a tedious journey over land and sea, which could be shortened no more than a little by traveling as far north as one dared.

All the inhabited countries of Shervane's world lay in the narrow belt between burning heat and insufferable cold. In every land, the far north was an unapproachable region smitten by the fury of Trilorne. And to the south of all countries lay the vast and gloomy Shadow Land, where Trilorne was never more than a pale disk on the horizon, and often was not visible at all.

These things Shervane learned in the years of his childhood, and in those years he had no wish to leave the wide lands between the mountains and the sea. Since the dawn of time his ancestors and the races before them had toiled to make these lands the fairest in the world; if they had failed, it was by a narrow margin. There were gardens bright with strange flowers, there were streams that trickled gently between moss-grown rocks to be lost in the pure waters of the tideless sea. There were fields of grain that rustled continually in the wind, as if the generations of seeds yet unborn were talking one to the other. In the wide meadows and beneath the trees the friendly cattle wandered aimlessly with foolish cries. And there was the great house, with its enormous rooms and its endless corridors, vast enough in reality but huger still to the mind of a child. This was the world in which Shervane had passed his years, the world he knew and loved. As yet, what lay beyond its borders had not concerned his mind.

But Shervane's universe was not one of those free from the domination of time. The harvest ripened and was gathered into the granaries; Trilorne rocked slowly through its little arc of sky, and with the passing seasons Shervane's mind and body grew. His land seemed smaller now: the mountains were nearer and the sea was only a brief walk from the great house. He began to learn of the world in which he lived, and to be made ready for the part he must play in its shaping.

Some of these things he learned from his father, Sherval, but most he was taught by Grayle, who had come across the mountains in the days of his father's father, and had now been tutor to three generations of Shervane's family. He was fond of Grayle, though the old man taught him many things he had no wish to learn, and the years of his boyhood passed pleasantly enough until the time came for him to go through the mountains into the lands beyond. Ages ago his family had come from the great countries of the east, and in every generation since, the eldest son had made that pilgrimage again to spend a year of his youth among his cousins. It was a wise custom, for beyond the mountains much of the knowledge of the past still lingered, and there one could meet men from other lands and study their ways.

In the last spring before his son's departure, Sherval collected three of his servants and certain animals it is convenient to call horses, and took Shervane to see those parts of the land he had never visited before. They rode west to the sea, and followed it for many days, until Trilorne was noticeably nearer the horizon. Still they went south, their shadows lengthening before them, turning again to the east only when the rays of the sun seemed to have lost all their power. They were now well within the limits of the Shadow Land, and it would not be wise to go farther south until the summer was at its height.

Shervane was riding beside his father, watching the changing landscape with all the eager curiosity of a boy seeing a new country for the first time. His father was talking about the soil, describing the crops that could be grown here and those that would fail if the attempt were made. But Shervane's attention was elsewhere: he was staring out across the desolate Shadow Land, wondering how far it stretched and what mysteries it held.

"Father," he said presently, "if you went south in a straight line, right across the Shadow Land, would you reach the other side of the world?"

His father smiled.

"Men have asked that question for centuries," he said, "but there are two reasons why they will never know the answer."

"What are they?"

"The first, of course, is the darkness and the cold. Even here, nothing can live during the winter months. But there is a better reason, though I see that Grayle has not spoken of it."

"I don't think he has: at least, I do not remember."

For a moment Sherval did not reply. He stood up in his stirrups and surveyed the land to the south.

"Once I knew this place well," he said to Shervane. "Come, —I have something to show you."

They turned away from the path they had been following, and for several hours rode once more with their backs to the sun. The land was rising slowly now, and Shervane saw that they were climbing a great ridge of rock that pointed like a dagger into the heart of the Shadow Land. They came presently to a hill too steep for the horses to ascend, and here they dismounted and left the animals in the servants' charge.

"There is a way around," said Sherval, "but it is quicker for us to climb than to take the horses to the other side."

The hill, though steep, was only a small one, and they reached its summit in a few minutes. At first Shervane could see nothing he had not met before; there was only the same undulating wilderness, which seemed to become darker and more forbidding with every yard that its distance from Trilorne increased.

He turned to his father with some bewilderment, but Sherval pointed to the far south and drew a careful line along the horizon.

"It is not easy to see," he said quietly. "My father showed it to me from this same spot, many years before you were born."

Shervane stared into the dusk. The southern sky was so dark as to be almost black, and it came down to meet the edge of the world. But not quite, for along the horizon, in a great curve dividing land from sky yet seeming to belong to neither, was a band of deeper darkness, black as the night which Shervane had never known.

He looked at it steadfastly for a long time, and perhaps some hint of the future may have crept into his soul, for the darkling land seemed suddenly alive and waiting. When at last he tore his eyes away, he know that nothing would ever be the same again, though he was still too young to recognize the challenge for what it was.

And so, for the first time in his life, Shervane saw the Wall.

In the early spring he said farewell to his people, and went with one servant over the mountains into the great lands of the eastern world. Here he met the men who shared his ancestry, and here he studied the history of his race, the arts that had grown from ancient times, and the sciences that ruled the lives of men. In the places of learning he made friends with boys who had come from lands even farther to the east: few of these was he likely to see again, but one was to play a greater part in his life than either could have imagined. Brayldon's father was a famous architect, but his son intended to eclipse him. He was traveling from land to land, always learning, watching, asking questions. Though he was only a few years older than Shervane, his knowledge of the world was infinitely greater—or so it seemed to the younger boy.

Between them they took the world to pieces and rebuilt it according to their desires. Brayldon dreamed of cities whose great avenues and stately towers would shame even the wonders of the past, but Shervane's interests lay more with the people who would dwell in those cities, and the way they ordered their lives.

They often spoke of the Wall, which Brayldon knew from the stories of his own people, though he himself had never seen it. Far to the south of every country, as Shervane had learned, it lay like a great barrier athwart the Shadow Land. In high summer it could be reached, though only with difficulty, but nowhere was there any way of passing it, and none knew what lay beyond. An entire world, never pausing even when it reached a hundred times the height of a man, it encircled the wintry sea that washed the shores of the Shadow Land. Travelers had stood upon those lonely beaches, scarcely warmed by the last thin rays of Trilorne, and had seen how the dark shadow of the Wall marched out to sea contemptuous of the waves beneath its feet. And on the far shores, other travelers had watched it come striding in across the ocean, to sweep past them on its journey round the world.

"One of my uncles," said Brayldon, "once reached the Wall when he was a young man. He did it for a wager, and he rode for ten days before he came beneath it. I think it frightened him—it was so huge and cold. He could not tell whether it was made of metal or of stone, and when he shouted, there was no echo at all, but his voice died away quickly as if the Wall were swallowing the sound. My people believe it is the end of the world, and there is nothing beyond."

"If that were true," Shervane replied, with irrefutable logic, "the ocean would have poured over the edge before the Wall was built."

"Not if Kyrone built it when He made the world."

Shervane did not agree.

"*My* people believe it is the work of man—perhaps the engineers of the First Dynasty, who made so many wonderful things. If they really had ships that could reach the Fire Lands—and even ships that could fly—they might have possessed enough wisdom to build the Wall."

Brayldon shrugged.

"They must have had a very good reason," he said. "We can never know the answer, so why worry about it?"

This eminently practical advice, as Shervane had discovered, was all that the ordinary man ever gave him. Only philosophers were interested in unanswerable questions: to most people, the enigma of the Wall, like the problem of existence itslf, was something that scarcely concerned their minds. And all the philosophers he had met had given him different answers.

First there had been Grayle, whom he had questioned on his return from the Shadow Land. The old man had looked at him quietly and said:

"There is only one thing behind the Wall, so I have heard. And that is madness."

Then there had been Artex, who was so old that he could scarcely hear Shervane's nervous questioning. He gazed at the boy through eyelids that seemed too tired to open fully, and had replied after a long time:

"Kyrone built the Wall in the third day of the making of the world. What is beyond, we shall discover when we die—for there go the souls of all the dead."

Yet Irgan, who lived in the same city, had flatly contradicted this.

"Only memory can answer your question, my son. For behind the Wall is the land in which we lived before our births."

Whom could he believe? The truth was that no one knew: if the knowledge had ever been possessed, it had been lost ages since.

Though this quest was unsuccessful, Shervane had learned many things in his year of study. With the returning spring he said farewell to Brayldon and the other friends he had known for such a little while, and set out along the ancient road that led him back to his own country. Once again he made the perilous journey through the great pass between the mountains, where walls of ice hung threatening against the sky. He came to the place where the road curved down once more toward the world of men, where there was warmth and running water and the breath no longer labored in the freezing air. Here, on the last rise of the road before it descended into the valley, one could see far out across the land to the distant gleam of the ocean. And there, almost lost in the mists at the edge of the world, Shervane could see the line of shadow that was his own country.

He went on down the great ribbon of stone until he came to the bridge that men had built across the cataract in the ancient days when the only other way had been destroyed by earthquake. But the bridge was gone: the storms and avalanches of early spring had swept away one of the mighty piers, and the beautiful metal rainbow lay a twisted ruin in the spray and foam a thousand feet below. The summer would have come and gone before the road could be opened once more: as Shervane sadly returned he knew that another year must pass ere he would see his home again.

He paused for many minutes on the last curve of the road, looking back toward the unattainable land that held all the things he loved. But the mists had closed over it, and he saw it no more. Resolutely he turned back along the road until the open lands had vanished and the mountains enfolded him again.

Brayldon was still in the city when Shervane returned. He was surprised and pleased to see his friend, and together they discussed what should be done in the year ahead. Shervane's cousins, who had grown fond of their guest, were not sorry to see him again, but their kindly suggestion that he should devote another year to study was not well received.

Shervane's plan matured slowly, in the face of considerable opposition. Even Brayldon was not enthusiastic at first, and much argument was needed before he would co-operate. Thereafter, the agreement of everyone else who mattered was only a question of time.

Summer was approaching when the two boys set out toward Brayldon's country. They rode swiftly, for the journey was a long one and must be completed before Trilorne began its winter fall. When they reached the lands that Brayldon knew, they made certain inquires which caused much shaking of heads. But the answers they obtained were accurate, and soon the Shadow Land was all around them, and presently for the second time in his life Shervane saw the Wall.

It seemed not far away when they first came upon it, rising from a bleak and lonely plain. Yet they rode endlessly across that plain before the Wall grew any nearer—and then they had almost reached its base before they realized how close they were, for there was no way of judging its distance until one could reach out and touch it.

When Shervane gazed up at the monstrous ebony sheet that had so troubled his mind, it seemed to be overhanging and about to crush him beneath its falling weight. With difficulty, he tore his eyes away from the hypnotic sight, and went nearer to examine the material of which the Wall was built.

It was true, as Brayldon had told him, that it felt cold to the touch—colder than it had any right to be even in this sun-starved land. It felt neither hard nor soft, for its texture eluded the hand in a way that was difficult to analyze. Shervane had the impression that something was preventing him from actual contact with the surface, yet he could see no space between the Wall and his fingers when he forced them against it. Strangest of all was the uncanny silence of which Brayldon's uncle had spoken: every word was deadened and all sounds died away with unnatural swiftness.

Brayldon had unloaded some tools and instruments from the pack horses, and had begun to examine the Wall's surface. He found very quickly that no drills or cutters would mark it in any way, and presently he came to the conclusion Shervane had already reached. The Wall was not merely adamant: it was unapproachable.

At last, in disgust, he took a perfectly straight metal rule and pressed its edge against the wall. While Shervane held a mirror to reflect the feeble light of Trilorne along the line of contact, Brayldon peered at the rule from the other side. It was as he had thought: an infinitely narrow streak of light showed unbroken between the two surfaces.

Brayldon looked thoughtfully at his friend.

"Shervane," he said, "I don't believe the Wall is made of matter, as we know it."

"Then perhaps the legends were right that said it was never built at all, but created as we see it now."

"I think so too," said Brayldon. "The engineers of the First Dynasty had such powers. There are some very ancient buildings in my land that seem to have been made in a single operation from a substance that shows absolutely no sign of weatherering. If it were black instead of colored, it would be very much like the material of the Wall."

He put away his useless tools and began to set up a simple portable theodolite.

"If I can do nothing else," he said with a wry smile, "at least I can find exactly how high it is!"

When they looked back for their last view of the Wall, Shervane wondered if he would ever see it again. There was nothing more he could learn: for the future, he must forget this foolish dream that he might one day master its secret. Perhaps there was no secret at all—perhaps beyond the Wall the Shadow Land stretched round the curve of the world until it met that same barrier again. That, surely, seemed the likeliest thing. But if it were so, then why had the Wall been built, and by what race?

With an almost angry effort of will, he put these thoughts aside and rode forward into the light of Trilorne, thinking of a future in which the Wall would play no more part than it did in the lives of other men.

So two years had passed before Shervane could return to his home. In two years, especially when one is young, much can be forgotten and even the things nearest to the heart lose their distinctness, so that they can no longer be clearly recalled. When Shervane came through the last foothills of the mountains and was again in the country of his childhood, the joy of his home-coming was mingled with a strange sadness. So many things were forgotten that he had once thought his mind would hold forever.

The news of his return had gone before him, and soon he saw far ahead a line of horses galloping along the road. He pressed forward eagerly, wondering if Sherval would be there to greet him, and was a little disappointed when he saw that Grayle was leading the procession.

Shervane halted as the old man rode up to his horse. Then Grayle put his hand upon his shoulder, but for a while he turned away his head and could not speak.

And presently Shervane learned that the storms of the year before had destroyed more than the ancient bridge, for the lightning had brought his own home in ruins to the ground Years before the appointed time, all the lands that Sherval had owned had passed into the possession of his son. Far more, indeed, than these, for the whole family had been assembled, according to its yearly custom, in the great house when the fire had come down upon it. In a single moment of time, everything between the mountains and the sea had passed into his keeping. He was the richest man his land had known for generations; and all these things he would have given to look again into the calm gray eyes of the father he would see no more.

Trilorne had risen and fallen in the sky many times since Shervane took leave of his childhood on the road before the mountains. The land had flourished in the passing years, and the possessions that had so suddenly become his had steadily increased their value. He had husbanded them well, and now he had time once more in which to dream. More than that— he had the wealth to make his dreams come true.

Often stories had come across the mountains of the work Brayldon was doing in the east, and although the two friends had never met since their youth they had exchanged messages regularly. Brayldon had achieved his ambitions: not only had he designed the two largest buildings erected since the ancient days, but a whole new city had been planned by him, though it would not be completed in his lifetime. Hearing of these things, Shervane remembered the aspirations of his own youth, and his mind went back across the years to the day when they had stood together beneath the majesty of the Wall. For a long time he wrestled with his thoughts, fearing to revive old longings that might not be assuaged. But at last he made his decision and wrote to Brayldon—for what was the use of wealth and power unless they could be used to shape one's dreams?

Then Shervane waited, wondering if Brayldon had forgotten the past in the years that had brought him fame. He had not long to wait: Brayldon could not come at once, for he had great works to carry to their completion, but when they were finished he would join his old friend. Shervane had thrown him a challenge that was worthy of his skill—one which if he could meet would bring him more satisfaction than anything he had yet done.

Early the next summer he came, and Shervane met him on the road below the bridge. They had been boys when they last parted, and now they were nearing middle age, yet as they greeted one another the years seemed to fall away and each was secretly glad to see how lightly Time had touched the friend he remembered.

They spent many days in conference together, considering the plans that Brayldon had drawn up. The work was an immense one, and would take many years to complete, but it was possible to a man of Shervane's wealth. Before he gave his final assent, he took his friend to see Grayle.

The old man had been living for some years in the little house that Shervane had built him. For a long time he had played no active part in the life of the great estates, but his advice was always ready when it was needed, and it was invariably wise.

Grayle knew why Brayldon had come to this land, and he expressed no surprise when the architect unrolled his sketches. The largest drawing showed the elevation of the Wall, with a great stairway rising along its side from the plain beneath. At six equally spaced intervals the slowly ascending ramp leveled out into wide platforms, the last of which was only a short distance below the summit of the Wall. Springing from the stairway at a score of places along its length were flying buttresses which to Grayle's eye seemed very frail and slender for the work they had to do. Then he realized that the great ramp would be largely self-supporting, and on one side all the lateral thrust would be taken by the Wall itself.

He looked at the drawing in silence for a while, and then remarked quietly:

"You always managed to have your way, Shervane. I might have guessed that this would happen in the end."

"Then you think it a good idea?" Shervane asked. He had never gone against the old man's advice, and was anxious to have it now. As usual Grayle came straight to the point.

"How much will it cost?" he said.

Brayldon told him, and for a moment there was a shocked silence.

"That includes," the architect said hastily, "the building of a good road across the Shadow Land, and the construction of a small town for the workmen. The stairway itself is made from about a million identical blocks which can be dovetailed together to form a rigid structure. We shall make these, I hope, from the minerals we find in the Shadow Land."

He sighed a little.

"I should have liked to have built it from metal rods, joined together, but that would have cost even more, for all the material would have to be brought over the mountains."

Grayle examined the drawing more closely.

"Why have you stopped short of the top?" he asked.

Brayldon looked at Shervane, who answered the question with a trace of embarrassment.

"I want to be the only one to make the final ascent," he replied. "The last stage will be by a lifting machine on the highest platform. There may be danger: that is why I am going alone."

That was not the only reason, but it was a good one. Behind the Wall, so Grayle had once said, lay madness. If that were true, no one else need face it.

Grayle was speaking once more in his quiet, dreamy voice.

"In that case," he said, "what you do is neither good nor bad, for it concerns you alone. If the Wall was built to keep something from our world, it will still be impassable from the other side."

Brayldon nodded.

"We had thought of that," he said with a touch of pride. "If the need should come, the ramp can be destroyed in a moment by explosives at selected spots."

"That is good," the old man replied. "Though I do not believe those stories, it is well to be prepared. When the work is finished, I hope I shall still be here. And now I shall try to remember what I heard of the Wall when I was as young as you were, Shervane, when you first questioned me about it."

Before the winter came, the road to the Wall had been marked out and the foundations of the temporary town had been laid. Most of the materials Brayldon needed were not hard to find, for the Shadow Land was rich in minerals. He had also surveyed the Wall itself and chosen the spot for the stairway. When Trilorne began to dip below the horizon, Brayldon was well content with the work that had been done.

By the next summer the first of the myriad concrete blocks had been made and tested to Brayldon's satisfaction, and before winter came again some thousands had been produced and part of the foundations laid. Leaving a trusted assistant in charge of the production, Brayldon could now return to his interrupted work. When enough of the blocks had been made, he would be back to supervise the building, but until then his guidance would not be needed.

Two or three times in the course of every year, Shervane rode out to the Wall to watch the stockpiles growing into great pyramids, and four years later Brayldon returned with him. Layer by layer the lines of stone started to creep up the flanks of the Wall, and the slim buttresses began to arch out into space. At first the stairway rose slowly, but as its summit narrowed the increase became more and more rapid. For a third of every year the work had to be abandoned, and there were anxious months in the long winter when Shervane stood on the borders of the Shadow Land, listening to the storms that thundered past him into the reverberating darkness. But Brayldon had built well, and every spring the work was standing unharmed as though it would outlive the Wall itself.

The last stones were laid seven years after the beginning of the work. Standing a mile away, so that he could see the structure in its entirety, Shervane remembered with wonder how all this had sprung from the few sketches Brayldon had shown him years ago, and he knew something of the emotion the artist must feel when his dreams become reality. And he remembered, too, the day when, as a boy by his father's side, he had first seen the Wall far off against the dusky sky of the Shadow Land.

There were guardrails around the upper platform, but Shervane did not care to go near its edge. The ground was at a dizzying distance, and he tried to forget his height by helping Brayldon and the workmen erect the simple hoist that would lift him the remaining twenty feet. When it was ready he stepped into the machine and turned to his friend with all the assurance he could muster.

"I shall be gone only a few minutes," he said with elaborate casualness. "Whatever I find, I'll return immediately."

He could hardly have guessed how small a choice was his.

Grayle was now almost blind and would not know another spring. But he recognized the approaching footsteps and greeted Brayldon by name before his visitor had time to speak.

"I am glad you came," he said. "I've been thinking of everything you told me, and I believe I know the truth at last. Perhaps you have guessed it already."

"No," said Brayldon. "I have been afraid to think of it."

The old man smiled a little.

"Why should one be afraid of something merely because it is strange? The Wall is wonderful, yes—but there's nothing terrible about it, to those who will face its secret without flinching.

"When I was a boy, Brayldon, my old master once said that time could never destroy the truth—it could only hide it among legends. He was right. From all the fables that have gathered around the Wall, I can now select the ones that are part of history.

"Long ago, Brayldon, when the First Dynasty was at its height, Trilorne was hotter than it is now and the Shadow Land was fertile and inhabited—as perhaps one day the Fire Lands may be when Trilorne is old and feeble. Men could go southward as they pleased, for there was no Wall to bar the way. Many must have done so, looking for new lands in which to settle. What happened to Shervane happened to them also, and it must have wrecked many minds—so many that the scientists of the First Dynasty built the Wall to prevent madness from spreading through the land. I cannot believe that this is true, but the legend says that it was made in a single day, with no labor, out of a cloud that encircled the world."

He fell into a reverie, and for a moment Brayldon did not disturb him. His mind was far in the past, picturing his world as a perfect globe floating in space while the Ancient Ones threw that band of darkness around the equator. False though that picture was in its most important detail, he could never wholly erase it from his mind.

As the last few feet of the Wall moved slowly past his eyes, Shervane needed all his courage lest he cry out to be lowered again. He remembered certain terrible stories he had once dismissed with laughter, for he came of a race that was singularly free from superstition. But what if, after all, those stories had been true, and the Wall had been built to keep some horror from the world?

He tried to forget these thoughts, and found it not hard to do so once he had passed the topmost level of the Wall. At first he could not interpret the picture his eyes brought him: then he saw that he was looking across an unbroken black sheet whose width he could not judge.

The little platform came to a stop, and he noted with half-conscious admiration how accurate Brayldon's calculations had been. Then, with a last word of assurance to the group below, he stepped onto the Wall and began to walk steadily forward.

At first it seemed as if the plain before him was infinite, for he could not even tell where it met the sky. But he walked on unfaltering, keeping his back to Trilorne. He wished he could have used his own shadow as a guide, but it was lost in the deeper darkness beneath his feet.

There was something wrong: it was growing darker with every footstep he took. Startled, he turned around and saw that the disk of Trilorne had now become pale and dusky, as if seen through a darkened glass. With mounting fear, he realized that this was by no means all that had happened— *Trilorne was smaller than the sun he had known all his life.*

He shook his head in an angry gesture of defiance. These things were fancies; he was imagining them. Indeed, they were so contrary to all experience that somehow he no longer felt frightened but strode resolutely forward with only a glance at the sun behind.

When Trilorne had dwindled to a point, and the darkness was all around him, it was time to abandon pretense. A wiser man would have turned back there and then, and Shervane had a sudden nightmare vision of himself lost in this eternal twilight between earth and sky, unable to retrace the path that led to safety. Then he remembered that as long as he could see Trilorne at all he could be in no real danger.

A little uncertainly now, he continued his way with many backward glances at the faint guiding light behind him. Trilorne itself had vanished, but there was still a dim glow in the sky to mark its place. And presently he needed its aid no longer, for far ahead a second light was appearing in the heavens.

At first it seemed only the faintest of glimmers, and when he was sure of its existence he noticed that Trilorne had already disappeared. But he felt more confident now, and as he moved onward, the returning light did something to subdue his fears.

When he saw that he was indeed approaching another sun, when he could tell beyond any doubt that it was expanding as a moment ago he had seen Trilorne contract, he forced all amazement down into the depths of his mind. He would only observe and record: later there would be time to understand these things. That his world might possess two suns, one shining upon it from either side, was not, after all, beyond imagination.

Now at last he could see, faintly through the darkness, the ebon line that marked the Wall's other rim. Soon he would be the first man in thousands of years, perhaps in eternity, to look upon the lands that it had sundered from his world. Would they be as fair as his own, and would there be people there whom he would be glad to greet?

But that they would be waiting, and in such a way, was more than he had dreamed.

Grayle stretched his hand out toward the cabinet beside him and fumbled for a large sheet of paper that was lying upon it. Brayldon watched him in silence, and the old man continued.

"How often we have all heard arguments about the size of the Universe, and whether it has any boundaries! We can imagine no ending to space, yet our minds rebel at the idea of infinity. Some philosophers have imagined that space is limited by curvature in a higher dimension—I suppose you know the theory. It may be true of other universes, if they exist, but for ours the answer is more subtle.

"Along the line of the Wall, Brayldon, our Universe comes to an end—and yet does not. There was no boundary, nothing to stop one going onward before the Wall was built. The Wall itself is merely a man-made barrier, sharing the properties of the space in which it lies. Those properties were always there, and the Wall added nothing to them."

He held the sheet of paper toward Brayldon and slowly rotated it.

"Here," he said, "is a plain sheet. It has, of course, two sides. *Can you imagine one that has not?*"

Brayldon stared at him in amazement.

"That's impossible—ridiculous!"

"But is it?" said Grayle softly. He reached toward the cabinet again and his fingers groped in its recesses. Then he drew out a long, flexible strip of paper and turned vacant eyes to the silently waiting Brayldon.

"We cannot match the intellects of the First Dynasty, but what their minds could grasp directly we can approach by analogy. This simple trick, which seems so trivial, may help you to glimpse the truth."

He ran his fingers along the paper strip, then joined the two ends together to make a circular loop.

"Here I have a shape which is perfectly familiar to you— the section of a cylinder. I run my finger around the inside, so—and now along the outside. The two surfaces are quite distinct: you can go from one to the other only by moving through the thickness of the strip. Do you agree?"

"Of course," said Brayldon, still puzzled. "But what does it prove?"

"Nothing," said Grayle. "But now watch—"

This sun, Shervane thought, was Trilorne's identical twin. The darkness had now lifted completely, and there was no longer the sensation, which he would not try to understand, of walking across an infinite plain.

He was moving slowly now, for he had no desire to come too suddenly upon that vertiginous precipice. In a little while he could see a distant horizon of low hills, as bare and lifeless as those he had left behind him. This did not disappoint him unduly, for the first glimpse of his own land would be no more attractive than this.

So he walked on: and when presently an icy hand fastened itself upon his heart, he did not pause as a man of lesser courage would have done. Without flinching, he watched that shockingly familiar landscape rise around him, until he could see the plain from which his journey had started, and the great stairway itself, and at last Brayldon's anxious, waiting face.

Again Grayle brought the two ends of the strip together, but now he had given it a half-twist so that the band was kinked. He held it out to Brayldon.

"Rut your finger around it now," he said quietly.

Brayldon did not do so: he could see the old man's meaning.

"I understand," he said. "You no longer have two separate surfaces. It now forms a single continuous sheet—*a one-sided surface*—something that at first sight seems utterly impossible."

"Yes," replied Grayle very softly. "I thought you would understand. *A one-sided surface*. Perhaps you realize now why this symbol of the twisted loop is so common in the ancient religions, though its meaning has been completely lost. Of course, it is no more than a crude and simple analogy—an example in two dimensions of what must really occur in three. But it is as near as our minds can ever get to the truth."

There was a long, brooding silence. Then Grayle sighed deeply and turned to Brayldon as if he could still see his face.

"Why did you come back before Shervane?" he asked, though he knew the answer well enough.

"We had to do it," said Brayldon sadly, "but I did not wish to see my work destroyed."

Grayle nodded in sympathy.

"I understand," he said.

Shervane ran his eye up the long flight of steps on which no feet would ever tread again. He felt few regrets: he had striven, and no one could have done more. Such victory as was possible had been his.

Slowly he raised his hand and gave the signal. The Wall swallowed the explosion as it had absorbed all other sounds, but the unhurried grace with which the long tiers of masonry curtsied and fell was something he would remember all his life. For a moment he had a sudden, inexpressibly poignant vision of another stairway, watched by another Shervane, falling in identical ruins on the far side of the Wall.

But that, he realized, was a foolish thought: for none knew better than he that the Wall possessed no other side.

Bishop's Lydeard, Somerset   *August 1946*

No Morning After

Tales of cosmic doom have long been a science-fiction staple, and are now a glut on the market. But here is one with a difference: offhand, I can't remember another humorous story about the End of the World.

———— ◆ ————

"But this is terrible!" said the Supreme Scientist. "Surely there is *something* we can do!"

"Yes, Your Cognizance, but it will be extremely difficult. The planet is more than five hundred light-years away, and it is very hard to maintain contact. However, we believe we can establish a bridgehead. Unfortunately, that is not the only problem. So far, we have been quite unable to communicate with these beings. Their telepathic powers are exceedingly rudimentary—perhaps even nonexistent. And if we cannot talk to them, there is no way in which we can help."

There was a long mental silence while the Supreme Scientist analyzed the situation and arrived, as he always did, at the correct answer.

"Any intelligent race must have *some* telepathic individuals," he mused. "We must send out hundreds of observers, tuned to catch the first hint of stray thought. When you find a single responsive mind, concentrate all your efforts upon it. We *must* get our message through."

"Very good, Your Cognizance. It shall be done."

Across the abyss, across the gulf which light itself took half a thousand years to span, the questing intellects of the planet Thaar sent out their tendrils of thought, searching desperately for a single human being whose mind could perceive their presence. And as luck would have it, they encountered William Cross.

At least, they thought it was luck at the time, though later

112

they were not so sure. In any case, they had little choice. The combination of circumstances that opened Bill's mind to them lasted only for seconds, and was not likely to occur again this side of eternity.

There were three ingredients in the miracle: it is hard to say if one was more important than another. The first was the accident of position. A flask of water, when sunlight falls upon it, can act as a crude lens, concentrating the light into a small area. On an immeasurably larger scale, the dense core of the Earth was converging the waves that came from Thaar. In the ordinary way, the radiations of thought are unaffected by matter—they pass through it as effortlessly as light through glass. But there is rather a lot of matter in a planet, and the whole Earth was acting as a gigantic lens. As it turned, it was carrying Bill through its focus, where the feeble thought impulses from Thaar were concentrated a hundred-fold.

Yet millions of other men were equally well placed: they received no message. But they were not rocket engineers: they had not spent years thinking and dreaming of space until it had become part of their very being.

And they were not, as Bill was, blind drunk, teetering on the last knife-edge of consciousness, trying to escape from reality into the world of dreams, where there were no disappointments and setbacks.

Of course, he could see the Army's point of view. "You are paid, Dr. Cross," General Potter had pointed out with unnecessary emphasis, "to design missiles, *not*—ah—spaceships. What you do in your space time is your own concern, but I must ask you not to use the facilities of the establishment for your hobby. From now on, all projects for the computing section will have to be cleared by me. That is all."

They couldn't sack him, of course: he was too important. But he was not sure that he wanted to stay. He was not really sure of anything except that the job had backfired on him, and that Brenda had finally gone off with Johnny Gardner—putting events in their order of importance.

Wavering slightly, Bill cupped his chin in his hands and stared at the whitewashed brick wall on the other side of the table. The only attempt at ornamentation was a calendar from Lockheed and a glossy six-by-eight from Aerojet showing L'il Abner Mark I making a boosted take-off. Bill gazed morosely at a spot midway between the two pictures, and emptied his mind of thought. The barriers went down. . . .

At that moment, the massed intellects of Thaar gave a soundless cry of triumph, and the wall in front of Bill slowly dissolved into a swirling mist. He appeared to be looking down a tunnel that stretched to infinity. As a matter of fact, he was.

Bill studied the phenomenon with mild interest. It had a certain novelty, but was not up to the standard of previous hallucinations. And when the voice started to speak in his mind, he let it ramble on for some time before he did anything about it. Even when drunk, he had an old-fashioned prejudice against starting conversations with himself.

"Bill," the voice began, "listen carefully. We have had great difficulty in contacting you, and this is extremely important."

Bill doubted this on general principles. *Nothing* was important any more.

"We are speaking to you from a very distant planet," continued the voice in a tone of urgent friendliness. "You are the only human being we have been able to contact, so you *must* understand what we are saying."

Bill felt mildly worried, though in an impersonal sort of way, since it was now rather hard to focus on his own problems. How serious was it, he wondered, when you started to hear voices? Well, it was best not to get excited. You can take it or leave it, Dr. Cross, he told himself. Let's take it until it gets to be a nuisance.

"OK," he answered with bored indifference. "Go right ahead and talk to me. I won't mind as long as it's interesting."

There was a pause. Then the voice continued, in a slightly worried fashion.

"We don't quite understand. Our message isn't merely *interesting*. It's vital to your entire race, and you must notify your government immediately."

"I'm waiting," said Bill. "It helps to pass the time."

Five hundred light-years away, the Thaars conferred hastily among themselves. Something seemed to be wrong, but they could not decide precisely what. There was no doubt that they had established contact, yet this was not the sort of reaction they had expected. Well, they could only proceed and hope for the best.

"Listen, Bill," they continued. "Our scientists have just discovered that your sun is about to explode. It will happen three days from now—seventy-four hours, to be exact. Nothing can stop it. But there's no need to be alarmed. We can save you, if you'll do what we say."

"Go on," said Bill. This hallucination was ingenious.

"We can create what we call a bridge—it's a kind of tunnel through space, like the one you're looking into now. The theory is far too complicated to explain, even to one of your mathematicians."

"Hold on a minute!" protested Bill. "I *am* a mathematician, and a darn good one, even when I'm sober. And I've read all about this kind of thing in the science-fiction magazines. I presume you're talking about some kind of short cut through a higher dimension of space. That's old stuff—pre-Einstein."

A sensation of distinct surprise seeped into Bill's mind.

"We had no idea you were so advanced scientifically," said the Thaarns. "But we haven't time to talk about the theory. All that matters is this—if you were to step into that opening in front of you, you'd find yourself instantly on another planet. It's a short cut, as you said—in this case through the thirty-seventh dimension."

"And it leads to your world?"

"Oh no—you couldn't live here. But there are plenty of planets like Earth in the Universe, and we've found one that will suit you. We'll establish bridgeheads like this all over Earth, so your people will only have to walk through them to be saved. Of course, they'll have to start building up civilization again when they reach their new homes, but it's their only hope. You have to pass on this message, and tell them what to do."

"I can just see them listening to me," said Bill. "Why don't you go and talk to the President?"

"Because yours was the only mind we were able to contact. Others seemed closed to us: we don't understand why."

"I could tell you," said Bill, looking at the nearly empty bottle in front of him. He was certainly getting his money's worth. What a remarkable thing the human mind was! Of course, there was nothing at all original in this dialogue: it was easy to see where the ideas came from. Only last week he'd been reading a story about the end of the world, and all this wishful thinking about bridges and tunnels through space was pretty obvious compensation for anyone who'd spent five years wrestling with recalcitrant rockets.

"If the sun does blow up," Bill asked abruptly—trying to catch his hallucination unawares—"what would happen?"

"Why, your planet would be melted instantly. All the planets, in fact, right out to Jupiter."

Bill had to admit that this was quite a grandiose conception. He let his mind play with the thought, and the more he considered it, the more he liked it.

"My dear hallucination," he remarked pityingly, "if I believed you, d'you know what I'd say?"

"But you *must* believe us!" came the despairing cry across the light-years.

Bill ignored it. He was warming to his theme.

"I'd tell you this. *It would be the best thing that could possibly happen.* Yes, it would save a whole lot of misery. No one would have to worry about the Russians and the atom bomb and the high cost of living. Oh, it would be wonderful! It's just what everybody really wants. Nice of you to come along and tell us, but just you go back home and pull your old bridge after you."

There was consternation on Thaar. The Supreme Scientist's brain, floating like a great mass of coral in its tank of nutrient solution, turned slightly yellow about the edges—something it had not done since the Xantil invasion, five thousand years ago. At least fifteen psychologists had nervous breakdowns and were never the same again. The main computer in the College of Cosmophysics started dividing every number in its memory circuits by zero, and promptly blew all its fuses.

And on Earth, Bill Cross was really hitting his stride.

"Look at *me*," he said, pointing a wavering finger at his chest. "I've spent years trying to make rockets do something useful, and they tell me I'm only allowed to build guided missiles, so that we can all blow each other up. The sun will make a neater job of it, and if you did give us another planet we'd only start the whole damn thing all over again."

He paused sadly, marshaling his morbid thoughts.

"And now Brenda heads out of town without even leaving a note. So you'll pardon my lack of enthusiasm for your Boy Scout act."

He couldn't have said "enthusiasm" aloud, Bill realized. But he could still think it, which was an interesting scientific discovery. As he got drunker and drunker, would his cogitation—whoops, *that* nearly threw him!—finally drop down to words of one syllable?

In a final despairing exertion, the Thaarns sent their thoughts along the tunnel between the stars.

"You can't really mean it, Bill! Are *all* human beings like you?"

Now that was an interesting philosophical question! Bill considered it carefully—or as carefully as he could in view of the warm, rosy glow that was now beginning to envelop him. After all, things might be worse. He could get another job, if only for the pleasure of telling General Potter what he could do with his three stars. And as for Brenda—well, women were like streetcars: there'd always be another along in a minute.

Best of all, there was a second bottle of whisky in the Top Secret file. Oh, frabjous day! He rose unsteadily to his feet and wavered across the room.

For the last time, Thaar spoke to Earth.

"Bill!" it repeated desperately. "Surely all human beings can't be like you!"

Bill turned and looked into the swirling tunnel. Strangē— it seemed to be lighted with flecks of starlight, and was really rather pretty. He felt proud of himself: not many people could imagine *that*.

"Like me?" he said. "No, they're not." He smiled smugly across the light-years, as the rising tide of euphoria lifted him out of his despondency. "Come to think of it," he added, "there are a lot of people much worse off than me. Yes, I guess I must be one of the lucky ones, after all."

He blinked in mild surprise, for the tunnel had suddenly collapsed upon itself and the whitewashed wall was there again, exactly as it had always been. Thaar knew when it was beaten.

"So much for *that* hallucination," thought Bill. "I was getting tired of it, anyway. Let's see what the next one's like."

As it happened, there wasn't a next one, for five seconds later he passed out cold, just as he was setting the combination of the file cabinet.

The next two days were rather vague and bloodshot, and he forgot all about the interview.

On the third day something was nagging at the back of his mind: he might have remembered if Brenda hadn't turned up again and kept him busy being forgiving.

And there wasn't a fourth day, of course.

London *August 1953*

The Possessed

And now the sun ahead was so close that the hurricane of radiation was forcing the Swarm back into the dark night of space. Soon it would be able to come no closer; the gales of light on which it rode from star to star could not be faced so near their source. Unless it encountered a planet very soon, and could fall down into the peace and safety of its shadow, this sun must be abandoned as had so many before.

Six cold outer worlds had already been searched and discarded. Either they were frozen beyond all hope of organic life, or else they harbored entities of types that were useless to the Swarm. If it was to survive, it must find hosts not too unlike those it had left on its doomed and distant home. Millions of years ago the Swarm had begun its journey, swept starward by the fires of its own exploding sun. Yet even now the memory of its lost birthplace was still sharp and clear, an ache that would never die.

There was a planet ahead, swinging its cone of shadow through the flame-swept night. The senses that the Swarm had developed upon its long journey reached out toward the approaching world, reached out and found it good.

The merciless buffeting of radiation ceased as the black disc of the planet eclipsed the sun. Falling freely under gravity, the Swarm dropped swiftly until it hit the outer fringe of the atmosphere. The first time it had made planetfall it had almost met its doom, but now it contracted its tenuous substance with the unthinking skill of long practice, until it formed a tiny, close-knit sphere. Slowly its velocity slackened, until at last it was floating motionless between earth and sky.

For many years it rode the winds of the stratosphere from Pole to Pole, or let the soundless fusillades of dawn blast it westward from the rising sun. Everywhere it found life, but nowhere intelligence. There were things that crawled and flew and leaped, but there were no things that talked or built. Ten million years hence there might be creatures here with minds

118

that the Swarm could possess and guide for its own purposes; there was no sign of them now. It could not guess which of the countless life-forms on this planet would be the heir to the future, and without such a host it was helpless—a mere pattern of electric charges, a matrix of order and self-awareness in a universe of chaos. By its own resources the Swarm had no control over matter, yet once it had lodged in the mind of a sentient race there was nothing that lay beyond its powers.

It was not the first time, and it would not be the last, that the planet had been surveyed by a visitant from space—though never by one in such peculiar and urgent need. The Swarm was faced with a tormenting dilemma. It could begin its weary travels once more, hoping that ultimately it might find the conditions it sought, or it could wait here on this world, biding its time until a race had arisen which would fit its purpose.

It moved like mist through the shadows, letting the vagrant winds take it where they willed. The clumsy, ill-formed reptiles of this young world never saw its passing, but it observed them, recording, analyzing, trying to extrapolate into the future. There was so little to choose between all these creatures; not one showed even the first faint glimmerings of conscious mind. Yet if it left this world in search of another, it might roam the Universe in vain until the end of time.

At last it made its decision. By its very nature, it could choose both alternatives. The greater part of the Swarm would continue its travels among the stars, but a portion of it would remain on this world, like a seed planted in the hope of future harvest.

It began to spin upon its axis, its tenuous body flattening into a disc. Now it was wavering at the frontiers of visibility —it was a pale ghost, a faint will-o'-the-wisp that suddenly fissured into two unequal fragments. The spinning slowly died away: the Swarm had become two, each an entity with all the memories of the original, and all its desires and needs.

There was a last exchange of thoughts between parent and child who were also identical twins. If all went well with them both, they would meet again in the far future here at this valley in the mountains. The one who was staying would return to this point at regular intervals down the ages; the one who continued the search would send back an emissary if ever a better world was found. And then they would be united again, no longer homeless exiles vainly wandering among the indifferent stars.

The light of dawn was spilling over the raw, new mountains when the parent swarm rose up to meet the sun. At the edge of the atmosphere the gales of radiation caught it and swept it unresisting out beyond the planets, to start again upon the endless search.

The one that was left began its almost equally hopeless task. It needed an animal that was not so rare that disease or accident could make it extinct, nor so tiny that it could never acquire any power over the physical world. And it must breed rapidly, so that its evolution could be directed and controlled as swiftly as possible.

The search was long and the choice difficult, but at last the Swarm selected its host. Like rain sinking into thirsty soil, it entered the bodies of certain small lizards and began to direct their destiny.

It was an immense task, even for a being which could never know death. Generation after generation of the lizards was swept into the past before there came the slightest improvement in the race. And always, at the appointed time, the Swarm returned to its rendezvous among the mountains. Always it returned in vain: there was no messenger from the stars, bringing news of better fortune elsewhere.

The centuries lengthened into millennia, the millennia into eons. By the standards of geological time, the lizards were now changing rapidly. Presently they were lizards no more, but warm-blooded, fur-covered creatures that brought forth their young alive. They were still small and feeble, and their minds were rudimentary, but they contained the seeds of future greatness.

Yet not only the living creatures were altering as the ages slowly passed. Continents were being rent asunder, mountains being worn down by the weight of the unwearying rain. Through all these changes, the Swarm kept to its purpose; and always, at the appointed times, it went to the meeting place that had been chosen so long ago, waited patiently for a while, and came away. Perhaps the parent swarm was still searching or perhaps—it was a hard and terrible thought to grasp—some unknown fate had overtaken it and it had gone the way of the race it had once ruled. There was nothing to do but to wait and see if the stubborn life-stuff of this planet could be forced along the path to intelligence.

And so the eons passed. . . .

Somewhere in the labyrinth of evolution the Swarm made its fatal mistake and took the wrong turning. A hundred million years had gone since it came to Earth, and it was very weary. It could not die, but it could degenerate. The memories of its ancient home and of its destiny were fading: its intelligence was waning even while its hosts climbed the long slope that would lead to self-awareness.

By a cosmic irony, in giving the impetus which would one day bring intelligence to this world, the Swarm had exhausted itself. It had reached the last stage of parasitism; no longer could it exist apart from its hosts. Never again could it ride free above the world, driven by wind and sun. To make the pilgrimage to the ancient rendezvous, it must travel slowly and painfully in a thousand little bodies. Yet it continued the immemorial custom, driven on by the desire for reunion which burned all the more fiercely now that it knew the bitterness of failure. Only if the parent swarm returned and reabsorbed it could it ever know new life and vigor.

The glaciers came and went; by a miracle the little beasts that now housed the waning alien intelligence escaped the clutching fingers of the ice. The oceans overwhelmed the land, and still the race survived. It even multiplied, but it could do no more. This world would never be its heritage, for far away in the heart of another continent a certain monkey had come down from the trees and was looking at the stars with the first glimmerings of curiosity.

The mind of the Swarm was dispersing, scattering among a million tiny bodies, no longer able to unite and assert its will. It had lost all cohesion; its memories were fading. In a million years, at most, they would all be gone.

Only one thing remained—the blind urge which still, at intervals which by some strange aberration were becoming ever shorter, drove it to seek its consummation in a valley that long ago had ceased to exist.

Quietly riding the lane of moonlight, the pleasure steamer passed the island with its winking beacon and entered the fjord. It was a calm and lovely night, with Venus sinking in the west out beyond the Faroes, and the lights of the harbor reflected with scarcely a tremor in the still waters far ahead.

Nils and Christina were utterly content. Standing side by side against the boat rail, their fingers locked together, they watched the wooded slopes drift silently by. The tall trees were motionless in the moonlight, their leaves unruffled by even the merest breath of wind, their slender trunks rising whitely from pools of shadow. The whole world was asleep; only the moving ship dared to break the spell that had bewitched the night.

Then suddenly, Christina gave a little gasp and Nils felt her fingers tighten convulsively on his. He followed her gaze: she was staring out across the water, looking toward the silent sentinels of the forest.

"What is it, darling?" he asked anxiously.

"Look!" she replied, in a whisper Nils could scarcely hear. "There—under the pines!"

Nils stared, and as he did so the beauty of the night ebbed slowly away and ancestral terrors came crawling back from exile. For beneath the trees the land was alive: a dappled brown tide was moving down the slopes of the hill and merging into the dark waters. Here was an open patch on which the moonlight fell unbroken by shadow. It was changing even as he watched: the surface of the land seemed to be rippling downward like a slow waterfall seeking union with the sea.

And then Nils laughed and the world was sane once more. Christina looked at him, puzzled but reassured.

"Don't you remember?" he chuckled. "We read all about it in the paper this morning. They do this every few years, and always at night. It's been going on for days."

He was teasing her, sweeping away the tension of the last few minutes. Christina looked back at him, and a slow smile lit up her face.

"Of course!" she said. "How stupid of me!" Then she turned once more toward the land and her expression became sad, for she was very tenderhearted.

"Poor little things!" she sighed. "I wonder why they do it?"

Nils shrugged his shoulders indifferently.

"No one knows," he answered. "It's just one of those mysteries. I shouldn't think about it if it worries you. Look— we'll soon be in harbor!"

They turned toward the beckoning lights where their future lay, and Christina glanced back only once toward the tragic, mindless tide that was still flowing beneath the moon.

Obeying an urge whose meaning they had never known, the doomed legions of the lemmings were finding oblivion beneath the waves.

Death and the Senator

Washington had never looked lovelier in the spring; and this was the last spring, thought Senator Steelman bleakly, that he would ever see. Even now, despite all that Dr. Jordan had told him, he could not fully accept the truth. In the past there had always been a way of escape; no defeat had been final. When men had betrayed him, he had discarded them—even ruined them, as a warning to others. But now the betrayal was within himself; already, it seemed, he could feel the labored beating of the heart that would soon be stilled. No point in planning now for the Presidential election of 1976; he might not even live to see the nominations. . . .

It was an end of dreams and ambition, and he could not console himself with the knowledge that for all men these must end someday. For him it was too soon; he thought of Cecil Rhodes, who had always been one of his heroes, crying "So much to do—so little time to do it in!" as he died before his fiftieth birthday. He was already older than Rhodes, and had done far less.

The car was taking him away from the Capitol; there was symbolism in that, and he tried not to dwell upon it. Now he was abreast of the New Smithsonian—that vast complex of museums he had never had time to visit, though he had watched it spread along the Mall throughout the years he had been in Washington. How much he had missed, he told himself bitterly, in his relentless pursuit of power. The whole universe of art and culture had remained almost closed to him, and that was only part of the price that he had paid. He had become a stranger to his family and to those who were once his friends. Love had been sacrificed on the altar of ambition, and the sacrifice had been in vain. Was there anyone in all the world who would weep at his departure?

Yes, there was. The feeling of utter desolation relaxed its grip upon his soul. As he reached for the phone, he felt ashamed that he had to call the office to get this number, when his mind was cluttered with memories of so many less important things.

(There was the White House, almost dazzling in the spring sunshine. For the first time in his life he did not give it a second glance. Already it belonged to another world—a world that would never concern him again.)

The car circuit had no vision, but he did not need it to sense Irene's mild surprise—and her still milder pleasure.

"Hello, Renee—how are you all?"

"Fine, Dad. When are we going to see you?"

It was the polite formula his daughter always used on the rare occasions when he called. And invariably, except at Christmas or birthdays, his answer was a vague promise to drop around at some indefinite future date.

"I was wondering," he said slowly, almost apologetically, "if I could borrow the children for an afternoon. It's a long time since I've taken them out, and I felt like getting away from the office."

"But of course," Irene answered, her voice warming with pleasure. "They'll love it. When would you like them?"

"Tomorrow would be fine. I could call around twelve, and take them to the Zoo or the Smithsonian, or anywhere else they felt like visiting."

Now she was really startled, for she knew well enough that he was one of the busiest men in Washington, with a schedule planned weeks in advance. She would be wondering what had happened; he hoped she would not guess the truth. No reason why she should, for not even his secretary knew of the stabbing pains that had driven him to seek this long-overdue medical checkup.

"That would be wonderful. They were talking about you only yesterday, asking when they'd see you again."

His eyes misted, and he was glad that Renee could not see him.

"I'll be there at noon," he said hastily, trying to keep the emotion out of his voice. "My love to you all." He switched off before she could answer, and relaxed against the upholstery with a sigh of relief. Almost upon impulse, without conscious planning, he had taken the first step in the reshaping of his life. Though his own children were lost to him, a bridge across the generations remained intact. If he did nothing else, he must guard and strengthen it in the months that were left.

Taking two lively and inquisitive children through the natural-history building was not what the doctor would have ordered, but it was what he wanted to do. Joey and Susan had grown so much since their last meeting, and it required both physical and mental alertness to keep up with them. No sooner had they entered the rotunda than they broke away from him, and scampered toward the enormous elephant dominating the marble hall.

"What's that?" cried Joey.

"It's an elephant, stupid," answered Susan with all the crushing superiority of her seven years.

"I know it's an effelant," retorted Joey. "But what's its name?"

Senator Steelman scanned the label, but found no assistance there. This was one occasion when the risky adage "Sometimes wrong, never uncertain" was a safe guide to conduct.

"He was called—er—Jumbo," he said hastily. "Just look at those tusks!"

"Did he ever get toothache?"

"Oh no."

"Then how did he clean his teeth? Ma says that if I don't clean mine . . ."

Steelman saw where the logic of this was leading, and thought it best to change the subject.

"There's a lot more to see inside. Where do you want to start—birds, snakes, fish, mammals?"

"Snakes!" clamored Susan. "I wanted to keep one in a box, but Daddy said no. Do you think he'd change his mind if you asked him?"

"What's a mammal?" asked Joey, before Steelman could work out an answer to that.

"Come along," he said firmly. "I'll show you."

As they moved through the halls and galleries, the children darting from one exhibit to another, he felt at peace with the world. There was nothing like a museum for calming the mind, for putting the problems of everyday life in their true perspective. Here, surrounded by the infinite variety and wonder of Nature, he was reminded of truths he had forgotten. He was only one of a million million creatures that shared this planet Earth. The entire human race, with its hopes and fears, its triumphs and its follies, might be no more than an incident in the history of the world. As he stood before the monstrous bones of Diplodocus (the children for

once awed and silent), he felt the winds of Eternity blowing
through his soul. He could no longer take so seriously the
gnawing of ambition, the belief that he was the man the
nation needed. *What* nation, if it came to that? A mere two
centuries ago this summer, the Declaration of Independence
had been signed; but this old American had lain in the Utah
rocks for a hundred million years. . . .

He was tired when they reached the Hall of Oceanic Life,
with its dramatic reminder that Earth still possessed animals
greater than any that the past could show. The ninety-foot
blue whale plunging into the ocean, and all the other swift
hunters of the sea, brought back memories of hours he had
once spent on a tiny, glistening deck with a white sail billow-
ing above him. That was another time when he had known
contentment, listening to the swish of water past the prow,
and the sighing of the wind through the rigging. He had not
sailed for thirty years; this was another of the world's pleasures he had put aside.

"I don't like fish," complained Susan. "When do we get to
the snakes?"

"Presently," he said. "But what's the hurry? There's plenty
of time."

The words slipped out before he realized it. He checked his
step, while the children ran on ahead. Then he smiled, without bitterness. For in a sense, it was true enough. There *was*
plenty of time. Each day, each hour could be a universe of
experience, if one used it properly. In the last weeks of his
life, he would begin to live.

As yet, no one at the office suspected anything. Even his
outing with the children had not caused much surprise; he
had done such things before, suddenly canceling his appoint-
ments and leaving his staff to pick up the pieces. The pattern
of his behavior had not yet changed, but in a few days it
would be obvious to all his associates that something had happened. He owed it to them—and to the Party—to break the
news as soon as possible; there were, however, many personal decisions he had to make first, which he wished to
settle in his own mind before he began the vast unwinding
of his affairs.

There was another reason for his hesitancy. During his
career, he had seldom lost a fight, and in the cut and thrust
of political life he had given quarter to none. Now, facing his
ultimate defeat, he dreaded the sympathy and the con-

dolences that his many enemies would hasten to shower upon him. The attitude, he knew, was a foolish one—a remnant of his stubborn pride which was too much a part of his personality to vanish even under the shadow of death.

He carried his secret from committee room to White House to Capitol, and through all the labyrinths of Washington society, for more than two weeks. It was the finest performance of his career, but there was no one to appreciate it. At the end of that time he had completed his plan of action; it remained only to dispatch a few letters he had written in his own hand, and to call his wife.

The office located her, not without difficulty, in Rome. She was still beautiful, he thought, as her features swam on to the screen; she would have made a fine First Lady, and that would have been some compensation for the lost years. As far as he knew, she had looked forward to the prospect; but had he ever really understood what she wanted?

"Hello, Martin," she said, "I was expecting to hear from you. I suppose you want me to come back."

"Are you willing to?" he asked quietly. The gentleness of his voice obviously surprised her.

"I'd be a fool to say no, wouldn't I? But if they don't elect you, I want to go my own way again. You must agree to that."

"They won't elect me. They won't even nominate me. You're the first to know this, Diana. In six months, I shall be dead."

The directness was brutal, but it had a purpose. That fraction-of-a-second delay while the radio waves flashed up to the communications satellites and back again to Earth had never seemed so long. For once, he had broken through the beautiful mask. Her eyes widened with disbelief, her hand flew to her lips.

"You're joking!"

"About *this?* It's true enough. My heart's worn out. Dr. Jordan told me, a couple of weeks ago. It's my own fault, of course, but let's not go into that."

"So that's why you've been taking out the children: I wondered what had happened."

He might have guessed that Irene would have talked with her mother. It was a sad reflection on Martin Steelman, if so commonplace a fact as showing an interest in his own grandchildren could cause curiosity.

"Yes," he admitted frankly. "I'm afraid I left it a little

late. Now I'm trying to make up for lost time. Nothing else seems very important."

In silence, they looked into each other's eyes across the curve of the Earth, and across the empty desert of the dividing years. Then Diana answered, a little unsteadily, "I'll start packing right away."

Now that the news was out, he felt a great sense of relief. Even the sympathy of his enemies was not as hard to accept as he had feared. For overnight, indeed, he had no enemies. Men who had not spoken to him in years, except with invective, sent messages whose sincerity could not be doubted. Ancient quarrels evaporated, or turned out to be founded on misunderstandings. It was a pity that one had to die to learn these things. . . .

He also learned that, for a man of affairs, dying was a full-time job. There were successors to appoint, legal and financial mazes to untangle, committee and state business to wind up. The work of an energetic lifetime could not be terminated suddenly, as one switches off an electric light. It was astonishing how many responsibilities he had acquired, and how difficult it was to divest himself of them. He had never found it easy to delegate power (a fatal flaw, many critics had said, in a man who hoped to be Chief Executive), but now he must do so, before it slipped forever from his hands.

It was as if a great clock was running down, and there was no one to rewind it. As he gave away his books, read and destroyed old letters, closed useless accounts and files, dictated final instructions, and wrote farewell notes, he sometimes felt a sense of complete unreality. There was no pain; he could never have guessed that he did not have years of active life ahead of him. Only a few lines on a cardiogram lay like a roadblock across his future—or like a curse, written in some strange language the doctors alone could read.

Almost every day now Diana, Irene, or her husband brought the children to see him. In the past he had never felt at ease with Bill, but that, he knew, had been his own fault. You could not expect a son-in-law to replace a son, and it was unfair to blame Bill because he had not been cast in the image of Martin Steelman, Jr. Bill was a person in his own right; he had looked after Irene, made her happy, and fathered her children. That he lacked ambition was a flaw—if flaw indeed it was—that the Senator could at last forgive.

He could even think, without pain or bitterness, of his own son, who had traveled this road before him and now lay, one cross among many, in the United Nations cemetery at Capetown. He had never visited Martin's grave; in the days when he had the time, white men were not popular in what was left of South Africa. Now he could go if he wished, but he was uncertain if it would be fair to harrow Diana with such a mission. His own memories would not trouble him much longer, but she would be left with hers.

Yet he would like to go, and felt it was his duty. Moreover, it would be a last treat for the children. To them it would be only a holiday in a strange land, without any tinge of sorrow for an uncle they had never known. He had started to make the arrangements when, for the second time within a month, his whole world was turned upside down.

Even now, a dozen or more visitors would be waiting for him each morning when he arrived at his office. Not as many as in the old days, but still a sizable crowd. He had never imagined, however, that Dr. Harkness would be among them.

The sight of that thin, gangling figure made him momentarily break his stride. He felt his cheeks flush, his pulse quicken at the memory of ancient battles across committee-room tables, of angry exchanges that had reverberated along the myriad channels of the ether. Then he relaxed; as far as he was concerned, all that was over.

Harkness rose to his feet, a little awkwardly, as he approached. Senator Steelman knew that initial embarrassment —he had seen it so often in the last few weeks. Everyone he now met was automatically at a disadvantage, always on the alert to avoid the one subject that was taboo.

"Well, Doctor," he said. "This is a surprise—I never expected to see *you* here."

He could not resist that little jab, and derived some satisfaction at watching it go home. But it was free from bitterness, as the other's smile acknowledged.

"Senator," replied Harkness, in a voice that was pitched so low that he had to lean forward to hear it, "I've some extremely important information for you. Can we speak alone for a few minutes? It won't take long."

Steelman nodded; he had his own ideas of what was important now, and felt only a mild curiosity as to why the scientist had come to see him. The man seemed to have changed a good deal since their last encounter, seven years ago. He was much more assured and self-confident, and had lost the nervous mannerisms that had helped to make him such an unconvincing witness.

"Senator," he began, when they were alone in the private office, "I've some news that may be quite a shock to you. I believe that you can be cured."

Steelman slumped heavily in his chair. This was the one thing he had never expected; from the first, he had not encumbered himself with the burden of vain hopes. Only a fool fought against the inevitable, and he had accepted his fate.

For a moment he could not speak; then he looked up at his old adversary and gasped: "Who told you that? All my doctors—"

"Never mind them; it's not their fault they're ten years behind the times. Look at this."

"What does it mean? I can't read Russian."

"It's the latest issue of the USSR *Journal of Space Medicine*. It arrived a few days ago, and we did the usual routine translation. This note here—the one I've marked—refers to some recent work at the Mechnikov Station."

"What's that?"

"You don't *know?* Why, that's their Satellite Hospital, the one they've built just below the Great Radiation Belt."

"Go on," said Steelman, in a voice that was suddenly dry and constricted. "I'd forgotten they'd called it that." He had hoped to end his life in peace, but now the past had come back to haunt him.

"Well, the note itself doesn't say much, but you can read a lot between the lines. It's one of those advance hints that scientists put out before they have time to write a full-fledged paper, so they can claim priority later. The title is: 'Therapeutic Effects of Zero Gravity on Circulatory Diseases.' What they've done is to induce heart disease artificially in rabbits and hamsters, and then take them up to the space station. In orbit, of course, nothing has any weight; the heart and muscles have practically no work to do. And the result is exactly what I tried to tell you, years ago. Even extreme cases can be arrested, and many can be cured."

The tiny, paneled office that had been the center of his world, the scene of so many conferences, the birthplace of so many plans, became suddenly unreal. Memory was much more vivid: he was back again at those hearings, in the fall of 1969, when the National Aeronautics and Space Administration's first decade of activity had been under review —and, frequently, under fire.

He had never been chairman of the Senate Committee on Astronautics, but he had been its most vocal and effective member. It was here that he had made his reputation as a guardian of the public purse, as a hardheaded man who could not be bamboozled by utopian scientific dreamers. He had done a good job; from that moment, he had never been far from the headlines. It was not that he had any particular feeling for space and science, but he knew a live issue when he saw one. Like a tape-recorder unrolling in his mind, it all came back. . . .

"Dr. Harkness, you are Technical Director of the National Aeronautics and Space Administration?"

"That is correct."

"I have here the figures for NASA's expenditure over the period 1959-69; they are quite impressive. At the moment the total is $82,547,540,000, and the estimate for fiscal '69-'70 is well over ten billions. Perhaps you could give us some indication of the return we can expect from all this."

"I'll be glad to do so, Senator."

That was how it had started, on a firm but not unfriendly note. The hostility had crept in later. That it was unjustified, he had known at the time; any big organization had weaknesses and failures, and one which literally aimed at the stars could never hope for more than partial success. From the beginning, it had been realized that the conquest of space would be at least as costly in lives and treasure as the conquest of the air. In ten years, almost a hundred men had died—on Earth, in space, and upon the barren surface of the Moon. Now that the urgency of the early sixties was over, the public was asking "Why?" Steelman was shrewd enough to see himself as mouthpiece for those questioning voices. His performance had been cold and calculated; it was convenient to have a scapegoat, and Dr. Harkness was unlucky enough to be cast for the role.

"Yes, Doctor, I understand all the benefits we've received from space research in the way of improved communications and weather forecasting, and I'm sure everyone appreciates them. But almost all this work has been done with automatic, unmanned vehicles. What I'm worried about—what many people are worried about—is the mounting expense of the Man-in-Space program, and its very marginal utility. Since the original Dyna-Soar and Apollo projects, almost a decade ago, we've shot billions of dollars into space. And with what result? So that a mere handful of men can spend a few uncomfortable hours outside the atmosphere, achieving nothing that television cameras and automatic equipment couldn't do—much better and cheaper. And the lives that have been lost! None of us will forget those screams we heard coming over the radio when the X-21 burned up on re-entry. What right have we to send men to such deaths?"

He could still remember the hushed silence in the committee chamber when he had finished. His questions were very reasonable ones, and deserved to be answered. What was unfair was the rhetorical manner in which he had framed them and, above all, the fact that they were aimed at a man who could not answer them effectively. Steelman would not have tried such tactics on a von Braun or a Rickover; they would have given him at least as good as they received. But Harkness was no orator; if he had deep personal feelings, he kept them to himself. He was a good scientist, an able administrator—and a poor witness. It had been like shooting fish in a barrel. The reporters had loved it; he never knew which of them coined the nickname "Hapless Harkness."

"Now this plan of yours, Doctor, for a fifty-man space laboratory—*how* much did you say it would cost?"

"I've already told you—just under one and a half billions."

"And the annual maintenance?"

"Not more than $250,000,000."

"When we consider what's happened to previous estimates, you will forgive us if we look upon these figures with some skepticism. But even assuming that they are right, what will we get for the money?"

"We will be able to establish our first large-scale research station in space. So far, we have had to do our experimenting in cramped quarters aboard unsuitable vehicles, usually when they were engaged on some other mission. A permanent, manned satellite laboratory is essential. Without it, further progress is out of the question. Astrobiology can hardly get started—"

"Astro what?"

"Astrobiology—the study of living organisms in space. The Russians really started it when they sent up the dog Laika in Sputnik II and they're still ahead of us in this field. But no one's done any serious work on insects or invertebrates—in fact, on any animals except dogs, mice, and monkeys."

"I see. Would I be correct in saying that you would like funds for building a zoo in space?"

The laughter in the committee room had helped to kill the project. And it had helped, Senator Steelman now realized, to kill him.

He had only himself to blame, for Dr. Harkness had tried, in his ineffectual way, to outline the benefits that a space laboratory might bring. He had particularly stressed the medical aspects, promising nothing; but pointing out the possibilities. Surgeons, he had suggested, would be able to develop new techniques in an environment where the organs had no weight; men might live longer, freed from the wear and tear of gravity, for the strain on heart and muscles would be enormously reduced. Yes, he had mentioned the heart; but that had been of no interest to Senator Steelman—healthy, and ambitious, and anxious to make good copy. . . .

"Why have you come to tell me this?" he said dully. "Couldn't you let me die in peace?"

"That's the point," said Harkness impatiently. "There's no need to give up hope."

"Because the Russians have cured some hamsters and rabbits?"

"They've done much more than that. The paper I showed you only quoted the preliminary results; it's already a year out of date. They don't want to raise false hopes, so they are keeping as quiet as possible."

"How do you know this?"

Harkness looked surprised.

"Why, I called Professor Stanyukovitch, my opposite number. It turned out that he was up on the Mechnikov Station, which proves how important they consider this work. He's an old friend of mine, and I took the liberty of mentioning your case."

The dawn of hope, after its long absence, can be as painful as its departure. Steelman found it hard to breathe and for a dreadful moment he wondered if the final attack had come. But it was only excitement; the constriction in his chest relaxed, the ringing in his ears faded away, and he heard Dr. Harkness' voice saying: "He wanted to know if you could come to Astrograd right away, so I said I'd ask you. If you can make it, there's a flight from New York at ten-thirty tomorrow morning."

Tomorrow he had promised to take the children to the Zoo; it would be the first time he had let them down. The thought gave him a sharp stab of guilt, and it required almost an effort of will to answer: "I can make it."

He saw nothing of Moscow during the few minutes that the big intercontinental ramjet fell down from the stratosphere. The view-screens were switched off during the descent, for the sight of the ground coming straight up as a ship fell vertically on its sustaining jets was highly disconcerting to passengers.

At Moscow he changed to a comfortable but old-fashioned turboprop, and as he flew eastward into the night he had his first real opportunity for reflection. It was a very strange question to ask himself, but was he altogether glad that the future was no longer wholly certain? His life, which a few hours ago had seemed so simple, had suddenly become complex again, as it opened out once more into possibilities he had learned to put aside. Dr. Johnson had been right when he said that nothing settles a man's mind more wonderfully than the knowledge that he will be hanged in the morning. For the converse was certainly true—nothing unsettled it so much as the thought of a reprieve.

He was asleep when they touched down at Astrograd, the space capital of the USSR. When the gentle impact of the landing shook him awake, for a moment he could not imagine where he was. Had he dreamed that he was flying halfway around the world in search of life? No; it was not a dream, but it might well be a wild-goose chase.

Twelve hours later, he was still waiting for the answer. The last instrument reading had been taken; the spots of light on the cardiograph display had ceased their fateful dance. The familiar routine of the medical examination and the gentle, competent voices of the doctors and nurses had done much to relax his mind. And it was very restful in the softly lit reception room, where the specialists had asked him to wait while they conferred together. Only the Russian magazines, and a few portraits of somewhat hirsute pioneers of Soviet medicine, reminded him that he was no longer in his own country.

He was not the only patient. About a dozen men and women, of all ages, were sitting around the wall, reading magazines and trying to appear at ease. There was no conversation, no attempt to catch anyone's eye. Every soul in this room was in his private limbo, suspended between life and death. Though they were linked together by a common misfortune, the link did not extend to communication. Each seemed as cut off from the rest of the human race as if he was already speeding through the cosmic gulfs where lay his only hope.

But in the far corner of the room, there was an exception. A young couple—neither could have been more than twenty-five—were huddling together in such desperate misery that at first Steelman found the spectacle annoying. No matter how bad their own problems, he told himself severely, people should be more considerate. They should hide their emotions—especially in a place like this, where they might upset others.

His annoyance quickly turned to pity, for no heart can remain untouched for long at the sight of simple, unselfish love in deep distress. As the minutes dripped away in a silence broken only by the rustling of papers and the scraping of chairs, his pity grew almost to an obsession.

What was their story, he wondered. The boy had sensitive, intelligent features; he might have been an artist, a scientist, a musician—there was no way of telling. The girl was pregnant; she had one of those homely peasant faces so common among Russian women. She was far from beautiful, but sorrow and love had given her features a luminous sweetness. Steelman found it hard to take his eyes from her—for somehow, though there was not the slightest physical resemblance, she reminded him of Diana. Thirty years ago, as they had walked from the church together, he had seen that same glow in the eyes of his wife. He had almost forgotten it; was the fault his, or hers, that it had faded so soon?

Without any warning, his chair vibrated beneath him. A swift, sudden tremor had swept through the building, as if a giant hammer had smashed against the ground, many miles away. An earthquake? Steelman wondered; then he remembered where he was, and started counting seconds.

He gave up when he reached sixty; presumably the sound-proofing was so good that the slower, air-borne noise had not reached him, and only the shock wave through the ground recorded the fact that a thousand tons had just leapt into the sky. Another minute passed before he heard, distant but clear, a sound as of a thunderstorm raging below the edge of the world. It was even more miles away than he had dreamed; what the noise must be like at the launching site was beyond imagination.

Yet that thunder would not trouble him, he knew, when he also rose into the sky; the speeding rocket would leave it far behind. Nor would the thrust of acceleration be able to touch his body, as it rested in its bath of warm water—more comfortable even than this deeply padded chair.

That distant rumble was still rolling back from the edge of space when the door of the waiting room opened and the nurse beckoned to him. Though he felt many eyes following him, he did not look back as he walked out to receive his sentence.

The news services tried to get in contact with him all the way back from Moscow, but he refused to accept the calls. "Say I'm sleeping and mustn't be disturbed," he told the stewardess. He wondered who had tipped them off, and felt annoyed at this invasion of his privacy. Yet privacy was something he had avoided for years, and had learned to appreciate only in the last few weeks. He could not blame the reporters and commentators if they assumed that he had reverted to type.

They were waiting for him when the ramjet touched down at Washington. He knew most of them by name, and some were old friends, genuinely glad to hear the news that had raced ahead of him.

"What does it feel like, Senator," said Macauley, of the *Times*, "to know you're back in harness? I take it that it's true—the Russians can cure you?"

"They *think* they can," he answered cautiously. "This is a new field of medicine, and no one can promise anything."

"When do you leave for space?"

"Within the week, as soon as I've settled some affairs here."

"And when will you be back—if it works?"

"That's hard to say. Even if everything goes smoothly, I'll be up there at least six months."

Involuntarily, he glanced at the sky. At dawn or sunset—even during the daytime, if one knew where to look—the Mechnikov Station was a spectacular sight, more brilliant than any of the stars. But there were now so many satellites of which this was true that only an expert could tell one from another.

"Six months," said a newsman thoughtfully. "That means you'll be out of the picture for '76."

"But nicely in it for 1980," said another.

"*And* 1984," added a third. There was a general laugh; people were already making jokes about 1984, which had once seemed so far in the future, but would soon be a date no different from any other . . . it was hoped.

The ears and the microphones were waiting for his reply. As he stood at the foot of the ramp, once more the focus of attention and curiosity, he felt the old excitement stirring in his veins. What a comeback it would be, to return from space a new man! It would give him a glamour that no other candidate could match; there was something Olympian, almost godlike, about the prospect. Already he found himself trying to work it into his election slogans. . . .

"Give me time to make my plans," he said. "It's going to take me a while to get used to this. But I promise you a statement before I leave Earth."

Before I leave Earth. Now, there was a fine, dramatic phrase. He was still savoring its rhythm with his mind when he saw Diana coming toward him from the airport buildings.

Already she had changed, as he himself was changing; in her eyes was a wariness and reserve that had not been there two days ago. It said, as clearly as any words: "Is it going to happen all over again?" Though the day was warm, he felt suddenly cold, as if he had caught a chill on those far Siberian plains.

But Joey and Susan were unchanged, as they ran to greet him. He caught them up in his arms, and buried his face in their hair, so that the cameras would not see the tears that had started from his eyes. As they clung to him in the innocent, unself-conscious love of childhood, he knew what his choice would have to be.

They alone had known him when he was free from the itch for power; that was the way they must remember him, if they remembered him at all.

"Your conference call, Mr. Steelman," said his secretary. "I'm routing it on to your private screen."

He swiveled round in his chair and faced the gray panel on the wall. As he did so, it split into two vertical sections. On the right half was a view of an office much like his own, and only a few miles away. But on the left—

Professor Stanyukovitch, lightly dressed in shorts and

singlet, was floating in mid-air a good foot above his seat. He grabbed it when he saw that he had company, pulled himself down, and fastened a webbed belt around his waist. Behind him were ranged banks of communications equipment; and behind those, Steelman knew, was space.

Dr. Harkness spoke first, from the right-hand screen.

"We were expecting to hear from you, Senator. Professor Stanyukovitch tells me that everything is ready."

"The next supply ship," said the Russian, "comes up in two days. It will be taking me back to Earth, but I hope to see you before I leave the station."

His voice was curiously high-pitched, owing to the thin oxyhelium atmosphere he was breathing. Apart from that, there was no sense of distance, no background of interference. Though Stanyukovitch was thousands of miles away, and racing through space at four miles a second, he might have been in the same office. Steelman could even hear the faint whirring of electric motors from the equipment racks behind him.

"Professor," answered Steelman, "there are a few things I'd like to ask before I go."

"Certainly."

Now he could tell that Stanyukovitch was a long way off. There was an appreciable time lag before his reply arrived: the station must be above the far side of the Earth.

"When I was at Astrograd, I noticed many other patients at the clinic. I was wondering—on what basis do you select those for treatment?"

This time the pause was much greater than the delay due to the sluggish speed of radio waves. Then Stanyukovitch answered: "Why, those with the best chance of responding."

"But your accommodation must be very limited. You must have many other candidates besides myself."

"I don't quite see the point—" interrupted Dr. Harkness, a little too anxiously.

Steelman swung his eyes to the right-hand screen. It was quite difficult to recognize, in the man staring back at him, the witness who had squirmed beneath his needling only a few years ago. That experience had tempered Harkness, had given him his baptism in the art of politics. Steelman had taught him much, and he had applied his hard-won knowledge.

His motives had been obvious from the first. Harkness would have been less than human if he did not relish this sweetest of revenges, this triumphant vindication of his faith.

And as Space Administration Director, he was well aware that half his budget battles would be over when all the world knew that a potential President of the United States was in a Russian space hospital . . . because his own country did not possess one.

"Dr. Harkness," said Steelman gently, "this is *my* affair. I'm still waiting for your answer, Professor."

Despite the issues involved, he was quite enjoying this. The two scientists, of course, were playing for identical stakes. Stanyukovitch had his problems too; Steelman could guess the discussions that had taken place at Astrograd and Moscow, and the eagerness with which the Soviet astronauts had grasped this opportunity—which, it must be admitted, they had richly earned.

It was an ironic situation, unimaginable only a dozen years before. Here were NASA and the USSR Commission of Astronautics working hand in hand, using him as a pawn for their mutual advantage. He did not resent this, for in their place he would have done the same. But he had no wish to be a pawn; he was an individual who still had some control of his own destiny.

"It's quite true," said Stanyukovitch, very reluctantly, "that we can only take a limited number of patients here in Mechnikov. In any case, the station's a research laboratory, not a hospital."

"How many?" asked Steelman relentlessly.

"Well—fewer than ten," admitted Stanyukovitch, still more unwillingly.

It was an old problem, of course, though he had never imagined that it would apply to him. From the depths of memory there flashed a newspaper item he had come across long ago. When penicillin had been first discovered, it was so rare that if both Churchill and Roosevelt had been dying for lack of it, only one could have been treated. . . .

Fewer than ten. He had seen a dozen waiting at Astrograd, and how many were there in the whole world? Once again, as it had done so often in the last few days, the memory of those desolate lovers in the reception room came back to haunt him. Perhaps they were beyond his aid; he would never know.

But one thing he did know. He bore a responsibility that he could not escape. It was true that no man could foresee the future, and the endless consequences of his actions. Yet if it had not been for him, by this time his own country might have had a space hospital circling beyond the atmosphere.

How many American lives were upon his conscience? Could he accept the help he had denied to others? Once he might have done so—but not now.

"Gentlemen," he said, "I can speak frankly with you both, for I know your interests are identical." (His mild irony, he saw, did not escape them.) "I appreciate your help and the trouble you have taken; I am sorry it has been wasted. No—don't protest; this isn't a sudden, quixotic decision on my part. If I was ten years younger, it might be different. Now I feel that this opportunity should be given to someone else—especially in view of my record." He glanced at Dr. Harkness, who gave an embarrassed smile. "I also have other, personal reasons, and there's no chance that I will change my mind. Please don't think me rude or ungrateful, but I don't wish to discuss the matter any further. Thank you again, and good-by."

He broke the circuit; and as the image of the two astonished scientists faded, peace came flooding back into his soul.

Imperceptibly, spring merged into summer. The eagerly awaited Bicentenary celebrations came and went; for the first time in years, he was able to enjoy Independence Day as a private citizen. Now he could sit back and watch the others perform—or he could ignore them if he wished.

Because the ties of a lifetime were too strong to break, and it would be his last opportunity to see many old friends, he spent hours looking in on both conventions and listening to the commentators. Now that he saw the whole world beneath the light of Eternity, his emotions were no longer involved; he understood the issues, and appreciated the arguments, but already he was as detached as an observer from another planet. The tiny, shouting figures on the screen were amusing marionettes, acting out roles in a play that was entertaining, but no longer important—at least, to him.

But it was important to his grandchildren, who would one day move out onto this same stage. He had not forgotten that; they were his share of the future, whatever strange form it might take. And to understand the future, it was necessary to know the past.

He was taking them into that past, as the car swept along Memorial Drive. Diana was at the wheel, with Irene beside her, while he sat with the children, pointing out the familiar sights along the highway. Familiar to him, but not to them;

even if they were not old enough to understand all that they were seeing, he hoped they would remember.

Past the marble stillness of Arlington (he thought again of Martin, sleeping on the other side of the world) and up into the hills the car wound its effortless way. Behind them, like a city seen through a mirage, Washington danced and trembled in the summer haze, until the curve of the road hid it from view.

It was quiet at Mount Vernon; there were few visitors so early in the week. As they left the car and walked toward the house, Steelman wondered what the first President of the United States would have thought could he have seen his home as it was today. He could never have dreamed that it would enter its second century still perfectly preserved, a changeless island in the hurrying river of time.

They walked slowly through the beautifully proportioned rooms, doing their best to answer the children's endless questions, trying to assimilate the flavor of an infinitely simpler, infinitely more leisurely mode of life. (But had it seemed simple or leisurely to those who lived it?) It was so hard to imagine a world without electricity, without radio, without any power save that of muscle, wind, and water. A world where nothing moved faster than a running horse, and most men died within a few miles of the place where they were born.

The heat, the walking, and the incessant questions proved more tiring than Steelman had expected. When they had reached the Music Room, he decided to rest. There were some attractive benches out on the porch, where he could sit in the fresh air and feast his eyes upon the green grass of the lawn.

"Meet me outside," he explained to Diana, "when you've done the kitchen and the stables. I'd like to sit down for a while."

"You're sure you're quite all right?" she said anxiously.

"I never felt better, but I don't want to overdo it. Besides, the kids have drained me dry—I can't think of any more answers. You'll have to invent some; the kitchen's your department, anyway."

Diana smiled.

"I was never much good in it, was I? But I'll do my best— I don't suppose we'll be more than thirty minutes."

When they had left him, he walked slowly out onto the lawn. Here Washington must have stood, two centuries ago, watching the Potomac wind its way to the sea, thinking of past wars and future problems. And here Martin Steelman, thirty-eighth President of the United States, might have stood a few months hence, had the fates ruled otherwise.

He could not pretend that he had no regrets, but they were very few. Some men could achieve both power and happiness, but that gift was not for him. Sooner or later, his ambition would have consumed him. In the last few weeks he had known contentment, and for that no price was too great.

He was still marveling at the narrowness of his escape when his time ran out and Death fell softly from the summer sky.

Colombo   *July 1960*

Who's There?

When Satellite Control called me, I was writing up the day's progress report in the Observation Bubble—the glass-domed office that juts out from the axis of the space station like the hubcap of a wheel. It was not really a good place to work, for the view was too overwhelming. Only a few yards away I could see the construction teams performing their slow-motion ballet as they put the station together like a giant jigsaw puzzle. And beyond them, twenty thousand miles below, was the blue-green glory of the full Earth, floating against the raveled star clouds of the Milky Way.

"Station Supervisor here," I answered. "What's the trouble?"

"Our radar's showing a small echo two miles away, almost stationary, about five degrees west of Sirius. Can you give us a visual report on it?"

Anything matching our orbit so precisely could hardly be a meteor; it would have to be something we'd dropped—perhaps an inadequately secured piece of equipment that had drifted away from the station. So I assumed; but when I pulled out my binoculars and searched the sky around Orion, I soon found my mistake. Though this space traveler was man-made, it had nothing to do with us.

"I've found it," I told Control. "It's someone's test satellite —cone-shaped, four antennas, and what looks like a lens system in its base. Probably U.S. Air Force, early nineteen-sixties, judging by the design. I know they lost track of several when their transmitters failed. There were quite a few attempts to hit this orbit before they finally made it."

After a brief search through the files, Control was able to confirm my guess. It took a little longer to find out that Washington wasn't in the least bit interested in our discovery of a twenty-year-old stray satellite, and would be just as happy if we lost it again.

"Well, we can't do *that*," said Control. "Even if nobody

wants it, the thing's a menace to navigation. Someone had better go out and haul it aboard."

That someone, I realized, would have to be me. I dared not detach a man from the closely knit construction teams, for we were already behind schedule—and a single day's delay on this job cost a million dollars. All the radio and TV networks on Earth were waiting impatiently for the moment when they could route their programs through us, and thus provide the first truly global service, spanning the world from Pole to Pole.

"I'll go out and get it," I answered, snapping an elastic band over my papers so that the air currents from the ventilators wouldn't set them wandering around the room. Though I tried to sound as if I was doing everyone a great favor, I was secretly not at all displeased. It had been at least two weeks since I'd been outside; I was getting a little tired of stores schedules, maintenance reports, and all the glamorous ingredients of a Space Station Supervisor's life.

The only member of the staff I passed on my way to the air lock was Tommy, our recently acquired cat. Pets mean a great deal to men thousands of miles from Earth, but there are not many animals that can adapt themselves to a weightless environment. Tommy mewed plaintively at me as I clambered into my space suit, but I was in too much of a hurry to play with him.

At this point, perhaps I should remind you that the suits we use on the station are completely different from the flexible affairs men wear when they want to walk around on the Moon. Ours are really baby spaceships, just big enough to hold one man. They are stubby cylinders, about seven feet long, fitted with low-powered propulsion jets, and have a pair of accordion-like sleeves at the upper end for the operator's arms. Normally, however, you keep your hands drawn inside the suit, working the manual controls in front of your chest.

As soon as I'd settled down inside my very exclusive spacecraft, I switched on power and checked the gauges on the tiny instrument panel. There's a magic word, "FORB," that you'll often hear spacemen mutter as they climb into their suits; it reminds them to test fuel, oxygen, radio, batteries. All my needles were well in the safety zone, so I lowered the transparent hemisphere over my head and sealed myself in. For a short trip like this, I did not bother to check the suit's internal lockers, which were used to carry food and special equipment for extended missions.

As the conveyor belt decanted me into the air lock, I felt like an Indian papoose being carried along on its mother's back. Then the pumps brought the pressure down to zero, the outer door opened, and the last traces of air swept me out into the stars, turning very slowly head over heels.

The station was only a dozen feet away, yet I was now an independent planet—a little world of my own. I was sealed up in a tiny, mobile cylinder, with a superb view of the entire Universe, but I had practically no freedom of movement inside the suit. The padded seat and safety belts prevented me from turning around, though I could reach all the controls and lockers with my hands or feet.

In space, the great enemy is the sun, which can blast you to blindness in seconds. Very cautiously, I opened up the dark filters on the "night" side of my suit, and turned my head to look out at the stars. At the same time I switched the helmet's external sunshade to automatic, so that whichever way the suit gyrated my eyes would be shielded from that intolerable glare.

Presently, I found my target—a bright fleck of silver whose metallic glint distinguished it clearly from the surrounding stars. I stamped on the jet-control pedal, and felt the mild surge of acceleration as the low-powered rockets set me moving away from the station. After ten seconds of steady thrust, I estimated that my speed was great enough, and cut off the drive. It would take me five minutes to coast the rest of the way, and not much longer to return with my salvage.

And it was at that moment, as I launched myself out into the abyss, that I knew that something was horribly wrong.

It is never completely silent inside a space suit; you can always hear the gentle hiss of oxygen, the faint whirr of fans and motors, the susurration of your own breathing—even, if you listen carefully enough, the rhythmic thump that is the pounding of your heart. These sounds reverberate through the suit, unable to escape into the surrounding void; they are the unnoticed background of life in space, for you are aware of them only when they change.

They had changed now; to them had been added a sound which I could not identify. It was an intermittent, muffled thudding, sometimes accompanied by a scraping noise, as of metal upon metal.

I froze instantly, holding my breath and trying to locate the alien sound with my ears. The meters on the control board gave no clues; all the needles were rock-steady on their scales, and there were none of the flickering red lights that would warn of impending disaster. That was some comfort, but not much. I had long ago learned to trust my instincts in such matters; their alarm signals were flashing now, telling me to return to the station before it was too late. . . .

Even now, I do not like to recall those next few minutes, as panic slowly flooded into my mind like a rising tide, overwhelming the dams of reason and logic which every man must erect against the mystery of the Universe. I knew then what it was like to face insanity; no other explanation fitted the facts.

For it was no longer possible to pretend that the noise disturbing me was that of some faulty mechanism. Though I was in utter isolation, far from any other human being or indeed any material object, I was not alone. The soundless void was bringing to my ears the faint but unmistakable stirrings of life.

In that first, heart-freezing moment it seemed that something was trying to get into my suit—something invisible, seeking shelter from the cruel and pitiless vacuum of space. I whirled madly in my harness, scanning the entire sphere of vision around me except for the blazing, forbidden cone toward the sun. There was nothing there. Of course. There could not be—yet that purposeful scrabbling was clearer than ever.

Despite the nonsense that has been written about us, it is not true that spacemen are superstitious. But can you blame me if, as I came to the end of logic's resources, I suddenly remembered how Bernie Summers had died, no farther from the station than I was at this very moment?

It was one of those "impossible" accidents; it always is. Three things had gone wrong at once. Bernie's oxygen regulator had run wild and sent the pressure soaring, the safety valve had failed to blow—and a faulty joint had given way instead. In a fraction of a second, his suit was open to space.

I had never known Bernie, but suddenly his fate became of overwhelming importance to me—for a horrible idea had come into my mind. One does not talk about these things, but a damaged space suit is too valuable to be thrown away, even if it has killed its wearer. It is repaired, renumbered—and issued to someone else. . . .

What happens to the soul of a man who dies between the stars, far from his native world? Are you still here, Bernie, clinging to the last object that linked you to your lost and distant home?

As I fought the nightmares that were swirling around me—for now it seemed that the scratchings and soft fumblings were coming from all directions—there was one last hope to which I clung. For the sake of my sanity, I had to prove that this wasn't Bernie's suit—that the metal walls so closely wrapped around me had never been another man's coffin.

It took me several tries before I could press the right button and switch my transmitter to the emergency wave length. "Station!" I gasped. "I'm in trouble! Get records to check my suit history and—"

I never finished; they say my yell wrecked the microphone. But what man alone in the absolute isolation of a space suit would *not* have yelled when something patted him softly on the back of the neck?

I must have lunged forward, despite the safety harness, and smashed against the upper edge of the control panel. When the rescue squad reached me a few minutes later, I was still unconscious, with an angry bruise across my forehead.

And so I was the last person in the whole satellite relay system to know what had happened. When I came to my senses an hour later, all our medical staff was gathered around my bed, but it was quite a while before the doctors bothered to look at me. They were much too busy playing with the three cute little kittens our badly misnamed Tommy had been rearing in the seclusion of my space suit's Number Five Storage Locker.

Dallas   *February 1958*

Before Eden

*Like "I Remember Babylon," this was intended as a caution-
ary tale, though, as usual, Wells was the first to warn of
planetary contamination in* The War of the Worlds.

*Today, there is an international committee (CETEX) study-
ing the subject, NASA has a "Planetary Quarantine" officer
on its headquarters staff, and Sir Bernard Lovell castigates the
Russians for dropping unsterilized probes on Venus.*

*The USSR has since claimed that its first Venus lander was
properly sterilized. If it is wrong, the events in this story may
already have happened.*

"I guess," said Jerry Garfield, cutting the engines, "that this
is the end of the line." With a gentle sigh, the underjets faded
out; deprived of its air cushion, the scout car *Rambling Wreck*
settled down upon the twisted rocks of the Hesperian Plateau.

There was no way forward; on neither its jets nor its tractors could S.5—to give the *Wreck* its official name—scale the
escarpment that lay ahead. The South Pole of Venus was only
thirty miles away, but it might have been on another planet.
They would have to turn back, and retrace their four-hun-
dred-mile journey through this nightmare landscape.

The weather was fantastically clear, with visibility of
almost a thousand yards. There was no need of radar to show
the cliffs ahead; for once, the naked eye was good enough.
The green auroral light, filtering down through clouds that
had rolled unbroken for a million years, gave the scene an
underwater appearance, and the way in which all distant objects blurred into the haze added to the impression. Sometimes it was easy to believe that they were driving across a
shallow sea bed, and more than once Jerry had imagined that
he had seen fish floating overhead.

148

"Shall I call the ship, and say we're turning back?" he asked.

"Not yet," said Dr. Hutchins. "I want to think."

Jerry shot an appealing glance at the third member of the crew, but found no moral support there. Coleman was just as bad; although the two men argued furiously half the time, they were both scientists and therefore, in the opinion of a hardheaded engineer-navigator, not wholly responsible citizens. If Cole and Hutch had bright ideas about going forward, there was nothing he could do except register a protest.

Hutchins was pacing back and forth in the tiny cabin, studying charts and instruments. Presently he swung the car's searchlight toward the cliffs, and began to examine them carefully with binoculars. Surely, thought Jerry, he doesn't expect me to drive up there! S.5 was a hover-track, not a mountain goat. . . .

Abruptly, Hutchins found something. He released his breath in a sudden explosive gasp, then turned to Coleman.

"Look!" he said, his voice full of excitement. "Just to the left of that black mark! Tell me what you see."

He handed over the glasses, and it was Coleman's turn to stare.

"Well I'm damned," he said at length. "You were right. There *are* rivers on Venus. That's a dried-up waterfall."

"So you owe me one dinner at the Bel Gourmet when we get back to Cambridge. With champagne."

"No need to remind me. Anyway, it's cheap at the price. But this still leaves your other theories strictly on the crackpot level."

"Just a minute," interjected Jerry. "What's all this about rivers and waterfalls? Everyone knows they can't exist on Venus. It never gets cold enough on this steam bath of a planet for the clouds to condense."

"Have you looked at the thermometer lately?" asked Hutchins with deceptive mildness.

"I've been slightly too busy driving."

"Then I've news for you. It's down to two hundred and thirty, and still falling. Don't forget—we're almost at the Pole, it's wintertime, and we're sixty thousand feet above the lowlands. All this adds up to a distinct nip in the air. If the temperature drops a few more degrees, we'll have rain. The water will be boiling, of course—but it will be water. And though George won't admit it yet, this puts Venus in a completely different light."

"Why?" asked Jerry, though he had already guessed.

"Where there's water, there may be life. We've been in too much of a hurry to assume that Venus is sterile, merely because the average temperature's over five hundred degrees. It's a lot colder here, and that's why I've been so anxious to get to the Pole. There are lakes up here in the highlands, and I want to look at them."

"But *boiling* water!" protested Coleman. "Nothing could live in that!"

"There are algae that manage it on earth. And if we've learned one thing since we started exploring the planets, it's this: wherever life has the slightest chance of surviving, you'll find it. This is the only chance it's ever had on Venus."

"I wish we could test your theory. But you can see for yourself—we can't go up that cliff."

"Perhaps not in the car. But it won't be too difficult to climb those rocks, even wearing thermosuits. All we need do is walk a few miles toward the Pole; according to the radar maps, it's fairly level once you're over the rim. We could manage in—oh, twelve hours at the most. Each of us has been out for longer than that, in much worse conditions."

That was perfectly true. Protective clothing that had been designed to keep men alive in the Venusian lowlands would have an easy job here, where it was only a hundred degrees hotter than Death Valley in midsummer.

"Well," said Coleman, "you know the regulations. You can't go by yourself, and someone has to stay here to keep contact with the ship. How do we settle it this time—chess or cards?"

"Chess takes too long," said Hutchins, "especially when you two play it." He reached into the chart table and produced a well-worn pack. Cut them, Jerry."

"Ten of spades. Hope you can beat it, George."

So do I. Damn—only five of clubs. Well, give my regards to the Venusians."

Despite Hutchins' assurance, it was hard work climbing the escarpment. The slope was not too steep, but the weight of oxygen gear, refrigerated thermosuit, and scientific equipment came to more than a hundred pounds per man. The lower gravity—thirteen per cent weaker than Earth's—gave a little help, but not much, as they toiled up screes, rested on ledges to regain breath, and then clambered on again through the submarine twilight. The emerald glow that washed around them was brighter than that of the full Moon on Earth. A moon would never have been wasted on Venus, Jerry told himself it could never have been seen from the surface, there were no oceans for it to rule—and the incessant aurora was a far more constant source of light.

They had climbed more than two thousand feet before the ground leveled out into a gentle slope, scarred here and there by channels that had clearly been cut by running water. After a little searching, they came across a gulley wide and deep enough to merit the name of river bed, and started to walk along it.

"I've just thought of something," said Jerry after they had traveled a few hundred yards. "Suppose there's a storm up ahead of us? I don't feel like facing a tidal wave of boiling water."

"If there's a storm," replied Hutchins a little impatiently, "we'll hear it. There'll be plenty of time to reach high ground."

He was undoubtedly right, but Jerry felt no happier as they continued to climb the gently shelving watercourse. His uneasiness had been growing ever since they had passed over the brow of the cliff and had lost radio contact with the scout car. In this day and age, to be out of touch with one's fellow men was a unique and unsettling experience. It had never happened to Jerry before in all his life; even aboard the *Morning Star*, when they were a hundred million miles from Earth, he could always send a message to his family and get a reply back within minutes. But now, a few yards of rock had cut him off from the rest of mankind; if anything happened to them here, no one would ever know, unless some later expedition found their bodies. George would wait for the agreed number of hours; then he would head back to the ship—alone. I guess I'm not really the pioneering type, Jerry told himself. I like running complicated machines, and that's how I got involved in space flight. But I never stopped to think where it would lead, and now it's too late to change my mind. . . .

They had traveled perhaps three miles toward the Pole, following the meanders of the river bed, when Hutchins stopped to make observations and collect specimens. "Still getting colder!" he said. "The temperature's down to one hundred and ninety-nine. That's far and away the lowest ever recorded on Venus. I wish we could call George and let him know."

Jerry tried all the wave bands; he even attempted to raise the ship—the unpredictable ups and downs of the planet's ionosphere sometimes made such long-distance reception possible—but there was not a whisper of a carrier wave above the roar and crackle of the Venusian thunderstorms.

"This is even better," said Hutchins, and now there was real excitement in his voice. "The oxygen concentration's way up—fifteen parts in a million. It was only five back at the car, and down in the lowlands you can scarcely detect it."

"But fifteen in a *million!*" protested Jerry. "Nothing could breathe that!"

"You've got hold of the wrong end of the stick," Hutchins explained. "Nothing does breathe it. Something *makes* it. Where do you think Earth's oxygen comes from? It's all produced by life—by growing plants. Before there were plants on Earth, our atmosphere was just like this one—a mess of carbon dioxide and ammonia and methane. Then vegetation evolved, and slowly converted the atmosphere into something that animals could breathe."

"I see," said Jerry, "and you think that the same process has just started here?"

"It looks like it. *Something* not far from here is producing oxygen—and plant life is the simplest explanation."

"And where there are plants," mused Jerry, "I suppose you'll have animals, sooner or later."

"Yes," said Hutchins, packing his gear and starting up the gulley, "though it takes a few hundred million years. We may be too soon—but I hope not."

"That's all very well," Jerry answered. "But suppose we meet something that doesn't like us? We've no weapons."

Hutchins gave a snort of disgust.

"And we don't need them. Have you stopped to think what we look like? Any animal would run a mile at the sight of us."

There was some trtuh in that. The reflecting metal foil of their thermosuits covered them from head to foot like flexible, glittering armor. No insects had more elaborate antennas than those mounted on their helmets and back packs, and the wide lenses through which they stared out at the world looked like blank yet monstrous eyes. Yes, there were few animals on Earth that would stop to argue with such apparitions; but any Venusians might have different ideas.

Jerry was still mulling this over when they came upon the lake. Even at that first glimpse, it made him think not of the life they were seeking, but of death. Like a black mirror, it lay amid a fold of the hills; its far edge was hidden in the eternal mist, and ghostly columns of vapor swirled and danced upon its surface. All it needed, Jerry told himself, was Charon's ferry waiting to take them to the other side—or the Swan of Tuonela swimming majestically back and forth as it guarded the entrance to the Underworld. . . .

Yet for all this, it was a miracle—the first free water that men had ever found on Venus. Hutchins was already on his knees, almost in an attitude of prayer. But he was only collecting drops of the precious liquid to examine through his pocket microscope.

"Anything there?" asked Jerry anxiously.

Hutchins shook his head.

"If there is, it's too small to see with this instrument. I'll tell you more when we're back at the ship." He sealed a test tube and placed it in his collecting bag, as tenderly as any prospector who had just found a nugget laced with gold. It might be—it probably was—nothing more than plain water. But it might also be a universe of unknown, living creatures on the first stage of their billion-year journey to intelligence.

Hutchins had walked no more than a dozen yards along the edge of the lake when he stopped again, so suddenly that Garfield nearly collided with him.

"What's the matter?" Jerry asked. "Seen something?"

"That dark patch of rock over there. I noticed it before we stopped at the lake."

"What about it? It looks ordinary enough to me."

"I think it's grown bigger."

All his life, Jerry was to remember this moment. Somehow he never doubted Hutchins' statement; by this time he could believe anything, even that rocks could grow. The sense of isolation and mystery, the presence of that dark and brooding lake, the never-ceasing rumble of distant storms and the green flickering of the aurora—all these had done something to his mind, had prepared it to face the incredible. Yet he felt no fear; that would come later.

He looked at the rock. It was about five hundred feet away, as far as he could estimate. In this dim, emerald light it was hard to judge distances or dimensions. The rock—or whatever it was—seemed to be a horizontal slab of almost black material, lying near the crest of a low ridge. There was a second, much smaller, patch of similar material near it; Jerry tried to measure and memorize the gap between them, so that he would have some yardstick to detect any change.

Even when he saw that the gap was slowly shrinking, he

still felt no alarm—only a puzzled excitement. Not until it had vanished completely, and he realized how his eyes had tricked him, did that awful feeling of helpless terror strike into his heart.

Here were no growing or moving rocks. What they were watching was a dark tide, a crawling carpet, sweeping slowly but inexorably toward them over the top of the ridge.

The moment of sheer, unreasoning panic lasted, mercifully, no more than a few seconds. Garfield's first terror began to fade as soon as he recognized its cause. For that advancing tide had reminded him, all too vividly, of a story he had read many years ago about the army ants of the Amazon, and the way in which they destroyed everything in their path. . . .

But whatever this tide might be, it was moving too slowly to be a real danger, unless it cut off their line of retreat. Hutchins was staring at it intently through their only pair of binoculars; he was the biologist, and he was holding his ground. No point in making a fool of myself, thought Jerry, by running like a scalded cat, if it isn't necessary.

"For heaven's sake," he said at last, when the moving carpet was only a hundred yards away and Hutchins had not uttered a word or stirred a muscle. "What *is* it?"

Hutchins slowly unfroze, like a statue coming to life.

"Sorry," he said, "I'd forgotten all about you. It's a plant, of course. At least, I suppose we'd better call it that."

"But it's *moving!*"

"Why should that surprise you? So do terrestrial plants. Ever seen speeded-up movies of ivy in action?"

"That still stays in one place—it doesn't crawl all over the landscape."

"Then what about the plankton plants of the sea? *They* can swim when they have to."

Jerry gave up; in any case, the approaching wonder had robbed him of words.

He still thought of the thing as a carpet—a deep-pile one, raveled into tassels at the edges. It varied in thickness as it moved; in some parts it was a mere film; in others, it heaped up to a depth of a foot or more. As it came closer and he could see its texture, Jerry was reminded of black velvet. He wondered what it felt like to the touch, then remembered that it would burn his fingers even if it did nothing else to them. He found himself thinking, in the lightheaded nervous reaction that often follows a sudden shock: "If there *are* any

Venusians, we'll never be able to shake hands with them. They'd burn us, and we'd give them frostbite."

So far, the thing had shown no signs that it was aware of their presence. It had merely flowed forward like the mindless tide that it almost certainly was. Apart from the fact that it climbed over small obstacles, it might have been an advancing flood of water.

And then, when it was only ten feet away, the velvet tide checked itself. On the right and the left, it still flowed forward; but dead ahead it slowed to a halt.

"We're being encircled," said Jerry anxiously. "Better fall back, until we're sure it's harmless."

To his relief, Hutchins stepped back at once. After a brief hesitation, the creature resumed its slow advance and the dent in its front line straightened out.

Then Hutchins stepped forward again—and the thing slowly withdrew. Half a dozen times the biologist advanced, only to retreat again, and each time the living tide ebbed and flowed in synchronism with his movements. I never imagined, Jerry told himself, that I'd live to see a man waltzing with a plant. . . .

"Thermophobia," said Hutchins. "Purely automatic reaction. It doesn't like our heat."

"*Our* heat!" protested Jerry. "Why, we're living icicles by comparison."

"Of course—but our suits aren't, and that's all it knows about."

Stupid of me, thought Jerry. When you were snug and cool inside your thermosuit, it was easy to forget that the refrigeration unit on your back was pumping a blast of heat out into the surrounding air. No wonder the Venusian plant had shied away. . . .

"Let's see how it reacts to light," said Hutchins. He switched on his chest lamp, and the green auroral glow was instantly banished by the flood of pure white radiance. Until man had come to this planet, no white light had ever shone upon the surface of Venus, even by day. As in the seas of Earth, there was only a green twilight, deepening slowly to utter darkness.

The transformation was so stunning that neither man could check a cry of astonishment. Gone in a flash was the deep, somber black of the thick-piled velvet carpet at their feet. Instead, as far as their lights carried, lay a blazing pattern of glorious, vivid reds, laced with streaks of gold. No Persian prince could ever have commanded so opulent a tapestry from his weavers, yet this was the accidental product of biological forces. Indeed, until they had switched on their floods, these superb colors had not even existed, and they would vanish once more when the alien light of Earth ceased to conjure them into being.

"Tikov was right," murmured Hutchins. "I wish he could have known."

"Right about what?" asked Jerry, though it seemed almost a sacrilege to speak in the presence of such loveliness.

"Back in Russia, fifty years ago, he found that plants living in very cold climates tended to be blue and violet, while those from hot ones were red or orange. He predicted that the Martian vegetation would be violet, and said that if there were plants on Venus they'd be red. Well, he was right on both counts. But we can't stand here all day—we've work to do."

"You're sure it's quite safe?" asked Jerry, some of his caution reasserting itself.

"Absolutely—it can't touch our suits even if it wants to. Anyway, it's moving past us."

That was true. They could see now that the entire creature —if it was a single plant, and not a colony—covered a roughly circular area about a hundred yards across. It was sweeping over the ground, as the shadow of a cloud moves before the wind—and where it had rested, the rocks were pitted with innumerable tiny holes that might have been etched by acid.

"Yes," said Hutchins, when Jerry remarked about this. "That's how some lichens feed; they secrete acids that dissolve rock. But no questions, please—not till we get back to the ship. I've several lifetimes' work here, and a couple of hours to do it in."

This was botany on the run. . . . The sensitive edge of the huge plant-thing could move with surprising speed when it tried to evade them. It was as if they were dealing with an animated flapjack, an acre in extent. There was no reaction— apart from the automatic avoidance of their exhaust heat— when Hutchins snipped samples or took probes. The creature flowed steadily onward over hills and valleys, guided by some strange vegetable instinct. Perhaps it was following some vein of mineral; the geologists could decide that, when they analyzed the rock samples that Hutchins had collected both before and after the passage of the living tapestry.

There was scarcely time to think or even to frame the countless questions that their discovery had raised. Presumably these creatures must be fairly common, for them to have found one so quickly. How did they reproduce? By shoots, spores, fission, or some other means? Where did they get their energy? What relatives, rivals, or parasites did they have? This could not be the only form of life on Venus—the very idea was absurd, for if you had one species, you must have thousands. . . .

Sheer hunger and fatigue forced them to a halt at last. The creature they were studying could eat its way around Venus —though Hutchins believed that it never went very far from the lake, because from time to time it approached the water and inserted a long, tubelike tendril into it—but the animals from Earth had to rest.

It was a great relief to inflate the pressurized tent, climb in through the air lock, and strip off their thermosuits. For the first time, as they relaxed inside their tiny plastic hemisphere, the true wonder and importance of the discovery forced itself upon their minds. This world around them was no longer the same; Venus was no longer dead—it had joined Earth and Mars.

For life called to life, across the gulfs of space. Everything that grew or moved upon the face of any planet was a portent, a promise that Man was not alone in this Universe of blazing suns and swirling nebulae. If as yet he had found no companions with whom he could speak, that was only to be expected, for the light-years and the ages still stretched before him, waiting to be explored. Meanwhile, he must guard and cherish the life he found, whether it be upon Earth or Mars or Venus.

So Graham Hutchins, the happiest biologist in the Solar System, told himself as he helped Garfield collect their refuse and seal it into a plastic disposal bag. When they deflated the tent and started on the homeward journey, there was no sign of the creature they had been examining. That was just as well; they might have been tempted to linger for more experiments, and already it was getting uncomfortably close to their deadline.

No matter; in a few months they would be back with a team of assistants, far more adequately equipped and with the eyes of the world upon them. Evolution had labored for a billion years to make this meeting possible; it could wait a little longer.

For a while nothing moved in the greenly glimmering, fog-bound landscape; it was deserted by man and crimson carpet alike. Then, flowing over the wind-carved hills, the creature reappeared. Or perhaps it was another of the same strange species; no one would ever know.

It flowed past the little cairn of stones where Hutchins and Garfield had buried their wastes. And then it stopped.

It was not puzzled, for it had no mind. But the chemical urges that drove it relentlessly over the polar plateau were crying: Here, here! Somewhere close at hand was the most precious of all the foods it needed—phosphorous, the element without which the spark of life could never ignite. It began to nuzzle the rocks, to ooze into the cracks and crannies, to scratch and scrabble with probing tendrils. Nothing that it did was beyond the capacity of any plant or tree on Earth— but it moved a thousand times more quickly, requiring only minutes to reach its goal and pierce through the plastic film.

And then it feasted, on food more concentrated than any it had ever known. It absorbed the carbohydrates and the proteins and the phosphates, the nicotine from the cigarette ends, the cellulose from the paper cups and spoons. All these it broke down and assimilated into its strange body, without difficulty and without harm.

Likewise it absorbed a whole microcosmos of living creatures—the bacteria and viruses which, upon an older planet, had evolved into a thousand deadly strains. Though only a very few could survive in this heat and this atmosphere, they were sufficient. As the carpet crawled back to the lake, it carried contagion to all its world.

Even as the Morning Star *set course for her distant home, Venus was dying. The films and photographs and specimens that Hutchins was carrying in triumph were more precious even than he knew. They were the only record that would ever exist of life's third attempt to gain a foothold in the Solar System.*

Beneath the clouds of Venus, the story of Creation was ended.

Colombo   *May 1960*

Superiority

Students of World War II will recognize the inspiration of this story. I hope that no one will be put off by the fact that it has been required reading for an M.I.T. engineering course.

———— ◆ ————

In making this statement—which I do of my own free will—I wish first to make it perfectly clear that I am not in any way trying to gain sympathy, nor do I expect any mitigation of whatever sentence the Court may pronounce. I am writing this in an attempt to refute some of the lying reports broadcast over the prison radio and published in the papers I have been allowed to see. These have given an entirely false picture of the true cause of our defeat, and as the leader of my race's armed forces at the cessation of hostilities I feel it my duty to protest against such libels upon those who served under me.

I also hope that this statement may explain the reasons for the application I have twice made to the Court, and will now induce it to grant a favor for which I can see no possible grounds of refusal.

The ultimate cause of our failure was a simple one: despite all statements to the contrary, it was not due to lack of bravery on the part of our men, or to any fault of the Fleet's. We were defeated by one thing only—by the inferior science of our enemies. I repeat—by the *inferior* science of our enemies.

When the war opened, we had no doubt of our ultimate victory. The combined fleets of our allies greatly exceeded in number and armament those which the enemy could muster against us, and in almost all branches of military science we were their superiors. We were sure that we could maintain this superiority. Our belief proved, alas, to be only too well founded.

At the opening of the war our main weapons were the long-range homing torpedo, dirigible ball-lightning and the various modifications of the Klydon beam. Every unit of the Fleet was equipped with these, and though the enemy possessed similar weapons their installations were generally of lesser power. Moreover, we had behind us a far greater military Research Organization, and with this initial advantage we could not possibly lose.

The campaign proceeded according to plan until the Battle of the Five Suns. We won this, of course, but the opposition proved stronger than we had expected. It was realized that victory might be more difficult, and more delayed, than had first been imagined. A conference of supreme commanders was therefore called to discuss our future strategy.

Present for the first time at one of our war conferences was Professor-General Norden, the new Chief of the Research Staff, who had just been appointed to fill the gap left by the death of Malvar, our greatest scientist. Malvar's leadership had been responsible, more than any other single factor, for the efficiency and power of our weapons. His loss was a very serious blow, but no one doubted the brilliance of his successor—though many of us disputed the wisdom of appointing a theoretical scientist to fill a post of such vital importance. But we had been overruled.

I can well remember the impression Norden made at that conference. The military advisers were worried, and as usual turned to the scientists for help. Would it be possible to improve our existing weapons, they asked, so that our present advantage could be increased still further?

Norden's reply was quite unexpected. Malvar had often been asked such a question—and he had always done what we requested.

"Frankly, gentlemen," said Norden, "I doubt it. Our existing weapons have practically reached finality. I don't wish to criticize my predecessor, or the excellent work done by the Research Staff in the last few generations, but do you realize that there has been no basic change in armaments for over a century? It is, I am afraid, the result of a tradition that has become conservative. For too long, the Research Staff has devoted itself to perfecting old weapons instead of developing new ones. It is fortunate for us that our opponents have been no wiser: we cannot assume that this will always be so."

Norden's words left an uncomfortable impression, as he had no doubt intended. He quickly pressed home the attack.

"What we want are *new* weapons—weapons totally different from any that have been employed before. Such weapons can be made: it will take time, of course, but since assuming charge I have replaced some of the older scientists by young men and have directed research into several unexplored fields which show great promise. I believe, in fact, that a revolution in warfare may soon be upon us."

We were skeptical. There was a bombastic tone in Norden's voice that made us suspicious of his claims. We did not know, then, that he never promised anything that he had not already almost perfected in the laboratory. *In the laboratory*—that was the operative phrase.

Norden proved his case less than a month later, when he demonstrated the Sphere of Annihilation, which produced complete disintegration of matter over a radius of several hundred meters. We were intoxicated by the power of the new weapon, and were quite prepared to overlook one fundamental defect—the fact that it *was* a sphere and hence destroyed its rather complicated generating equipment at the instant of formation. This meant, of course, that it could not be used on warships but only on guided missiles, and a great program was started to convert all homing torpedoes to carry the new weapon. For the time being all further offensives were suspended.

We realize now that this was our first mistake. I still think that it was a natural one, for it seemed to us then that all our existing weapons had become obsolete overnight, and we already regarded them as almost primitive survivals. What we did not appreciate was the magnitude of the task we were attempting, and the length of time it would take to get the revolutionary super-weapon into battle. Nothing like this had happened for a hundred years and we had no previous experience to guide us.

The conversion problem proved far more difficult than anticipated. A new class of torpedo had to be designed, because the standard model was too small. This meant in turn that only the larger ships could launch the weapon, but we were prepared to accept this penalty. After six months, the heavy units of the Fleet were being equipped with the Sphere. Training maneuvers and tests had shown that it was operating satisfactorily and we were ready to take it into action. Norden was already being hailed as the architect of victory, and had half promised even more spectacular weapons.

Then two things happened. One of our battleships disappeared completely on a training flight, and an investigation showed that under certain conditions the ship's long-range radar could trigger the Sphere immediately it had been launched. The modification needed to overcome this defect was trivial, but it caused a delay of another month and was the source of much bad feeling between the naval staff and the scientists. We were ready for action again—when Norden announced that the radius of effectiveness of the Sphere had now been increased by ten, thus multiplying by a thousand the chances of destroying an enemy ship.

So the modifications started all over again, but everyone agreed that the delay would be worth it. Meanwhile, however, the enemy had been emboldened by the absence of further attacks and had made an unexpected onslaught. Our ships were short of torpedoes, since none had been coming from the factories, and were forced to retire. So we lost the systems of Kyrane and Floranus, and the planetary fortress of Rhamsandron.

It was an annoying but not a serious blow, for the recaptured systems had been unfriendly, and difficult to administer. We had no doubt that we could restore the position in the near future, as soon as the new weapon became operational.

These hopes were only partially fulfilled. When we renewed our offensive, we had to do so with fewer of the Spheres of Annihilation than had been planned, and this was one reason for our limited success. The other reason was more serious.

While we had been equipping as many of our ships as we could with the irresistible weapon, the enemy had been building feverishly. His ships were of the old pattern with the old weapons—but they now outnumbered ours. When we went into action, we found that the numbers ranged against us were often one hundred per cent greater than expected, causing target confusion among the automatic weapons and resulting in higher losses than anticipated. The enemy losses were higher still, for once a Sphere had reached its objective, destruction was certain, but the balance had not swung as far in our favor as we had hoped.

Moreover, while the main fleets had been engaged, the enemy had launched a daring attack on the lightly held systems of Eriston, Duranus, Carmanidora and Pharanidon— recapturing them all. We were thus faced with a threat only fifty light-years from our home planets.

There was much recrimination at the next meeting of the supreme commanders. Most of the complaints were addressed to Norden—Grand Admiral Taxaris in particular maintaining that thanks to our admittedly irresistible weapon we were now considerably worse off than before. We should, he claimed, have continued to build conventional ships, thus preventing the loss of our numerical superiority.

Norden was equally angry and called the naval staff ungrateful bunglers. But I could tell that he was worried—as indeed we all were—by the unexpected turn of events. He hinted that there might be a speedy way of remedying the situation.

We now know that Research had been working on the Battle Analyzer for many years, but, at the time, it came as a revelation to us and perhaps we were too easily swept off our feet. Norden's argument, also, was seductively convincing. What did it matter, he said, if the enemy had twice as many ships as we—if the efficiency of ours could be doubled or even trebled? For decades the limiting factor in warfare had been not mechanical but biological—it had become more and more difficult for any single mind, or group of minds, to cope with the rapidly changing complexities of battle in three-dimensional space. Norden's mathematicians had analyzed some of the classic engagements of the past, and had shown that even when we had been victorious we had often operated our units at much less than half of their theoretical efficiency.

The Battle Analyzer would change all this by replacing the operations staff with electronic calculators. The idea was not new, in theory, but until now it had been no more than a utopian dream. Many of us found it difficult to believe that it was still anything but a dream: after we had run through several very complex dummy battles, however, we were convinced.

It was decided to install the Analyzer in four of our heaviest ships, so that each of the main fleets could be equipped with one. At this stage, the trouble began—though we did not know it until later.

The Analyzer contained just short of a million vacuum tubes and needed a team of five hundred technicians to maintain and operate it. It was quite impossible to accommodate the extra staff aboard a battleship, so each of the four units had to be accompanied by a converted liner to carry the technicians not on duty. Installation was also a very slow and tedious business, but by gigantic efforts it was completed in six months.

Then, to our dismay, we were confronted by another crisis.

Nearly five thousand highly skilled men had been selected to serve the Analyzers and had been given an intensive course at the Technical Training Schools. At the end of seven months, ten per cent of them had had nervous breakdowns and only forty per cent had qualified.

Once again, everyone started to blame everyone else. Norden, of course, said that the Research Staff could not be held responsible, and so incurred the enmity of the Personnel and Training Commands. It was finally decided that the only thing to do was to use two instead of four Analyzers and to bring the others into action as soon as men could be trained. There was little time to lose, for the enemy was still on the offensive and his morale was rising.

The first Analyzer fleet was ordered to recapture the system of Eriston. On the way, by one of the hazards of war, the liner carrying the technicians was struck by a roving mine. A warship would have survived, but the liner with its irreplaceable cargo was totally destroyed. So the operation had to be abandoned.

The other expedition was, at first, more successful. There was no doubt at all that the Analyzer fulfilled its designers' claims, and the enemy was heavily defeated in the first engagements. He withdrew, leaving us in possession of Saphran, Leucon and Hexanerax. But his Intelligence Staff must have noted the change in our tactics and the inexplicable presence of a liner in the heart of our battle Fleet. It must have noted, also, that our first Fleet had been accompanied by a similar ship—and had withdrawn when it had been destroyed.

In the next engagement, the enemy used his superior numbers to launch an overwhelming attack on the Analyzer ship and its unarmed consort. The attack was made without regard to losses—both ships were, of course, very heavily protected —and it succeeded. The result was the virtual decapitation of the Fleet, since an effectual transfer to the old operational methods proved impossible. We disengaged under heavy fire, and so lost all our gains and also the systems of Lormyia, Ismarnus, Beronis, Alphanidon and Sideneus.

At this stage, Grand Admiral Taxaris expressed his disapproval of Norden by committing suicide, and I assumed supreme command.

The situation was now both serious and infuriating. With stubborn conservatism and complete lack of imagination, the enemy continued to advance with his old-fashioned and inefficient but now vastly more numerous ships. It was galling to realize that if we had only continued building, without seeking new weapons, we would have been in a far more advantageous position. There were many acrimonious conferences at which Norden defended the scientists while everyone else blamed them for all that had happened. The difficulty was that Norden had proved every one of his claims: he had a perfect excuse for all the disasters that had occurred. And we could not now turn back—the search for an irresistible weapon must go on. At first it had been a luxury that would shorten the war. Now it was a necessity if we were to end it victoriously.

We were on the defensive, and so was Norden. He was more than ever determined to re-establish his prestige and that of the Research Staff. But we had been twice disappointed, and would not make the same mistake again. No doubt Norden's twenty thousand scientists would produce many further weapons: we would remain unimpressed.

We were wrong. The final weapon was something so fantastic that even now it seems difficult to believe that it ever existed. Its innocent, noncommittal name—The Exponential Field—gave no hint of its real potentialities. Some of Norden's mathematicians had discovered it during a piece of entirely theoretical research into the properties of space, and to everyone's great surprise their results were found to be physically realizable.

It seems very difficult to explain the operation of the Field to the layman. According to the technical description, it "produces an exponential condition of space, so that a finite distance in normal, linear space may become infinite in pseudo-space." Norden gave an analogy which some of us found useful. It was as if one took a flat disk of rubber—representing a region of normal space—and then pulled its center out to infinity. The circumference of the disk would be unaltered—but its "diameter" would be infinite. That was the sort of thing the generator of the Field did to the space around it.

As an example, suppose that a ship carrying the generator was surrounded by a ring of hostile machines. If it switched on the Field, *each* of the enemy ships would think that it—and the ships on the far side of the circle—had suddenly receded into nothingness. Yet the circumference of the circle would be the same as before: only the journey to the center would be of infinite duration, for as one proceeded, distances would appear to become greater and greater as the "scale" of space altered.

It was a nightmare condition, but a very useful one. Nothing could reach a ship carrying the Field: it might be englobed by an enemy fleet yet would be as inaccessible as if it were at the other side of the Universe. Against this, of course, it could not fight back without switching off the Field, but this still left it at a very great advantage, not only in defense but in offense. For a ship fitted with the Field could approach an enemy fleet undetected and suddenly appear in its midst.

This time there seemed to be no flaws in the new weapon. Needless to say, we looked for all the possible objections before we committed ourselves again. Fortunately the equipment was fairly simple and did not require a large operating staff. After much debate, we decided to rush it into production, for we realized that time was running short and the war was going against us. We had now lost about the whole of our initial gains, and enemy forces had made several raids into our own Solar System.

We managed to hold off the enemy while the Fleet was re-equipped and the new battle techniques were worked out. To use the Field operationally it was necessary to locate an enemy formation, set a course that would intercept it, and then switch on the generator for the calculated period of time. On releasing the Field again—if the calculations had been accurate—one would be in the enemy's midst and could do great damage during the resulting confusion, retreating by the same route when necessary.

The first trial maneuvers proved satisfactory and the equipment seemed quite reliable. Numerous mock attacks were made and the crews became accustomed to the new technique. I was on one of the test flights and can vividly remember my impressions as the Field was switched on. The ships around us seemed to dwindle as if on the surface of an expanding bubble: in an instant they had vanished completely. So had the stars—but presently we could see that the Galaxy was still visible as a faint band of light around the ship. The virtual radius of our pseudo-space was not really infinite, but some hundred thousand light-years, and so the distance to the farthest stars of our system had not been greatly increased—though the nearest had of course totally disappeared.

These training maneuvers, however, had to be canceled before they were complete owing to a whole flock of minor technical troubles in various pieces of equipment, notably the communications circuits. These were annoying, but not important, though it was thought best to return to Base to clear them up.

At that moment the enemy made what was obviously intended to be a decisive attack against the fortress planet of Iton at the limits of our Solar System. The Fleet had to go into battle before repairs could be made.

The enemy must have believed that we had mastered the secret of invisibility—as in a sense we had. Our ships appeared suddenly out of nowhere and inflicted tremendous damage—for a while. And then something quite baffling and inexplicable happened.

I was in command of the flagship *Hircania* when the trouble started. We had been operating as independent units, each against assigned objectives. Our detectors observed an enemy formation at medium range and the navigating officers measured its distance with great accuracy. We set course and switched on the generator.

The Exponential Field was released at the moment when we should have been passing through the center of the enemy group. To our consternation, we emerged into normal space at a distance of many hundred miles—and when we found the enemy, he had already found us. We retreated, and tried again. This time we were so far away from the enemy that he located us first.

Obviously, something was seriously wrong. We broke communicator silence and tried to contact the other ships of the Fleet to see if they had experienced the same trouble. Once again we failed—and this time the failure was beyond all reason, for the communication equipment appeared to be working perfectly. We could only assume, fantastic though it seemed, that the rest of the Fleet had been destroyed.

I do not wish to describe the scenes when the scattered units of the Fleet struggled back to Base. Our casualties had actually been negligible, but the ships were completely demoralized. Almost all had lost touch with one another and had found that their ranging equipment showed inexplicable errors. It was obvious that the Exponential Field was the cause of the troubles, despite the fact that they were only apparent when it was switched off.

The explanation came too late to do us any good, and Norden's final discomfiture was small consolation for the virtual loss of the war. As I have explained, the Field generators produced a radial distortion of space, distances appearing greater and greater as one approached the center of the artificial pseudo-space. When the Field was switched off, conditions returned to normal.

But not quite. It was never possible to restore the initial state *exactly*. Switching the Field on and off was equivalent to an elongation and contraction of the ship carrying the generator, but there was a hysteretic effect, as it were, and the initial condition was never quite reproducible, owing to all the thousands of electrical changes and movements of mass aboard the ship while the Field was on. These asymmetries and distortions were cumulative, and though they seldom amounted to more than a fraction of one per cent, that was quite enough. It meant that the precision ranging equipment and the tuned circuits in the communication apparatus were thrown completely out of adjustment. Any single ship could never detect the change—only when it compared its equipment with that of another vessel, or tried to communicate with it, could it tell what had happened.

It is impossible to describe the resultant chaos. Not a single component of one ship could be expected with certainty to work aboard another. The very nuts and bolts were no longer interchangeable, and the supply position became quite impossible. Given time, we might even have overcome these difficulties, but the enemy ships were already attacking in thousands with weapons which now seemed centuries behind those that we had invented. Our magnificent Fleet, crippled by our own science, fought on as best it could until it was overwhelmed and forced to surrender. The ships fitted with the Field were still invulnerable, but as fighting units they were almost helpless. Every time they switched on their generators to escape from enemy attack, the permanent distortion of their equipment increased. In a month, it was all over.

This is the true story of our defeat, which I give without prejudice to my defense before this Court. I make it, as I have said, to counteract the libels that have been circulating against the men who fought under me, and to show where the true blame for our misfortunes lay.

Finally, my request, which, as the Court will now realize, I make in no frivolous manner and which I hope will therefore be granted.

The Court will be aware that the conditions under which we are housed and the constant surveillance to which we are subjected night and day are somewhat distressing. Yet I am not complaining of this: nor do I complain of the fact that shortage of accommodation has made it necessary to house us in pairs.

But I cannot be held responsible for my future actions if I am compelled any longer to share my cell with Professor Norden, late Chief of the Research Staff of my armed forces.

London   *August 1948*

A Walk in the Dark

Robert Armstrong had walked just over two miles, as far as he could judge, when his torch failed. He stood still for a moment, unable to believe that such a misfortune could really have befallen him. Then, half maddened with rage, he hurled the useless instrument away. It landed somewhere in the darkness, disturbing the silence of this little world. A metallic echo came ringing back from the low hills: then all was quiet again.

This, thought Armstrong, was the ultimate misfortune. Nothing more could happen to him now. He was even able to laugh bitterly at his luck, and resolved never again to imagine that the fickle goddess had ever favored him. Who would have believed that the only tractor at Camp IV would have broken down when he was just setting off for Port Sanderson? He recalled the frenzied repair work, the relief when the second start had been made—and the final debacle when the caterpillar track had jammed.

It was no use then regretting the lateness of his departure: he could not have foreseen these accidents, and it was still a good four hours before the *Canopus* took off. He *had* to catch her, whatever happened; no other ship would be touching at this world for another month.

Apart from the urgency of his business, four more weeks on this out-of-the-way planet were unthinkable.

There had been only one thing to do. It was lucky that Port Sanderson was little more than six miles from the camp—not a great distance, even on foot. He had had to leave all his equipment behind, but it could follow on the next ship and he could manage without it. The road was poor, merely stamped out of the rock by one of the Board's hundred-ton crushers, but there was no fear of going astray.

Even now, he was in no real danger, though he might well be too late to catch the ship. Progress would be slow, for he dare not risk losing the road in this region of canyons and enigmatic tunnels that had never been explored. It was, of course, pitch-dark. Here at the edge of the Galaxy the stars were so few and scattered that their light was negligible. The strange crimson sun of this lonely world would not rise for many hours, and although five of the little moons were in the sky, they could barely be seen by the unaided eye. Not one of them could even cast a shadow.

Armstrong was not the man to bewail his luck for long. He began to walk slowly along the road, feeling its texture with his feet. It was, he knew, fairly straight except where it wound through Carver's Pass. He wished he had a stick or something to probe the way before him, but he would have to rely for guidance on the feel of the ground.

It was terribly slow at first, until he gained confidence. He had never known how difficult it was to walk in a straight line. Although the feeble stars gave him his bearings, again and again he found himself stumbling among the virgin rocks at the edge of the crude roadway. He was traveling in long zig-zags that took him to alternate sides of the road. Then he would stub his toes against the bare rock and grope his way back onto the hard-packed surface once again.

Presently it settled down to a routine. It was impossible to estimate his speed; he could only struggle along and hope for the best. There were four miles to go—four miles and as many hours. It should be easy enough, unless he lost his way. But he dared not think of that.

Once he had mastered the technique he could afford the luxury of thought. He could not pretend that he was enjoying the experience, but he had been in much worse positions before. As long as he remained on the road, he was perfectly safe. He had been hoping that as his eyes became adapted to the starlight he would be able to see the way, but he now knew that the whole journey would be blind. The discovery gave him a vivid sense of his remoteness from the heart of the Galaxy. On a night as clear as this, the skies of almost any other planet would have been blazing with stars. Here at this outpost of the Universe the sky held perhaps a hundred faintly gleaming points of light, as useless as the five ridiculous moons on which no one had ever bothered to land.

A slight change in the road interrupted his thoughts. Was there a curve here, or had he veered off to the right again? He moved very slowly along the invisible and ill-defined border. Yes, there was no mistake: the road was bending to the left. He tried to remember its appearance in the daytime, but he had only seen it once before. Did this mean that he was nearing the Pass? He hoped so, for the journey would then be half completed.

He peered ahead into the blackness, but the ragged line of the horizon told him nothing. Presently he found that the road had straightened itself again and his spirits sank. The entrance to the Pass must still be some way ahead: there were at least four miles to go.

Four miles—how ridiculous the distance seemed! How long would it take the *Canopus* to travel four miles? He doubted if man could measure so short an interval of time. And how many trillions of miles had he, Robert Armstrong, traveled in his life? It must have reached a staggering total by now, for in the last twenty years he had scarcely stayed more than a month at a time on any single world. This very year, he had twice made the crossing of the Galaxy, and that was a notable journey even in these days of the phantom drive.

He tripped over a loose stone, and the jolt brought him back to reality. It was no use, here, thinking of ships that could eat up the light-years. He was facing Nature, with no weapons but his own strength and skill.

It was strange that it took him so long to identify the real cause of his uneasiness. The last four weeks had been very full, and the rush of his departure, coupled with the annoyance and anxiety caused by the tractor's breakdowns, had driven everything else from his mind. Moreover, he had always prided himself on his hardheadedness and lack of imagination. Until now, he had forgotten all about that first evening at the Base, when the crews had regaled him with the usual tall yarns concocted for the benefit of newcomers.

It was then that the old Base clerk had told the story of his walk by night from Port Sanderson to the camp, and of what had trailed him through Carver's Pass, keeping always beyond the limit of his torchlight. Armstrong, who had heard such tales on a score of worlds, had paid it little attention at the time. This planet, after all, was known to be uninhabited. But logic could not dispose of the matter as easily as that. Suppose, after all, there was some truth in the old man's fantastic tale . . . ?

It was not a pleasant thought, and Armstrong did not intend to brood upon it. But he knew that if he dismissed it out of hand it would continue to prey on his mind. The only way to conquer imaginary fears was to face them boldly; he would have to do that now.

His strongest argument was the complete barrenness of this world and its utter desolation, though against that one could set many counterarguments, as indeed the old clerk had done. Man had only lived on this planet for twenty years, and much of it was still unexplored. No one could deny that the tunnels out in the wasteland were rather puzzling, but everyone believed them to be volcanic vents. Though, of course, life often crept into such places. With a shudder he remembered the giant polyps that had snared the first explorers of Vargon III.

It was all very inconclusive. Suppose, for the sake of argument, one granted the existence of life here. What of that?

The vast majority of life forms in the Universe were completely indifferent to man. Some, of course, like the gas-beings of Alcoran or the roving wave-lattices of Shandaloon, could not even detect him but passed through or around him as if he did not exist. Others were merely inquisitive, some embarrassingly friendly. There were few indeed that would attack unless provoked.

Nevertheless, it was a grim picture that the old stores clerk had painted. Back in the warm, well-lighted smoking room, with the drinks going around, it had been easy enough to laugh at it. But here in the darkness, miles from any human settlement, it was very different.

It was almost a relief when he stumbled off the road again and had to grope with his hands until he found it once more. This seemed a very rough patch, and the road was scarcely distinguishable from the rocks around. In a few minutes, however, he was safely on his way again.

It was unpleasant to see how quickly his thoughts returned to the same disquieting subject. Clearly it was worrying him more than he cared to admit.

He drew consolation from one fact: it had been quite obvious that no one at the Base had believed the old fellow's story. Their questions and banter had proved that. At the time, he had laughed as loudly as any of them. After all, what *was* the evidence? A dim shape, just seen in the darkness, that might well have been an oddly formed rock. And the curious clicking noise that had so impressed the old man—anyone could imagine such sounds at night if they were sufficiently overwrought. If it had been hostile, why hadn't the creature come any closer? "Because it was afraid of my light," the old chap had said. Well, that was plausible enough: it would explain why nothing had ever been seen in the daylight. Such a creature might live underground, only emerging at night—

damn it, why was he taking the old idiot's ravings so seriously! Armstrong got control of his thoughts again. If he went on this way, he told himself angrily, he would soon be seeing and hearing a whole menagerie of monsters.

There was, of course, one factor that disposed of the ridiculous story at once. It was really very simple; he felt sorry he hadn't thought of it before. *What would such a creature live on?* There was not even a trace of vegetation on the whole of the planet. He laughed to think that the bogy could be disposed of so easily—and in the same instant felt annoyed with himself for not laughing aloud. If he was so sure of his reasoning, why not whistle, or sing, or do anything to keep up his spirits? He put the question fairly to himself as a test of his manhood. Half-ashamed, he had to admit that he was still afraid—afraid because "there *might* be something in it, after all." But at least his analysis had done him some good.

It would have been better if he had left it there, and remained half-convinced by his argument. But a part of his mind was still busily trying to break down his careful reasoning. It succeeded only too well, and when he remembered the plant-beings of Xantil Major the shock was so unpleasant that he stopped dead in his tracks.

Now the plant-beings of Xantil were not in any way horrible. They were in fact extremely beautiful creatures. But what made them appear so distressing now was the knowledge that they could live for indefinite periods with no food whatsoever. All the energy they needed for their strange lives they extracted from cosmic radiation—and that was almost as intense here as anywhere else in the Universe.

He had scarcely thought of one example before others crowded into his mind and he remembered the life form on Trantor Beta, which was the only one known capable of directly utilizing atomic energy. That too had lived on an utterly barren world, very much like this. . . .

Armstrong's mind was rapidly splitting into two distinct portions, each trying to convince the other and neither wholly succeeding. He did not realize how far his morale had gone until he found himself holding his breath lest it conceal any sound from the darkness about him. Angrily, he cleared his mind of the rubbish that had been gathering there and turned once more to the immediate problem.

There was no doubt that the road was slowly rising, and the silhouette of the horizon seemed much higher in the sky. The road began to twist, and suddenly he was aware of great rocks on either side of him. Soon only a narrow ribbon of sky was still visible, and the darkness became, if possible, even more intense.

Somehow, he felt safer with the rock walls surrounding him: it meant that he was protected except in two directions. Also, the road had been leveled more carefully and it was easy to keep it. Best of all, he knew now that the journey was more than half completed.

For a moment his spirits began to rise. Then, with maddening perversity, his mind went back into the old grooves again. He remembered that it was on the far side of Carver's Pass that the old clerk's adventure had taken place—if it had ever happened at all.

In half a mile, he would be out in the open again, out of the protection of these sheltering rocks. The thought seemed doubly horrible now and he already felt a sense of nakedness. He could be attacked from any direction, and he would be utterly helpless. . . .

Until now, he had still retained some self-control. Very resolutely he had kept his mind away from the one fact that gave some color to the old man's tale—the single piece of evidence that had stopped the banter in the crowded room back at the camp and brought a sudden hush upon the company. Now, as Armstrong's will weakened, he recalled again the words that had struck a momentary chill even in the warm comfort of the Base building.

The little clerk had been very insistent on one point. He had never heard any sound of pursuit from the dim shape sensed, rather than seen, at the limit of his light. There was no scuffling of claws or hoofs on rock, nor even the clatter of displaced stones. It was as if, so the old man had declared in that solemn manner of his, "as if the thing that was following could see perfectly in the darkness, and had many small legs or pads so that it could move swiftly and easily over the rocks—like a giant caterpillar or one of the carpet-things of Kralkor II."

Yet, although there had been no noise of pursuit, there had been one sound that the old man had caught several times. It was so unusual that its very strangeness made it doubly ominous. It was a faint but horribly persistent *clicking*.

The old fellow had been able to describe it very vividly—much too vividly for Armstrong's liking now.

"Have you ever listened to a large insect crunching its

prey?" he said. "Well, it was just like that. I imagine that a crab makes exactly the same noise with its claws when it clashes them together. It was a—what's the word?—a *chitinous* sound."

At this point, Armstrong remembered laughing loudly. (Strange, how it was all coming back to him now.) But no one else had laughed, though they had been quick to do so earlier. Sensing the change of tone, he had sobered at once and asked the old man to continue his story. How he wished now that he had stifled his curiosity!

It had been quickly told. The next day, a party of skeptical technicians had gone into the no man's land beyond Carver's Pass. They were not skeptical enough to leave their guns behind, but they had no cause to use them, for they found no trace of any living thing. There were the inevitable pits and tunnels, glistening holes down which the light of the torches rebounded endlessly until it was lost in the distance—but the planet was riddled with them.

Though the party found no sign of life, it discovered one thing it did not like at all. Out in the barren and unexplored land beyond the Pass they had come upon an even larger tunnel than the rest. Near the mouth of that tunnel was a massive rock, half embedded in the ground. And the sides of that rock had been worn away *as if it had been used as an enormous whetstone.*

No less than five of those present had seen this disturbing rock. None of them could explain it satisfactorily as a natural formation, but they still refused to accept the old man's story. Armstrong had asked them if they had ever put it to the test. There had been an uncomfortable silence. Then big Andrew Hargraves had said: "Hell, who'd walk out to the Pass at night just for fun!" and had left it at that. Indeed, there was no other record of anyone walking from Port Sanderson to the camp by night, or for that matter by day. During the hours of light, no unprotected human being could live in the open beneath the rays of the enormous, lurid sun that seemed to fill half the sky. And no one would walk six miles, wearing radiation armor, if the tractor was available.

Armstrong felt that he was leaving the Pass. The rocks on either side were falling away, and the road was no longer as firm and well packed as it had been. He was coming out into the open plain once more, and somewhere not far away in the darkness was that enigmatic pillar that might have been used for sharpening monstrous fangs or claws. It was not a reassuring thought, but he could not get it out of his mind.

Feeling distinctly worried now, Armstrong made a great effort to pull himself together. He would try to be rational again; he would think of business, the work he had done at the camp—anything but this infernal place. For a while, he succeeded quite well. But presently, with a maddening persistence, every train of thought came back to the same point. He could not get out of his mind the picture of that inexplicable rock and its appalling possibilities. Over and over again he found himself wondering how far away it was, whether he had already passed it, and whether it was on his right or his left. . . .

The ground was quite flat again, and the road drove on straight as an arrow. There was one gleam of consolation: Port Sanderson could not be much more than two miles away. Armstrong had no idea how long he had been on the road. Unfortunately his watch was not illuminated and he could only guess at the passage of time. With any luck, the *Canopus* should not take off for another two hours at least. But he could not be sure, and now another fear began to enter his mind—the dread that he might see a vast constellation of lights rising swiftly into the sky ahead, and know that all this agony of mind had been in vain.

He was not zigzagging so badly now, and seemed to be able to anticipate the edge of the road before stumbling off it. It was probable, he cheered himself by thinking, that he was traveling almost as fast as if he had a light. If all went well, he might be nearing Port Sanderson in thirty minutes —a ridiculously small space of time. How he would laugh at his fears when he strolled into his already reserved stateroom in the *Canopus,* and felt that peculiar quiver as the phantom drive hurled the great ship far out of this system, back to the clustered star-clouds near the center of the Galaxy—back toward Earth itself, which he had not seen for so many years. One day, he told himself, he really must visit Earth again. All his life he had been making the promise, but always there had been the same answer —lack of time. Strange, wasn't it, that such a tiny planet should have played so enormous a part in the development of the Universe, should even have come to dominate worlds far wiser and more intelligent than itself!

Armstrong's thoughts were harmless again, and he felt calmer. The knowledge that he was nearing Port Sanderson was immensely reassuring, and he deliberately kept his mind on familiar, unimportant matters. Carver's Pass was already far behind, and with it that thing he no longer intended to recall. One day, if he ever returned to this world, he would visit the Pass in the daytime and laugh at his fears, In twenty minutes now, they would have joined the nightmares of his childhood.

It was almost a shock, though one of the most pleasant he had ever known, when he saw the lights of Port Sanderson come up over the horizon. The curvature of this little world was very deceptive: it did not seem right that a planet with a gravity almost as great as Earth's should have a horizon so close at hand. One day, someone would have to discover what lay at this world's core to give it so great a density. Perhaps the many tunnels would help—it was an unfortunate turn of thought, but the nearness of his goal had robbed it of terror now. Indeed, the thought that he might really be in danger seemed to give his adventure a certain piquancy and heightened interest. Nothing could happen to him now, with ten minutes to go and the lights of the Port already in sight.

A few minutes later, his feelings changed abruptly when he came to the sudden bend in the road. He had forgotten the chasm that caused his detour, and added half a mile to the journey. Well, what of it? he thought stubbornly. An extra half-mile would make no difference now—another ten minutes, at the most.

It was very disappointing when the lights of the city vanished. Armstrong had not remembered the hill which the road was skirting; perhaps it was only a low ridge, scarcely noticeable in the daytime. But by hiding the lights of the Port it had taken away his chief talisman and left him again at the mercy of his fears.

Very unreasonably, his intelligence told him, he began to think how horrible it would be if anything happened now, so near the end of the journey. He kept the worst of his fears at bay for a while, hoping desperately that the lights of the city would soon reappear. But as the minutes dragged on, he realized that the ridge must be longer than he imagined. He tried to cheer himself by the thought that the city would be all the nearer when he saw it again, but somehow logic seemed to have failed him now. For presently he found himself doing something he had not stooped to, even out in the waste by Carver's Pass.

He stopped, turned slowly round, and with bated breath listened until his lungs were nearly bursting.

The silence was uncanny, considering how near he must be to the Port. There was certainly no sound from behind him. Of course there wouldn't be, he told himself angrily. But he was immensely relieved. The thought of that faint and insistent clicking had been haunting him for the last hour.

So friendly and familiar was the noise that did reach him at last that the anticlimax almost made him laugh aloud. Drifting through the still air from a source clearly not more than a mile away came the sound of a landing-field tractor, perhaps one of the machines loading the *Canopus* itself. In a matter of seconds, thought Armstrong, he would be around this ridge with the Port only a few hundred yards ahead. The journey was nearly ended. In a few moments, this evil plain would be no more than a fading nightmare.

It seemed terribly unfair: so little time, such a small fraction of a human life, was all he needed now. But the gods have always been unfair to man, and now they were enjoying their little jest. For there could be no mistaking the rattle of monstrous claws in the darkness *ahead of him.*

Stratford-on-Avon   *April 1945*

The Call of the Stars

Down there on Earth the twentieth century is dying. As I look across at the shadowed globe blocking the stars, I can see the lights of a hundred sleepless cities, and there are moments when I wish that I could be among the crowds now surging and singing in the streets of London, Capetown, Rome, Paris, Berlin, Madrid. . . . Yes, I can see them all at a single glance, burning like fireflies against the darkened planet. The line of midnight is now bisecting Europe: in the eastern Mediterranean a tiny, brilliant star is pulsing as some exuberant pleasure ship waves her searchlights to the sky. I think she is deliberately aiming at us; for the past few minutes the flashes have been qiute regular and startlingly bright. Presently I'll call the communications center and find out who she is, so that I can radio back our own greetings.

Passing into history now, receding forever down the stream of time, is the most incredible hundred years the world has ever seen. It opened with the conquest of the air, saw at its mid-point the unlocking of the atom—and now ends with the bridging of space.

(For the past five minutes I've been wondering what's happening to Nairobi; now I realize that they are putting on a mammoth fireworks display. Chemically fueled rockets may be obsolete out here—but they're still using lots of them down on Earth tonight.)

The end of a century—and the end of a millennium. What will the hundred years that begin with two and zero bring? The planets, of course; floating there in space, only a mile away, are the ships of the first Martian expedition. For two years I have watched them grow, assembled piece by piece, as the space station itself was built by the men I worked with a generation ago.

Those ten ships are ready now, with all their crews aboard, waiting for the final instrument check and the signal for departure. Before the first day of the new century has passed its noon, they will be tearing free from the reins of Earth, to head out toward the strange world that may one day be man's second home.

As I look at the brave little fleet that is now preparing to challenge infinity, my mind goes back forty years, to the days when the first satellites were launched and the Moon still seemed very far away. And I remember—indeed, I have never forgotten—my father's fight to keep me down on Earth.

There were not many weapons he had failed to use. Ridicule had been the first: "Of course they can do it," he had sneered, "but what's the point? Who wants to go out into space while there's so much to be done here on Earth? There's not a single planet in the Solar System where men can live. The Moon's a burnt-out slag heap, and everywhere else is even worse. *This* is where we were meant to live."

Even then (I must have been eighteen or so at the time) I could tangle him up on points of logic. I can remember answering, "How do you know where we were meant to live, Dad? After all, we were in the sea for about a billion years before we decided to tackle the land. Now we're making the next big jump: I don't know where it will lead—nor did that first fish when it crawled up on the beach, and started to sniff the air."

So when he couldn't outargue me, he had tried subtler pressures. He was always talking about the dangers of space travel, and the short working life of anyone foolish enough to get involved in rocketry. At that time, people were still scared of meteors and cosmic rays; like the "Here Be Dragons" of the old map makers, they were the mythical monsters on the still-blank celestial charts. But they didn't worry me; if anything, they added the spice of danger to my dreams.

While I was going through college, Father was comparatively quiet. My training would be valuable whatever profession I took up in later life, so he could not complain—though he occasionally grumbled about the money I wasted buying all the books and magazines on astronautics that I could find. My college record was good, which naturally pleased him; perhaps he did not realize that it would also help me to get my way.

All through my final year I had avoided talking of my plans. I had even given the impression (though I am sorry for that now) that I had abandoned my dream of going into space. Without saying anything to him, I put in my application to Astrotech, and was accepted as soon as I had graduated.

The storm broke when that long blue envelope with the embossed heading "Institute of Astronautical Technology" dropped into the mailbox. I was accused of deceit and ingratitude, and I do not think I ever forgave my father for destroying the pleasure I should have felt at being chosen for the most exclusive—and most glamorous—apprenticeship the world has ever known.

The vacations were an ordeal; had it not been for Mother's sake, I do not think I would have gone home more than once a year, and I always left again as quickly as I could. I had hoped that Father would mellow as my training progressed and as he accepted the inevitable, but he never did.

Then had come that stiff and awkward parting at the spaceport, with the rain streaming down from leaden skies and beating against the smooth walls of the ship that seemed so eagerly waiting to climb into the eternal sunlight beyond the reach of storms. I know now what it cost my father to watch the machine he hated swallow up his only son: for I understand many things today that were hidden from me then.

He knew, even as we parted at the ship, that he would never see me again. Yet his old, stubborn pride kept him from saying the only words that might have held me back. I knew that he was ill, but how ill, he had told no one. That was the only weapon he had not used against me, and I respect him for it.

Would I have stayed had I known? It is even more futile to speculate about the unchangeable past than the unforeseeable future; all I can say now is that I am glad I never had to make the choice. At the end he let me go; he gave up his fight against my ambition, and a little while later his fight with Death.

So I said good-by to Earth, and to the father who loved me but knew no way to say it. He lies down there on the planet I can cover with my hand; how strange it is to think that of the countless billion human beings whose blood runs in my veins, I was the very first to leave his native world. . . .

The new day is breaking over Asia; a hairline of fire is rimming the eastern edge of Earth. Soon it will grow into a burning crescent as the sun comes up out of the Pacific—yet Europe is preparing for sleep, except for those revelers who will stay up to greet the dawn.

And now, over there by the flagship, the ferry rocket is

coming back for the last visitors from the station. Here comes the message I have been waiting for: CAPTAIN STEVENS PRESENTS HIS COMPLIMENTS TO THE STATION COMMANDER. BLAST-OFF WILL BE IN NINETY MINUTES; HE WILL BE GLAD TO SEE YOU ABOARD NOW.

Well, Father, now I know how you felt: time has gone full circle. Yet I hope that I have learned from the mistakes we both made, long ago. I shall remember you when I go over there to the flagship *Starfire* and say good-by to the grandson you never knew.

New York *January 1957*

The Reluctant Orchid

Science fiction, it has often been pointed out, is sadly lacking in humor. But something is worthwhile only if one can make fun of it, and this I set out to do in Tales *from the "White Hart." There is nothing fictitious about the White Hart, or most of its clientele.*

Imitation is the sincerest form of flattery, and I would like to pay here a tribute to the memory of Lord Dunsany, who was very kind to me in the early nineteen-fifties. There is undoubtedly a family resemblance between Harry Purvis and his Mr. Jorkens.

———◆—◆◆—◆———

Though few people in the "White Hart" will concede that any of Harry Purvis' stories are actually *true*, everyone agrees that some are much more probable than others. And on any scale of probability, the affair of the Reluctant Orchid must rate very low indeed.

I don't remember what ingenious gambit Harry used to launch this narrative: maybe some orchid fanicer brought his latest monstrosity into the bar, and that set him off. No matter. I do remember the story, and after all that's what counts.

The adventure did not, this time, concern any of Harry's numerous relatives, and he avoided explaining just how he managed to know so many of the sordid details. The hero—if you can call him that—of this hothouse epic was an inoffensive little clerk named Hercules Keating. And if you think *that* is the most unlikely part of the story, just stick round a while.

Hercules is not the sort of name you can carry off lightly at the best of times, and when you are four foot nine and look as if you'd have to take a physical-culture course before you can even become a ninety-seven-pound weakling, it is a positive embarrassment. Perhaps it helped to explain why

Hercules had very little social life, and all his real friends grew in pots in a humid conservatory at the bottom of his garden. His needs were simple and he spent very little money on himself; consequently his collection of orchids and cacti was really rather remarkable. Indeed, he had a wide reputation among the fraternity of cactophiles, and often received from remote corners of the globe parcels smelling of mold and tropical jungles.

Hercules had only one living relative, and it would have been hard to find a greater contrast than Aunt Henrietta. She was a massive six-footer, usually wore a rather loud line in Harris tweeds, drove a Jaguar with reckless skill, and chain-smoked cigars. Her parents had set their hearts on a boy, and had never been able to decide whether or not their wish had been granted. Henrietta earned a living, and quite a good one, breeding dogs of various shapes and sizes. She was seldom without a couple of her latest models, and they were not the type of portable canine which ladies like to carry in their handbags. The Keating Kennels specialized in Great Danes, Alsatians, and Saint Bernards. . . .

Henrietta, rightly despising men as the weaker sex, had never married. However, for some reason she took an avuncular (yes, that is definitely the right word) interest in Hercules, and called to see him almost every weekend. It was a curious kind of relationship: probably Henrietta found that Hercules bolstered up her feelings of superiority. If he was a good example of the male sex, then they were certainly a pretty sorry lot. Yet, if this was Henrietta's motivation, she was unconscious of it and seemed genuinely fond of her nephew. She was patronizing, but never unkind.

As might be expected, her attentions did not exactly help Hercules' own well-developed inferiority complex. At first he had tolerated his aunt; then he came to dread her regular visits, her booming voice, and her bone-crushing handshake; and at last he grew to hate her. Eventually, indeed, his hate was the dominant emotion in his life, exceeding even his love for his orchids. But he was careful not to show it, realizing that if Aunt Henrietta discovered how he felt about her, she would probably break him in two and throw the pieces to her wolf pack.

There was no way, then, in which Hercules could express his pent-up feelings. He had to be polite to Aunt Henrietta even when he felt like murder. And he often did feel like murder, though he knew that there was nothing he would ever do about it. Until one day . . .

According to the dealer, the orchid came from "somewhere in the Amazon region"—a rather vague postal address. When Hercules first saw it, it was not a very prepossessing sight, even to anyone who loved orchids as much as he did. A shapeless root, about the size of a man's fist—that was all. It was redolent of decay, and there was the faintest hint of a rank, carrion smell. Hercules was not even sure that it was viable, and told the dealer as much. Perhaps that enabled him to purchase it for a trifling sum, and he carried it home without much enthusiasm.

It showed no signs of life for the first month, but that did not worry Hercules. Then, one day, a tiny green shoot appeared and started to creep up to the light. After that, progress was rapid. Soon there was a thick, fleshy stem as big as a man's forearm, and colored a positively virulent green. Near the top of the stem a series of curious bulges circled the plant: otherwise it was completely featureless. Hercules was now quite excited: he was sure that some entirely new species had swum into his ken.

The rate of growth was now really fantastic: soon the plant was taller than Hercules, not that that was saying a great deal. Moreover, the bulges seemed to be developing, and it looked as if at any moment the orchid would burst into bloom. Hercules waited anxiously, knowing how short-lived some flowers can be, and spent as much time as he possibly could in the hothouse. Despite all his watchfulness, the transformation occurred one night while he was asleep.

In the morning, the orchid was fringed by a series of eight dangling tendrils, almost reaching to the ground. They must have developed inside the plant and emerged with—for the vegetable world—explosive speed. Hercules stared at the phenomenon in amazement, and went very thoughtfully to work.

That evening, as he watered the plant and checked its soil, he noticed a still more peculiar fact. The tendrils were thickening, and they were not completely motionless. They had a slight but unmistakable tendency to vibrate, as if possessing a life of their own. Even Hercules, for all his interest and enthusiasm, found this more than a little disturbing.

A few days later, there was no doubt about it at all. When he approached the orchid, the tendrils swayed toward him in an unpleasantly suggestive fashion. The impression of hunger was so strong that Hercules began to feel very uncomfortable indeed, and something started to nag at the back of his mind. It was quite a while before he could recall what it was: then he said to himself, "Of course! How stupid of me!" and went along to the local library. Here he spent a most interesting half hour rereading a little piece by one H. G. Wells entitled, "The Flowering of the Strange Orchid."

"My goodness!" thought Hercules, when he had finished the tale. As yet there had been no stupefying odor which might overpower the plant's intended victim, but otherwise the characteristics were all too similar. Hercules went home in a very unsettled mood indeed.

He opened the conservatory door and stood looking along the avenue of greenery toward his prize specimen. He judged the length of the tendrils—already he found himself calling them tentacles—with great care and walked to within what appeared a safe distance. The plant certainly had an impression of alertness and menace far more appropriate to the animal than the vegetable kingdom. Hercules remembered the unfortunate history of Doctor Frankenstein, and was not amused.

But, really, this was ridiculous! Such things didn't happen in real life. Well, there was one way to put matters to the test. . . .

Hercules went into the house and came back a few minutes later with a broomstick, to the end of which he had attached a piece of raw meat. Feeling a considerable fool, he advanced toward the orchid as a lion tamer might approach one of his charges at mealtime.

For a moment, nothing happened. Then two of the tendrils developed an agitated twitch. They began to sway back and forth, as if the plant was making up its mind. Abruptly, they whipped out with such speed that they practically vanished from view. They wrapped themselves round the meat, and Hercules felt a powerful tug at the end of his broomstick. Then the meat was gone: the orchid was clutching it, if one may mix metaphors slightly, to its bosom.

"Jumping Jehosophat!" yelled Hercules. It was very seldom indeed that he used such strong language.

The orchid showed no further signs of life for twenty-four hours. It was waiting for the meat to become high, and it was also developing its digestive system. By the next day, a network of what looked like short roots had covered the still-visible chunk of meat. By nightfall, the meat was gone.

The plant had tasted blood.

Hercules' emotions as he watched over his prize were curiously mixed. There were times when it almost gave him nightmares, and he foresaw a whole range of horrid possibilities.

The orchid was now extremely strong, and if he got within its clutches he would be done for. But, of course, there was not the slightest danger of that. He had arranged a system of pipes so that it could be watered from a safe distance, and its less orthodox food he simply tossed within range of its tentacles. It was now eating a pound of raw meat a day, and he had an uncomfortable feeling that it could cope with much larger quantities if given the opportunity.

Hercules' natural qualms were, on the whole, outweighed by his feeling of triumph that such a botanical marvel had fallen into his hands. Whenever he chose, he could become the most famous orchid-grower in the world. It was typical of his somewhat restricted viewpoint that it never occurred to him that other people besides orchid fanciers might be interested in his pet.

The creature was now about six feet tall, and apparently still growing—though much more slowly than it had been. All the other plants had been moved from its end of the conservatory, not so much because Hercules feared that it might be cannibalistic as to enable him to tend them without danger. He had stretched a rope across the central aisle so that there was no risk of his accidentally walking within range of those eight dangling arms.

It was obvious that the orchid had a highly developed nervous system, and something very nearly approaching intelligence. It knew when it was going to be fed, and exhibited unmistakable signs of pleasure. Most fantastic of all—though Hercules was still not sure about this—it seemed capable of producing sounds. There were times, just before a meal, when he fancied he could hear an incredibly high-pitched whistle, skirting the edge of audibility. A newborn bat might have had such a voice: he wondered what purpose it served. Did the orchid somehow lure its prey into its clutches by sound? If so, he did not think the technique would work on him.

While Hercules was making these interesting discoveries, he continued to be fussed over by Aunt Henrietta and assaulted by her hounds, which were never as house-trained as she claimed them to be. She would usually roar up the street on a Sunday afternoon with one dog in the seat beside her and another occupying most of the baggage compartment. Then she would bound up the steps two at a time, nearly deafen Hercules with her greeting, half paralyze him with her handshake, and blow cigar smoke in his face. There had been a time when he was terrified that she would kiss him, but he had long since realized that such effeminate behavior was foreign to her nature.

Aunt Henrietta looked upon Hercules' orchids with some scorn. Spending one's spare time in a hothouse was, she considered, a very effete recreation. When *she* wanted to let off steam, she went big-game hunting in Kenya. This did nothing to endear her to Hercules, who hated blood sports. But despite his mounting dislike for his overpowering aunt, every Sunday afternoon he dutifully prepared tea for her and they had a tête-à-tête together which, on the surface at least, seemed perfectly friendly. Henrietta never guessed that as he poured the tea Hercules often wished it was poisoned: she was, far down beneath her extensive fortifications, a fundamentally goodhearted person and the knowledge would have upset her deeply.

Hercules did not mention his vegetable octopus to Aunt Henrietta. He had occasionally shown her his most interesting specimens, but this was something he was keeping to himself. Perhaps, even before he had fully formulated his diabolical plan, his subconscious was already preparing the ground. . . .

It was late one Sunday evening, when the roar of the Jaguar had died away into the night and Hercules was restoring his shattered nerves in the conservatory, that the idea first came fully fledged into his mind. He was staring at the orchid, noting how the tendrils were now as thick around as a man's thumb, when a most pleasing fantasy suddenly flashed before his eyes. He pictured Aunt Henrietta struggling helplessly in the grip of the monster, unable to escape from its carnivorous clutches. Why, it would be the perfect crime. The distraught nephew would arrive on the scene too late to be of assistance, and when the police answered his frantic call they would see at a glance that the whole affair was a deplorable accident. True, there would be an inquest, but the coroner's censure would be toned down in view of Hercules' obvious grief. . . .

The more he thought of the idea, the more he liked it. He could see no flaws, as long as the orchid co-operated. That, clearly, would be the greatest problem. He would have to plan a course of training for the creature. It already looked sufficiently diabolical; he must give it a disposition to suit its appearance.

Considering that he had no prior experience in such matters, and that there were no authorities he could consult, Hercules proceeded along very sound and businesslike lines. He would use a fishing rod to dangle pieces of meat just outside the orchid's range, until the creature lashed its tentacles in a frenzy. At such times its high-pitched squeak was clearly audible, and Hercules wondered how it managed to produce the sound. He also wondered what its organs of perception were, but this was yet another mystery that could not be solved without close examination. Perhaps Aunt Henrietta, if all went well, would have a brief opportunity of discovering these interesting facts—though she would probably be too busy to report them for the benefit of posterity.

There was no doubt that the beast was quite powerful enough to deal with its intended victim. It had once wrenched a broomstick out of Hercules' grip, and although that in itself proved very little, the sickening "crack" of the wood a moment later brought a smile of satisfaction to its trainer's thin lips. He began to be much more pleasant and attentive to his aunt. In every respect, indeed, he was the model nephew.

When Hercules considered that his picador tactics had brought the orchid into the right frame of mind, he wondered if he should test it with live bait. This was a problem that worried him for some weeks, during which time he would look speculatively at every dog or cat he passed in the street, but he finally abandoned the idea, for a rather peculiar reason. He was simply too kindhearted to put it into practice. Aunt Henrietta would have to be the first victim.

He starved the orchid for two weeks before he put his plan into action. This was as long as he dared risk—he did not wish to weaken the beast—merely to whet its appetite, that the outcome of the encounter might be more certain. And so, when he had carried the teacups back into the kitchen and was sitting upwind of Aunt Henrietta's cigar, he said casually: "I've got something I'd like to show you, Auntie. I've been keeping it as a surprise. It'll tickle you to death."

That, he thought, was not a completely accurate description, but it gave the general idea.

Auntie took the cigar out of her mouth and looked at Hercules with frank surprise.

"Well!" she boomed. "Wonders will never cease! What *have* you been up to, you rascal?" She slapped him playfully on the back and shot all the air out of his lungs.

"You'll never believe it," gritted Hercules, when he had recovered his breath. "It's in the conservatory."

"Eh?" said Auntie, obviously puzzled.

"Yes—come along and have a look. It's going to create a real sensation."

Auntie gave a snort that might have indicated disbelief, but followed Hercules without further question. The two Alsatians now busily chewing up the carpet looked at her anxiously and half rose to their feet, but she waved them away.

"All right, boys," she ordered gruffly. "I'll be back in a minute." Hercules thought this unlikely.

It was a dark evening, and the lights in the conservatory were off. As they entered, Auntie snorted, "Gad, Hercules—the place smells like a slaughterhouse. Haven't met such a stink since I shot that elephant in Bulawayo and we couldn't find it for a week."

"Sorry, Auntie," apologized Hercules, propelling her forward through the gloom. "It's a new fertilizer I'm using. It produces the most stunning results. Go on—another couple of yards. I want this to be a *real* surprise."

"I hope this isn't a joke," said Auntie suspiciously, as she stomped forward.

"I can promise you it's no joke," replied Hercules, standing with his hand on the light switch. He could just see the looming bulk of the orchid: Auntie was now within ten feet of it. He waited until she was well inside the danger zone, and threw the switch.

There was a frozen moment while the scene was transfixed with light. Then Aunt Henrietta ground to a halt and stood, arms akimbo, in front of the giant orchid. For a moment Hercules was afraid she would retreat before the plant could get into action: then he saw that she was calmly scrutinizing it, unable to make up her mind what the devil it was.

It was a full five seconds before the orchid moved. Then the dangling tentacles flashed into action—but not in the way that Hercules had expected. The plant clutched them tightly, protectively, *around itself*—and at the same time it gave a high-pitched scream of pure terror. In a moment of sickening disillusionment, Hercules realized the awful truth.

His orchid was an utter coward. It might be able to cope with the wild life of the Amazon jungle, but coming suddenly upon Aunt Henrietta had completely broken its nerve.

As for its proposed victim, she stood watching the creature with an astonishment which swiftly changed to another emotion. She spun around on her heels and pointed an accusing finger at her nephew.

"Hercules!" she roared. "The poor thing's scared to death. *Have you been bullying it?*"

Hercules could only stand with his head hanging low in shame and frustration.

"N-no, Auntie," he quavered. "I guess it's naturally nervous."

"Well, I'm used to animals. You should have called me before. You must treat them firmly—but gently. Kindness always works, as long as you show them you're the master. There, there, did-dums—don't be frightened of Auntie—she won't hurt you . . ."

It was, thought Hercules in his blank despair, a revolting sight. With surprising gentleness, Aunt Henrietta fussed over the beast, patting and stroking it until the tentacles relaxed and the shrill, whistling scream died away. After a few minutes of this pandering, it appeared to get over its fright. Hercules finally fled with a muffled sob when one of the tentacles crept forward and began to stroke Henrietta's gnarled fingers. . . .

From that day, he was a broken man. What was worse, he could never escape from the consequences of his intended crime. Henrietta had acquired a new pet, and was liable to call not only at weekends but two or three times in between as well. It was obvious that she did not trust Hercules to treat the orchid properly, and still suspected him of bullying it. She would bring tasty tidbits that even her dogs had rejected, but which the orchid accepted with delight. The smell, which had so far been confined to the conservatory, began to creep into the house. . . .

And there, concluded Harry Purvis, as he brought this improbable narrative to a close, the matter rests—to the satisfaction of two, at any rate, of the parties concerned. The orchid is happy, and Aunt Henrietta has something (query, someone?) else to dominate. From time to time the creature has a nervous breakdown when a mouse gets loose in the conservatory, and she rushes to console it.

As for Hercules, there is no chance that he will ever give any more trouble to either of them. He seems to have sunk into a kind of vegetable sloth: indeed, said Harry thoughtfully, every day he becomes more and more like an orchid himself.

The harmless variety, of course. . . .

Miami   *April 1954*

Encounter at Dawn

It was in the last days of the Empire. The tiny ship was far from home, and almost a hundred light-years from the great parent vessel searching through the loosely packed stars at the rim of the Milky Way. But even here it could not escape from the shadow that lay across civilization: beneath that shadow, pausing ever and again in their work to wonder how their distant homes were faring, the scientists of the Galactic Survey still labored at their never-ending task.

The ship held only three occupants, but among them they carried knowledge of many sciences, and the experience of half a lifetime in space. After the long interstellar night, the star ahead was warming their spirits as they dropped down toward its fires. A little more golden, a trifle more brilliant than the sun that now seemed a legend of their childhood. They knew from past experience that the chance of locating planets here was more than ninety per cent, and for the moment they forgot all else in the excitement of discovery.

They found the first planet within minutes of coming to rest. It was a giant, of a familiar type, too cold for proto-plasmic life and probably possessing no stable surface. So they turned their search sunward, and presently were rewarded.

It was a world that made their hearts ache for home, a world where everything was hauntingly familiar, yet never quite the same. Two great land masses floated in blue-green seas, capped by ice at both poles. There were some desert regions, but the larger part of the planet was obviously fertile. Even from this distance, the signs of vegetation were unmistakably clear.

They gazed hungrily at the expanding landscape as they fell down into the atmosphere, heading toward noon in the subtropics. The ship plummeted through cloudless skies toward a great river, checked its fall with a surge of soundless power, and came to rest among the long grasses by the water's edge.

No one moved: there was nothing to be done until the auto-

matic instruments had finished their work. Then a bell tinkled
softly and the lights on the control board flashed in a pattern
of meaningful chaos. Captain Altman rose to his feet with a
sigh of relief.

"We're in luck," he said. "We can go outside without protection, if the pathogenic tests are satisfactory. What did you
make of the place as we came in, Bertrond?"

"Geologically stable—no active volcanoes, at least. I didn't
see any trace of cities, but that proves nothing. If there's a
civilization here, it may have passed that stage."

"Or not reached it yet?"

Bertrond shrugged. "Either's just as likely. It may take us
some time to find out on a planet this size."

"More time than we've got," said Clindar, glancing at the
communications panel that linked them to the mother ship
and thence to the Galaxy's threatened heart. For a moment
there was a gloomy silence. Then Clindar walked to the control board and pressed a pattern of keys with automatic skill.

With a slight jar, a section of the hull slid aside and the
fourth member of the crew stepped out onto the new planet,
flexing metal limbs and adjusting servomotors to the unaccustomed gravity. Inside the ship, a television screen glimmered
into life, revealing a long vista of waving grasses, some trees
in the middle distance, and a glimpse of the great river. Clindar punched a button, and the picture flowed steadily across
the screen as the robot turned its head.

"Which way shall we go?" Clindar asked.

"Let's have a look at those trees," Altman replied. "If
there's any animal life we'll find it there."

"Look!" cried Bertrond. "A bird!"

Clindar's fingers flew over the keyboard: the picture cen-
tered on the tiny speck that had suddenly appeared on the left
of the screen, and expanded rapidly as the robot's telephoto
lens came into action.

"You're right," he said. "Feathers—beak—well up the evo-
lutionary ladder. This place looks promising. I'll start the
camera."

The swaying motion of the picture as the robot walked forward did not distract them: they had grown accustomed to it
long ago. But they had never become reconciled to this exploration by proxy when all their impulses cried out to them
to leave the ship, to run through the grass and to feel the wind

blowing against their faces. Yet it was too great a risk to take, even on a world that seemed as fair as this. There was always a skull hidden behind Nature's most smiling face. Wild beasts, poisonous reptiles, quagmires—death could come to the unwary explorer in a thousand disguises. And worst of all were the invisible enemies, the bacteria and viruses against which the only defense might often be a thousand light-years away.

A robot could laugh at all these dangers and even if, as sometimes happened, it encountered a beast powerful enough to destroy it—well, machines could always be replaced.

They met nothing on the walk across the grasslands. If any small animals were disturbed by the robot's passage, they kept outside its field of vision. Clindar slowed the machine as it approached the trees, and the watchers in the spaceship flinched involuntarily at the branches that appeared to slash across their eyes. The picture dimmed for a moment before the controls readjusted themselves to the weaker illumination; then it came back to normal.

The forest was full of life. It lurked in the undergrowth, clambered among the branches, flew through the air. It fled chattering and gibbering through the trees as the robot advanced. And all the while the automatic cameras were recording the pictures that formed on the screen, gathering material for the biologists to analyze when the ship returned to base.

Clindar breathed a sigh of relief when the trees suddenly thinned. It was exhausting work, keeping the robot from smashing into obstacles as it moved through the forest, but on open ground it could take care of itself. Then the picture trembled as if beneath a hammer blow, there was a grinding metallic thud, and the whole scene swept vertiginously upward as the robot toppled and fell.

"What's that?" cried Altman. "Did you trip?"

"No," said Clindar grimly, his fingers flying over the keyboard. "Something attacked from the rear. I hope . . . ah . . I've still got control."

He brought the robot to a sitting position and swiveled its head. It did not take long to find the cause of the trouble. Standing a few feet away, and lashing its tail angrily, was a large quadruped with a most ferocious set of teeth. At the moment it was, fairly obviously, trying to decide whether to attack again.

Slowly, the robot rose to its feet, and as it did so the great beast crouched to spring. A smile flitted across Clindar's face:

he knew how to deal with this situation. His thumb felt for the seldom-used key labeled "Siren."

The forest echoed with a hideous undulating scream from the robot's concealed speaker, and the machine advanced to meet its adversary, arms flailing in front of it. The startled beast almost fell over backward in its effort to turn, and in seconds was gone from sight.

"Now I suppose we'll have to wait a couple of hours until everything comes out of hiding again," said Bertrond ruefully.

"I don't know much about animal psychology," interjected Altman, "but is it usual for them to attack something completely unfamiliar?"

"Some will attack anything that moves, but that's unusual. Normally they attack only for food, or if they've already been threatened. What are you driving at? Do you suggest that there are other robots on this planet?"

"Certainly not. But our carnivorous friend may have mistaken our machine for a more edible biped. Don't you think that this opening in the jungle is rather unnatural? It could easily be a path."

"In that case," said Clindar promptly, "we'll follow it and find out. I'm tired of dodging trees, but I hope nothing jumps on us again: it's bad for my nerves."

"You were right, Altman," said Bertrond a little later. "It's certainly a path. But that doesn't mean intelligence. After all, animals—"

He stopped in mid-sentence, and at the same instant Clindar brought the advancing robot to a halt. The path had suddenly opened out into a wide clearing, almost completely occupied by a village of flimsy huts. It was ringed by a wooden palisade, obviously defense against an enemy who at the moment presented no threat. For the gates were wide open, and beyond them the inhabitants were going peacefully about their ways.

For many minutes the three explorers stared in silence at the screen. Then Clindar shivered a little and remarked: "It's uncanny. It might be our own planet, a hundred thousand years ago. I feel as if I've gone back in time."

"There's nothing weird about it," said the practical Altman. "After all, we've discovered nearly a hundred planets with our type of life on them."

"Yes," retorted Clindar. "A hundred in the whole Galaxy! I still think it's strange it had to happen to us."

"Well, it had to happen to *somebody*," said Bertrond philosophically. "Meanwhile, we must work out our contact procedure. If we send the robot into the village it will start a panic."

"That," said Altman, "is a masterly understatement. What we'll have to do is catch a native by himself and prove that we're friendly. Hide the robot, Clindar. Somewhere in the woods where it can watch the village without being spotted. We've a week's practical anthropology ahead of us!"

It was three days before the biological tests showed that it would be safe to leave the ship. Even then Bertrond insisted on going alone—alone, that is, if one ignored the substantial company of the robot. With such an ally he was not afraid of this planet's larger beasts, and his body's natural defenses could take care of the microorganisms. So, at least, the analyzers had assured him; and considering the complexity of the problem, they made remarkably few mistakes. . . .

He stayed outside for an hour, enjoying himself cautiously, while his companions watched with envy. It would be another three days before they could be quite certain that it was safe to follow Bertrond's example. Meanwhile, they kept busy enough watching the village through the lenses of the robot, and recording everything they could with the cameras. They had moved the spaceship at night so that it was hidden in the depths of the forest, for they did not wish to be discovered until they were ready.

And all the while the news from home grew worse. Though their remoteness here at the edge of the Universe deadened its impact, it lay heavily on their minds and sometimes overwhelmed them with a sense of futility. At any moment, they knew, the signal for recall might come as the Empire summoned up its last resources in its extremity. But until then they would continue their work as though pure knowledge were the only thing that mattered.

Seven days after landing, they were ready to make the experiment. They knew now what paths the villagers used when going hunting, and Bertrond chose one of the less frequented ways. Then he placed a chair firmly in the middle of the path and settled down to read a book.

It was not, of course, quite as simple as that: Bertrond had taken all imaginable precautions. Hidden in the undergrowth fifty yards away, the robot was watching through its telescopic lenses, and in its hand it held a small but deadly weapon. Controlling it from the spaceship, his fingers poised over the keyboard, Clindar waited to do what might be necessary.

That was the negative side of the plan: the positive side

was more obvious. Lying at Bertrond's feet was the carcass of a small, horned animal which he hoped would be an acceptable gift to any hunter passing this way.

Two hours later the radio in his suit harness whispered a warning. Quite calmly, though the blood was pounding in his veins, Bertrond laid aside his book and looked down the trail. The savage was walking forward confidently enough, swinging a spear in his right hand. He paused for a moment when he saw Bertrond, then advanced more cautiously. He could tell that there was nothing to fear, for the stranger was slightly built and obviously unarmed.

When only twenty feet separated them, Bertrond gave a reassuring smile and rose slowly to his feet. He bent down, picked up the carcass, and carried it forward as an offering. The gesture would have been understood by any creature on any world, and it was understood here. The savage reached forward, took the animal, and threw it effortlessly over his shoulder. For an instant he stared into Bertrond's eyes with a fathomless expression; then he turned and walked back toward the village. Three times he glanced round to see if Bertrond was following, and each time Bertrond smiled and waved reassurance. The whole episode lasted little more than a minute. As the first contact between two races it was completely without drama, though not without dignity.

Bertrond did not move until the other had vanished from sight. Then he relaxed and spoke into his suit microphone.

"That was a pretty good beginning," he said jubilantly. "He wasn't in the least frightened, or even suspicious. I think he'll be back."

"It still seems too good to be true," said Altman's voice in his ear. "I should have thought he'd have been either scared or hostile. Would *you* have accepted a lavish gift from a peculiar stranger with such little fuss?"

Bertrond was slowly walking back to the ship. The robot had now come out of cover and was keeping guard a few paces behind him.

"*I* wouldn't," he replied, "but I belong to a civilized community. Complete savages may react to strangers in many different ways, according to their past experience. Suppose this tribe has never had any enemies. That's quite possible on a large but sparsely populated planet. Then we may expect curiosity, but no fear at all."

"If these people have no enemies," put in Clindar, no longer fully occupied in controlling the robot, "why have they got a stockade round the village?"

"I meant no *human* enemies," replied Bertrond. "If that's true, it simplifies our task immensely."

"Do you think he'll come back?"

"Of coure. If he's as human as I think, curiosity and greed will make him return. In a couple of days we'll be bosom friends."

Looked at dispassionately, it became a fantastic routine. Every morning the robot would go hunting under Clindar's direction, until it was now the deadliest killer in the jungle. Then Bertrond would wait until Yaan—which was the nearest they could get to his name—came striding confidently along the path. He came at the same time every day, and he always came alone. They wondered about this: did he wish to keep his great discovery to himself and thus get all the credit for his hunting prowess? If so, it showed unexpected foresight and cunning.

At first Yaan had departed at once with his prize, as if afraid that the donor of such a generous gift might change his mind. Soon, however, as Bertrond had hoped, he could be induced to stay for a while by simple conjuring tricks and a display of brightly colored fabrics and crystals, in which he took a childlike delight. At last Bertrond was able to engage him in lengthy conversations, all of which were recorded as well as being filmed through the eyes of the hidden robot.

One day the philologists might be able to analyze this material; the best that Bertrond could do was to discover the meanings of a few simple verbs and nouns. This was made more difficult by the fact that Yaan not only used different words for the same thing, but sometimes the same word for different things.

Between these daily interviews, the ship traveled far, surveying the planet from the air and sometimes landing for more detailed examinations. Although several other human settlements were observed, Bertrond made no attempt to get in touch with them, for it was easy to see that they were all at much the same cultural level as Yaan's people.

It was, Bertrond often thought, a particularly bad joke on the part of Fate that one of the Galaxy's very few truly human races should have been discovered at this moment of time. Not long ago this would have been an event of supreme importance; now civilization was too hard-pressed to concern itself with these savage cousins waiting at the dawn of history.

Not until Bertrond was sure he had become part of Yaan's everyday life did he introduce him to the robot. He was showing Yaan the patterns in a kaleidoscope when Clindar brought the machine striding through the grass with its latest victim dangling across one metal arm. For the first time Yaan showed something akin to fear; but he relaxed at Bertrond's soothing words, though he continued to watch the advancing monster. It halted some distance away, and Bertrond walked forward to meet it. As he did so, the robot raised its arms and handed him the dead beast. He took it solemnly and carried it back to Yaan, staggering a little under the unaccustomed load.

Bertrond would have given a great deal to know just what Yaan was thinking as he accepted the gift. Was he trying to decide whether the robot was master or slave? Perhaps such conceptions as this were beyond his grasp: to him the robot might be merely another man, a hunter who was a friend of Bertrond.

Clindar's voice, slightly larger than life, came from the robot's speaker.

"It's astonishing how calmly he accepts us. Won't anything scare him?"

"You will keep judging him by your own standards," replied Bertrond. "Remember, his psychology is completely different, and much simpler. Now that he has confidence in me, anything that I accept won't worry him."

"I wonder if that will be true of all his race?" queried Altman. "It's hardly safe to judge by a single specimen. I want to see what happens when we send the robot into the village."

"Hello!" exclaimed Bertrond. "*That* surprised him. He's never met a person who could speak with two voices before."

"Do you think he'll guess the truth when he meets us?" said Clindar.

"No. The robot will be pure magic to him—but it won't be any more wonderful than fire and lightning and all the other forces he must already take for granted."

"Well, what's the next move?" asked Altman, a little impatiently. "Are you going to bring him to the ship, or will you go into the village first?"

Bertrond hesitated. "I'm anxious not to do too much too quickly. You know the accidents that have happened with strange races when that's been tried. I'll let him think this over, and when we get back tomorrow I'll try to persuade him to take the robot back to the village."

In the hidden ship, Clindar reactivated the robot and started it moving again. Like Altman, he was growing a little impatient of this excessive caution, but on all matters relating to alien life-forms Bertrond was the expert, and they had to obey his orders.

There were times now when he almost wished he were a robot himself, devoid of feelings or emotions, able to watch the fall of a leaf or the death agonies of a world with equal detachment. . . .

The sun was low when Yaan heard the great voice crying from the jungle. He recognized it at once, despite its inhuman volume: it was the voice of his friend, and it was calling him.

In the echoing silence, the life of the village came to a stop. Even the children ceased their play: the only sound was the thin cry of a baby frightened by the sudden silence.

All eyes were upon Yaan as he walked swiftly to his hut and grasped the spear that lay beside the entrance. The stockade would soon be closed against the prowlers of the night, but he did not hesitate as he stepped out into the lengthening shadows. He was passing through the gates when once again that mighty voice summoned him, and now it held a note of urgency that came clearly across all the barriers of language and culture.

The shining giant who spoke with many voices met him a little way from the village and beckoned him to follow. There was no sign of Bertrond. They walked for almost a mile before they saw him in the distance, standing not far from the river's edge and staring out across the dark, slowly moving waters.

He turned as Yaan approached, yet for a moment seemed unaware of his presence. Then he gave a gesture of dismissal to the shining one, who withdrew into the distance.

Yaan waited. He was patient and, though he could never have expressed it in words, contented. When he was with Bertrond he felt the first intimations of that selfless, utterly irrational devotion his race would not fully achieve for many ages.

It was a strange tableau. Here at the river's brink two men were standing. One was dressed in a closely fitting uniform equipped with tiny, intricate mechanisms. The other was wearing the skin of an animal and was carrying a flint-tipped spear. Ten thousand generations lay between them, ten thou-

sand generations and an immeasurable gulf of space. Yet
they were both human. As she must do often in Eternity,
Nature had repeated one of her basic patterns.

Presently Bertrand began to speak, walking to and fro in
short, quick steps as he did, and in his voice there was a trace
of madness.

"It's all over, Yaan. I'd hoped that with our knowledge we
could have brought you out of barbarism in a dozen generations, but now you will have to fight your way up from the
jungle alone, and it may take you a million years to do so.
I'm sorry—there's so much we could have done. Even now I
wanted to stay here, but Altman and Clindar talk of duty, and
I suppose that they are right. There is little enough that we
can do, but our world is calling and we must not forsake it.

"I wish you could understand me, Yaan. I wish you knew
what I was saying. I'm leaving you these tools: some of them
you will discover how to use, though as likely as not in a
generation they'll be lost or forgotten. See how this blade
cuts: it will be ages before your world can make its like.
And guard this well: when you press the button—look! If
you use it sparingly, it will give you light for years, though
sooner or later it will die. As for these other things—find what
use for them you can.

"Here come the first stars, up there in the east. Do you
ever look at the stars, Yaan? I wonder how long it will be
before you have discovered what they are, and I wonder what
will have happened to us by then. Those stars are our homes,
Yaan, and we cannot save them. Many have died already, in
explosions so vast that I can imagine them no more than you.
In a hundred thousand of your years, the light of those funeral pyres will reach your world and set its peoples wondering. By then, perhaps, your race will be reaching for the stars.
I wish I could warn you against the mistakes we made, and
which now will cost us all that we have won.

"It is well for your people, Yaan, that your world is here at
the frontier of the Universe. You may escape the doom that
waits for us. One day, perhaps, your ships will go searching
among the stars as we have done, and they may come upon
the ruins of our worlds and wonder who we were. But they
will never know that we met here by this river when your race
was young.

"Here come my friends; they would give me no more time.
Good-by, Yaan—use well the things I have left you. They are
your world's greatest treasures."

Something huge, something that glittered in the starlight, was sliding down from the sky. It did not reach the ground, but came to rest a little way above the surface, and in utter silence a rectangle of light opened in its side. The shining giant appeared out of the night and stepped through the golden door. Bertrond followed, pausing for a moment at the threshold to wave back at Yaan. Then the darkness closed behind him.

No more swiftly than smoke drifts upward from a fire, the ship lifted away. When it was so small that Yaan felt he could hold it in his hands, it seemed to blur into a long line of light slanting upward into the stars. From the empty sky a peal of thunder echoed over the sleeping land; and Yaan knew at last that the gods were gone and would never come again.

For a long time he stood by the gently moving waters, and into his soul there came a sense of loss he was never to forget and never to understand. Then, carefully and reverently, he collected together the gifts that Bertrond had left.

Under the stars, the lonely figure walked homeward across a nameless land. Behind him the river flowed softly to the sea, winding through the fertile plains on which, more than a thousand centuries ahead, Yaan's descendants would build the great city they were to call Babylon.

London   *November 1950*

"If I Forget Thee,
Oh Earth . . ."

When Marvin was ten years old, his father took him through
the long, echoing corridors that led up through Administration and Power, until at last they came to the uppermost levels
of all and were among the swiftly growing vegetation of the
Farmlands. Marvin liked it here: it was fun watching the
great, slender plants creeping with almost visible eagerness
toward the sunlight as it filtered down through the plastic
domes to meet them. The smell of life was everywhere, awak-
ening inexpressible longings in his heart: no longer was he
breathing the dry, cool air of the residential levels, purged of
all smells but the faint tang of ozone. He wished he could
stay here for a little while, but Father would not let him.
They went onward until they had reached the entrance to the
Observatory, which he had never visited: but they did not
stop, and Marvin knew with a sense of rising excitement that
there could be only one goal left. For the first time in his life,
he was going Outside.

There were a dozen of the surface vehicles, with their wide
balloon tires and pressurized cabins, in the great servicing
chamber. His father must have been expected, for they were
led at once to the little scout car waiting by the huge circular
door of the air lock. Tense with expectancy, Marvin settled
himself down in the cramped cabin while his father started
the motor and checked the controls. The inner door of the
lock slid open and then closed behind them: he heard the
roar of the great air pumps fade slowly away as the pressure
dropped to zero. Then the "Vacuum" sign flashed on, the
outer door parted, and before Marvin lay the land which he
had never yet entered.

He had seen it in photographs, of course: he had watched
it imaged on television screens a hundred times. But now it
was lying all around him, burning beneath the fierce sun that
crawled so slowly across the jet-black sky. He stared into the
west, away from the blinding splendor of the sun—and there

were the stars, as he had been told but had never quite believed. He gazed at them for a long time, marveling that anything could be so bright and yet so tiny. They were intense unscintillating points, and suddenly he remembered a rhyme he had once read in one of his father's books:

> *Twinkle, twinkle, little star,*
> *How I wonder what you are.*

Well, *he* knew what the stars were. Whoever asked that question must have been very stupid. And what did they mean by "twinkle"? You could see at a glance that all the stars shone with the same steady, unwavering light. He abandoned the puzzle and turned his attention to the landscape around him.

They were racing across a level plain at almost a hundred miles an hour, the great balloon tires sending up little spurts of dust behind them. There was no sign of the Colony: in the few minutes while he had been gazing at the stars, its domes and radio towers had fallen below the horizon. Yet there were other indications of man's presence, for about a mile ahead Marvin could see the curiously shaped structures clustering round the head of a mine. Now and then a puff of vapor would emerge from a squat smokestack and would instantly disperse.

They were past the mine in a moment: Father was driving with a reckless and exhilarating skill as if—it was a strange thought to come into a child's mind—he were trying to escape from something. In a few minutes they had reached the edge of the plateau on which the Colony had been built. The ground fell sharply away beneath them in a dizzying slope whose lower stretches were lost in shadow. Ahead, as far as the eye could reach, was a jumbled wasteland of craters, mountain ranges, and ravines. The crests of the mountains, catching the low sun, burned like islands of fire in a sea of darkness: and above them the stars still shone as steadfastly as ever.

There could be no way forward—yet there was. Marvin clenched his fists as the car edged over the slope and started the long descent. Then he saw the barely visible track leading down the mountainside, and relaxed a little. Other men, it seemed, had gone this way before.

Night fell with a shocking abruptness as they crossed the shadow line and the sun dropped below the crest of the plateau. The twin searchlights sprang into life, casting blue-white bands on the rocks ahead, so that there was scarcely need to check their speed. For hours they drove through valleys and past the foot of mountains whose peaks seemed to comb the stars, and sometimes they emerged for a moment into the sunlight as they climbed over higher ground.

And now on the right was a wrinkled, dusty plain, and on the left, its ramparts and terraces rising mile after mile into the sky, was a wall of mountains that marched into the distance until its peaks sank from sight below the rim of the world. There was no sign that men had ever explored this land, but once they passed the skeleton of a crashed rocket, and beside it a stone cairn surmounted by a metal cross.

It seemed to Marvin that the mountains stretched on forever: but at last, many hours later, the range ended in a towering, precipitous headland that rose steeply from a cluster of little hills. They drove down into a shallow valley that curved in a great arc toward the far side of the mountains: and as they did so, Marvin slowly realized that something very strange was happening in the land ahead.

The sun was now low behind the hills on the right: the valley before them should be in total darkness. Yet it was awash with a cold white radiance that came spilling over the crags beneath which they were driving. Then, suddenly, they were out in the open plain, and the source of the light lay before them in all its glory.

It was very quiet in the little cabin now that the motors had stopped. The only sound was the faint whisper of the oxygen feed and an occasional metallic crepitation as the outer walls of the vehicle radiated away their heat. For no warmth at all came from the great silver crescent that floated low above the far horizon and flooded all this land with pearly light. It was so brilliant that minutes passed before Marvin could accept its challenge and look steadfastly into its glare, but at last he could discern the outlines of continents, the hazy border of the atmosphere, and the white islands of cloud. And even at this distance, he could see the glitter of sunlight on the polar ice.

It was beautiful, and it called to his heart across the abyss of space. There in that shining crescent were all the wonders that he had never known—the hues of sunset skies, the moaning of the sea on pebbled shores, the patter of falling rain, the unhurried benison of snow. These and a thousand others should have been his rightful heritage, but he knew them only from the books and ancient records, and the thought filled him with the anguish of exile.

Why could they not return? It seemed so peaceful beneath those lines of marching cloud. Then Marvin, his eyes no longer blinded by the glare, saw that the portion of the disk that should have been in darkness was gleaming faintly with an evil phosphorescence: and he remembered. He was looking upon the funeral pyre of a world—upon the radioactive aftermath of Armageddon. Across a quarter of a million miles of space, the glow of dying atoms was still visible, a perennial reminder of the ruinous past. It would be centuries yet before that deadly glow died from the rocks and life could return again to fill that silent, empty world.

And now Father began to speak, telling Marvin the story which until this moment had meant no more to him than the fairy tales he had once been told. There were many things he could not understand: it was impossible for him to picture the glowing, multicolored pattern of life on the planet he had never seen. Nor could he comprehend the forces that had destroyed it in the end, leaving the Colony, preserved by its isolation, as the sole survivor. Yet he could share the agony of those final days, when the Colony had learned at last that never again would the supply ships come flaming down through the stars with gifts from home. One by one the radio stations had ceased to call: on the shadowed globe the lights of the cities had dimmed and died, and they were alone at last, as no men had ever been alone before, carrying in their hands the future of the race.

Then had followed the years of despair, and the long-drawn battle for survival in this fierce and hostile world. That battle had been won, though barely: this little oasis of life was safe against the worst that Nature could do. But unless there was a goal, a future toward which it could work, the Colony would lose the will to live, and neither machines nor skill nor science could save it then.

So, at last, Marvin understood the purpose of this pilgrimage. He would never walk beside the rivers of that lost and legendary world, or listen to the thunder raging above its softly rounded hills. Yet one day—how far ahead?—his children's children would return to claim their heritage. The winds and the rains would scour the poisons from the burning lands and carry them to the sea, and in the depths of the sea they would waste their venom until they could harm no living things. Then the great ships that were still waiting here on the silent, dusty plains could lift once more into space, along the road that led to home.

That was the dream: and one day, Marvin knew with a sudden flash of insight, he would pass it on to his own son, here at this same spot with the mountains behind him and the silver light from the sky streaming into his face.

He did not look back as they began the homeward journey. He could not bear to see the cold glory of the crescent Earth fade from the rocks around him, as he went to rejoin his people in their long exile.

London   *December 1950*

Patent Pending

There are no subjects that have not been discussed, at some time or other, in the saloon bar of the "White Hart"—and whether or not there are ladies present makes no difference whatsoever. After all, they came in at their own risk. Three of them, now I come to think of it, have eventually gone out again with husbands. So perhaps the risk isn't on their side at all. . . .

I mention this because I would not like you to think that all our conversations are highly erudite and scientific, and our activities purely cerebral. Though chess is rampant, darts and shove-ha'penny also flourish. The *Times Literary Supplement*, the *Saturday Review*, the *New Statesman*, and the *Atlantic Monthly* may be brought in by some of the customers, but the same people are quite likely to leave with the latest issue of *Staggering Stories of Pseudoscience*.

A great deal of business also goes on in the obscurer corners of the pub. Copies of antique books and magazines frequently change hands at astronomical prices, and on almost any Wednesday at least three well-known dealers may be seen smoking large cigars as they lean over the bar, swapping stories with Drew. From time to time a vast guffaw announces the denouement of some anecdote and provokes a flood of anxious inquiries from patrons who are afraid they may have missed something. But, alas, delicacy forbids that I should repeat any of these interesting tales here. Unlike most things in this island, they are not for export. . . .

Luckily, no such restrictions apply to the tales of Mr. Harry Purvis, B.Sc. (at least), Ph.D. (probably), F.R.S. (personally I don't think so, though it *has* been rumored). None of them would bring a blush to the cheeks of the most delicately nurtured maiden aunts, should any still survive in these days.

I must apologize. This is too sweeping a statement. There was one story which might, in some circles, be regarded as a little daring. Yet I do not hesitate to repeat it, for I know that you, dear reader, will be sufficiently broad-minded to take no offense.

It started in this fashion. A celebrated Fleet Street reviewer had been pinned into a corner by a persuasive publisher, who was about to bring out a book of which he had high hopes. It was one of the riper productions of the deep and decadent South—a prime example of the "and-then-the-house-gave-another-lurch-as-the-termites-finished-the-east-wing" school of fiction. Eire had already banned it, but that is an honor which few books escape nowadays, and certainly could not be considered a distinction. However, if a leading British newspaper could be induced to make a stern call for its suppression, it would become a best seller overnight. . . .

Such was the logic of its publisher, and he was using all his wiles to induce co-operation. I heard him remark, apparently to allay any scruples his reviewer friend might have, "Of course not! If they can understand it, they *can't* be corrupted any further!" And then Harry Purvis, who has an uncanny knack of following half a dozen conversations simultaneously, so that he can insert himself in the right one at the right time, said in his peculiarly penetrating and noninterruptable voice: "Censorship does raise some very difficult problems doesn't it? I've always argued that there's an inverse correlation between a country's degree of civilization and the restraints it puts on its press."

A New England voice from the back of the room cut in: "On *that* argument, Paris is a more civilized place than Boston."

"Precisely," answered Purvis. For once, he waited for a reply.

"OK," said the New England voice mildly. "I'm not arguing. I just wanted to check."

"To continue," said Purvis, wasting no more time in doing so, "I'm reminded of a matter which has not yet concerned the censor, but which will certainly do so before long. It began in France, and so far has remained there. When it *does* come out into the open, it may have a greater impact on our civilization than the atom bomb.

"Like the atom bomb, it arose out of equally academic research. *Never*, gentlemen, underestimate science. I doubt if there is a single field of study so theoretical, so remote from what is laughingly called everyday life, that it may not one day produce something that will shake the world.

"You will appreciate that the story I am telling you is, for once in a while, secondhand. I got it from a colleague at the Sorbonne last year while I was over there at a scientific conference. So the names are all fictitious: I was told them at the time, but I can't remember them now.

"Professor—ah—Julian was an experimental physiologist at one of the smaller, but less impecunious, French universities. Some of you may remember that rather unlikely tale we heard here the other week from that fellow Hinckelberg, about his colleague who'd learned how to control the behavior of animals through feeding the correct currents into their nervous systems. Well, if there *was* any truth in that story—and frankly I doubt it—the whole project was probably inspired by Julian's papers in *Comptes Rendus*.

"Professor Julian, however, never published his most remarkable results. When you stumble on something which is really terrific, you don't rush into print. You wait until you have overwhelming evidence—unless you're afraid that someone else is hot on the track. Then you may issue an ambiguous report that will establish your priority at a later date, without giving too much away at the moment—like the famous cryptogram that Huygens put out when he detected the rings of Saturn.

"You may well wonder what Julian's discovery was, so I won't keep you in suspense. It was simply the natural extension of what man has been doing for the last hundred years. First the camera gave us the power to capture scenes. Then Edison invented the phonograph, and sound was mastered. Today, in the talking film, we have a kind of mechanical memory which would be inconceivable to our forefathers. But surely the matter cannot rest there. Eventually science must be able to catch and store thoughts and sensations themselves, and feed them back into the mind so that, whenever it wishes, it can repeat any experience in life, down to its minutest detail."

"That's an old idea!" snorted someone. "See the 'feelies' in *Brave New World*."

"All good ideas have been thought of by somebody before they are realized," said Purvis severely. "The point is that what Huxley and others had talked about, Julian actually did. My goodness, there's a pun there! Aldous—Julian—oh, let it pass!

"It was done electronically, of course. You all know how the encephalograph can record the minute electrical impulses in the living brain—the so-called 'brain waves,' as the popular press calls them. Julian's device was a much subtler elaboration of this well-known instrument. And, having recorded cerebral impulses, he could play them back again. It sounds simple, doesn't it? So was the phonograph, but it took the genius of Edison to think of it.

"And now, enter the villain. Well, perhaps that's too strong a word, for Professor Julian's assistant Georges—Georges Dupin—is really quite a sympathetic character. It was just that, being a Frenchman of a more practical turn of mind than the Professor, he saw at once that there were some milliards of francs involved in this laboratory toy.

"The first thing was to get it out of the laboratory. The French have an undoubted flair for elegant engineering, and after some weeks of work—with the full co-operation of the Professor—Georges had managed to pack the "playback" side of the apparatus into a cabinet no larger than a television set, and containing not very many more parts.

"Then Georges was ready to make his first experiment. It would involve considerable expense, but, as someone so rightly remarked, you cannot make omelettes without breaking eggs. And the analogy is, if I may say so, an exceedingly apt one.

"For Georges went to see the most famous gourmet in France, and made an interesting proposition. It was one that the great man could not refuse, because it was so unique a tribute to his eminence. Georges explained patiently that he had invented a device for registering (he said nothing about storing) sensations. In the cause of science, and for the honor of the French cuisine, could he be privileged to analyze the emotions, the subtle nuances of gustatory discrimination, that took place in Monsieur le Baron's mind when he employed his unsurpassed talents? Monsieur could name the restaurant, the chef, and the menu—everything would be arranged for his convenience. Of course, if he was too busy, no doubt that well-known epicure Le Comte de—

"The Baron, who was in some respects a surprisingly coarse man, uttered a word not to be found in most French dictionaries. 'That cretin!' he exploded. 'He would be happy on English cooking! No, I shall do it.' And forthwith he sat down to compose the menu, while Georges anxiously estimated the cost of the items and wondered if his bank balance would stand the strain. . . .

"It would be interesting to know what the chef and the waiters thought about the whole business. There was the

Baron, seated at his favorite table and doing full justice to his favorite dishes, not in the least inconvenienced by the tangle of wires that trailed from his head to that diabolical-looking machine in the corner. The restaurant was empty of all other occupants, for the last thing Georges wanted was premature publicity. This had added very considerably to the already distressing cost of the experiment. He could only hope that the results would be worth it.

"They were. The only way of *proving* that, of course, would be to play back Georges' 'recording.' We have to take his word for it, since the utter inadequacy of words in such matters is all too well known. The Baron *was* a genuine connoisseur, not one of those who merely pretend to powers of discrimination they do not possess. You know Thurber's 'Only a naïve domestic Burgundy, but I think you'll admire its presumption.' The Baron would have known at the first sniff whether it was domestic or not—and if it had been presumptuous he'd have smacked it down.

"I gather that Georges had his money's worth out of that recording, even though he had not intended it merely for personal use. It opened up new worlds to him, and clarified the ideas that had been forming in his ingenious brain. There was no doubt about it: all the exquisite sensations that had passed through the Baron's mind during the consumption of that Lucullan repast had been captured, so that anyone else, however untrained they might be in such matters, could savor them to the full. For, you see, the recording dealt purely with emotions: intelligence did not come into the picture at all. The Baron needed a lifetime of knowledge and training before he could *experience* these sensations. But once they were down on tape, anyone, even if in real life he had no sense of taste at all, could take over from there.

"Think of the glowing vistas that opened up before Georges's eyes! There were other meals, other gourmets. There were the collected impressions of all the vintages of Europe—what would connoisseurs not pay for them? When the last bottle of a rare wine had been broached, its incorporeal essence could be preserved, as the voice of Melba can travel down the centuries. For, after all, it was not the wine itself that mattered, but the sensations it evoked. . . .

"So mused Georges. But this, he knew, was only a beginning. The French claim to logic I have often disputed, but in Georges's case it cannot be denied. He thought the matter over for a few days: then he went to see his *petite dame*.

" 'Yvonne, *ma chérie*,' he said, 'I have a somewhat unusual request to make of you. . . .' "

Harry Purvis knew when to break off in a story. He turned to the bar and called, "Another Scotch, Drew." No one said a word while it was provided.

"To continue," said Purvis, at length, "the experiment, unusual though it was, even in France, was successfully carried out. As both discretion and custom demanded, all was arranged in the lonely hours of the night. You will have gathered already that Georges was a persuasive person, though I doubt if Mam'selle needed much persuading.

"Stifling her curiosity with a sincere but hasty kiss, Georges saw Yvonne out of the lab and rushed back to his apparatus. Breathlessly, he ran through the playback. It worked—not that he had ever had any real doubts. Moreover—do please remember I have only my informant's word for this—it was indistinguishable from the real thing. At that moment something approaching religious awe overcame Georges. This was, without a doubt, the greatest invention in history. He would be immortal as well as wealthy, for he had achieved something of which all men had dreamed, and had robbed old age of one of its terrors. . . .

"He also realized that he could now dispense with Yvonne, if he so wished. This raised implications that would require further thought. *Much* further thought.

"You will, of course, appreciate that I am giving you a highly condensed account of events. While all this was going on, Georges was still working as a loyal employee of the Professor, who suspected nothing. As yet, indeed, Georges had done little more than any research worker might have in similar circumstances. His performances had been somewhat beyond the call of duty, but could all be explained away if need be.

"The next step would involve some very delicate negotiations and the expenditure of further hard-won francs. Georges now had all the material he needed to prove, beyond a shadow of doubt, that he was handling a very valuable commercial property. There were shrewd businessmen in Paris who would jump at the opportunity. Yet a certain delicacy, for which we must give him full credit, restrained Georges from using his second—er—recording as a sample of the wares his machine could purvey. There was no way of disguising the personalities involved, and Georges was a modest man. 'Besides,' he argued, again with great good sense, 'when the gramophone company wishes to make a *disque,* it does not enregister the performance of some amateur musician. *That* is a matter for professionals. And so, *ma foi,* is *this.'* Whereupon, after a further call at his bank, he set forth again for Paris.

"He did not go anywhere near the Place Pigalle, because that was full of Americans and prices were accordingly exorbitant. Instead, a few discreet inquiries and some understanding cab drivers took him to an almost oppressively respectable suburb, where he presently found himself in a pleasant waiting room, by no means as exotic as might have been supposed.

"And there, somewhat embarrassed, Georges explained his mission to a formidable lady whose age one could have no more guessed than her profession. Used though she was to unorthodox requests, *this* was something she had never encountered in all her considerable experience. But the customer was always right, as long as he had the cash, and so in due course everything was arranged. One of the young ladies and her boy friend, an apache of somewhat overwhelming masculinity, traveled back with Georges to the provinces. At first they were, naturally, somewhat suspicious, but as Georges had already found, no expert can ever resist flattery. Soon they were all on excellent terms. Hercule and Susette promised Georges that they would give him every cause for satisfaction.

"No doubt some of you would be glad to have further details, but you can scarcely expect me to supply them. All I can say is that Georges—or, rather, his instrument—was kept very busy, and that by the morning little of the recording material was left unused. For it seems that Hercule was indeed appropriately named. . . .

"When this piquant episode was finished, Georges had very little money left, but he did possess two recordings that were quite beyond price. Once more he set off to Paris, where, with practically no trouble, he came to terms with some businessmen who were so astonished that they gave him a very generous contract before coming to their senses. I am pleased to report this, because so often the scientist emerges second best in his dealings with the world of finance. I'm equally pleased to record that Georges had made provision for Professor Julian in the contract. You may say cynically that it was, after all, the Professor's invention, and that sooner or later Georges would have had to square him. But I like to think that there was more to it than that.

"The full details of the scheme for exploiting the device

are, of course, unknown to me. I gather that Georges had been expansively eloquent—not that much eloquence was needed to convince anyone who had once experienced one or both of his playbacks. The market would be enormous, unlimited. The export trade alone could put France on her feet again and would wipe out her dollar deficit overnight—once certain snags had been overcome. Everything would have to be managed through somewhat clandestine channels, for think of the hubbub from the hypocritical Anglo-Saxons when they discovered just what was being imported into their countries. The Mothers' Union, the Daughters of the American Revolution, the Housewives League, and *all* the religious organizations would rise as one. The lawyers were looking into the matter very carefully, and as far as could be seen the regulations that still excluded *Tropic of Capricorn* from the mails of the English-speaking countries could not be applied to this case—for the simple reason that no one had thought of it. But there would be such a shout for new laws that Parliament and Congress would have to do something, so it was best to keep under cover as long as possible.

"In fact, as one of the directors pointed out, if the recordings were banned, so much the better. They could make much more money on a smaller output, because the price would promptly soar and all the vigilance of the customs officials couldn't block every leak. It would be Prohibition all over again.

"You will scarcely be surprised to hear that by this time Georges had somewhat lost interest in the gastronomical angle. It was an interesting but definitely minor possibility of the invention. Indeed, this had been tacitly admitted by the directors as they drew up the articles of association, for they had included the pleasures of the cuisine among 'subsidiary rights.'

"Georges returned home with his head in the clouds, and a substantial check in his pocket. A charming fancy had struck his imagination. He thought of all the trouble to which the gramophone companies had gone to so that the world might have the complete recordings of the forty-eight preludes and fugues or the nine symphonies. Well, *his* new company would put out a complete and definite set of recordings, performed by experts versed in the most esoteric knowledge of East and West. How many opus numbers would be required? That, of course, had been a subject of profound debate for some thousands of years. The Hindu textbooks, Georges had heard, got well into three figures. It would be a most interesting research, combining profit with pleasure in an unexampled manner. . . . He had already begun some preliminary studies, using treatises which even in Paris were none too easy to obtain.

"If you think that while all this was going on, Georges had neglected his usual interests, you are all too right. He was working literally night and day, for he had not yet revealed his plans to the Professor and almost everything had to be done when the lab was closed. And one of the interests he had had to neglect was Yvonne.

"Her curiosity had already been aroused, as any girl's would have been. But now she was more than intrigued—she was distracted. For Georges had become so remote and cold. He was no longer in love with her.

"It was a result that might have been anticipated. Publicans have to guard against the danger of sampling their own wares too often—I'm sure *you* don't, Drew—and Georges had fallen into this seductive trap. He had been through that recording too many times, with somewhat debilitating results. Moreover, poor Yvonne was not to be compared with the experienced and talented Susette. It was the old story of the professional versus the amateur.

"All that Yvonne knew was that Georges was in love with someone else. That was true enough. She suspected that he had been unfaithful to her. And *that* raises profound philosophical questions we can hardly go into here.

"This being France, in case you had forgotten, the outcome was inevitable. Poor Georges! He was working late one night at the lab, as usual, when Yvonne finished him off with one of those ridiculous ornamental pistols which are *de rigueur* for such occasions. Let us drink to his memory."

- "That's the trouble with all your stories," said John Beynon. "You tell us about wonderful inventions, and then at the end it turns out that the discoverer was killed, so no one can do anything about it. For I suppose, as usual, the apparatus was destroyed?"

"But no," replied Purvis. "Apart from Georges, this is one of the stories that has a happy ending. There was no trouble at all about Yvonne, of course. Georges's grieving sponsors arrived on the scene with great speed and prevented any adverse publicity. Being men of sentiment as well as men of business, they realized that they would have to secure Yvonne's freedom. They promptly did this by playing the recording to *le Maire* and *le Préfet*, thus convincing them that the poor girl had experienced irresistible provocation. A few shares in the new company clinched the deal, with expressions of the utmost cordiality on both sides. Yvonne even got her gun back."

"Then when—" began someone else.

"Ah, these things take time. There's the question of mass production, you know. It's quite possible that distribution has already commenced through private—*very* private— channels. Some of those dubious little shops and notice boards around Leicester Square may soon start giving hints."

"Of course," said the New England voice disrespectfully, "you wouldn't know the *name* of the company."

You can't help admiring Purvis at times like this. He scarcely hesitated.

"*Le Société Anonyme d'Aphrodite,*" he replied. "And I've just remembered something that will cheer *you* up. They hope to get round your sticky mails regulations and establish themselves before the inevitable congressional inquiry starts. They're opening up a branch in Nevada: apparently you can still get away with anything there." He raised his glass.

"To Georges Dupin," he said solemnly. "Martyr to science. Remember him when the fireworks start. And one other thing—"

"Yes?" we all asked.

"Better start saving now. And sell your TV sets before the bottom drops out of the market."

London   *January 1953*

The Sentinel

"The Sentinel" is the foundation upon which Stanley Kubrick and I later erected "2001: A Space Odyssey." In the years since this story was originally published, a number of scientists—e.g., Carl Sagan—have started to take the basic concept quite seriously.

Perhaps the real science of exoarchaeology will be born when we reach the Moon, or perhaps it is waiting for us on Mars, as suggested in "Trouble with Time." The odds are all against it—but the possible prizes are so great that there are few better reasons for exploring space.

If there is nothing like the "Sentinel" anywhere in the Solar System—there should be.

————◆————

The next time you see the full Moon high in the south, look carefully at its right-hand edge and let your eye travel upward along the curve of the disk. Round about two o'clock you will notice a small, dark oval: anyone with normal eyesight can find it quite easily. It is the great walled plain, one of the finest on the Moon, known as the Mare Crisium—the Sea of Crises. Three hundred miles in diameter, and almost completely surrounded by a ring of magnificent mountains, it had never been explored until we entered it in the late summer of 1996.

Our expedition was a large one. We had two heavy freighters which had flown our supplies and equipment from the main lunar base in the Mare Serenitatis, five hundred miles away. There were also three small rockets which were intended for short-range transport over regions which our surface vehicles couldn't cross. Luckily, most of the Mare Crisium is very flat. There are none of the great crevasses so

219 -

common and so dangerous elsewhere, and very few craters or mountains of any size. As far as we could tell, our powerful caterpillar tractors would have no difficulty in taking us wherever we wished to go.

I was geologist—or selenologist, if you want to be pedantic —in charge of the group exploring the southern region of the Mare. We had crossed a hundred miles of it in a week, skirting the foothills of the mountains along the shore of what was once the ancient sea, some thousand million years before. When life was beginning on Earth, it was already dying here. The waters were retreating down the flanks of those stupendous cliffs, retreating into the empty heart of the Moon. Over the land which we were crossing, the tideless ocean had once been half a mile deep, and now the only trace of moisture was the hoarfrost one could sometimes find in caves which the searing sunlight never penetrated.

We had begun our journey early in the slow lunar dawn, and still had almost a week of Earth time before nightfall. Half a dozen times a day we would leave our vehicle and go outside in the space suits to hunt for interesting minerals, or to place markers for the guidance of future travelers. It was an uneventful routine. There is nothing hazardous or even particularly exciting about lunar exploration. We could live comfortably for a month in our pressurized tractors, and if we ran into trouble we could always radio for help and sit tight until one of the spaceships came to our rescue.

I said just now that there was nothing exciting about lunar exploration, but of course that isn't true. One could never grow tired of those incredible mountains, so much more rugged than the gentle hills of Earth. We never knew, as we rounded the capes and promontories of that vanished sea, what new splendors would be revealed to us. The whole southern curve of the Mare Crisium is a vast delta where a score of rivers once found their way into the ocean, fed perhaps by the torrential rains that must have lashed the mountains in the brief volcanic age when the Moon was young. Each of these ancient valleys was an invitation, challenging us to climb into the unknown uplands beyond. But we had a hundred miles still to cover, and could only look longingly at the heights which others must scale.

We kept Earth time aboard the tractor, and precisely at 2200 hours the final radio message would be sent out to Base and we would close down for the day. Outside, the rocks would still be burning beneath the almost vertical sun, but to us it was night until we awoke again eight hours later. Then one of us would prepare breakfast, there would be a great buzzing of electric razors, and someone would switch on the short-wave radio from Earth. Indeed, when the smell of frying sausages began to fill the cabin, it was sometimes hard to believe that we were not back on our own world—everything was so normal and homely, apart from the feeling of decreased weight and the unnatural slowness with which objects fell.

It was my turn to prepare breakfast in the corner of the main cabin that served as a galley. I can remember that moment quite vividly after all these years, for the radio had just played one of my favorite melodies, the old Welsh air "David of the White Rock." Our driver was already outside in his space suit, inspecting our caterpillar treads. My assistant, Louis Garnett, was up forward in the control position, making some belated entries in yesterday's log.

As I stood by the frying pan waiting, like any terrestrial housewife, for the sausages to brown, I let my gaze wander idly over the mountain walls which covered the whole of the southern horizon, marching out of sight to east and west below the curve of the Moon. They seemed only a mile or two from the tractor, but I knew that the nearest was twenty miles away. On the Moon, of course, there is no loss of detail with distance—none of that almost imperceptible haziness which softens and sometimes transfigures all far-off things on Earth.

Those mountains were ten thousand feet high, and they climbed steeply out of the plain as if ages ago some subterranean eruption had smashed them skyward through the molten crust. The base of even the nearest was hidden from sight by the steeply curving surface of the plain, for the Moon is a very little world, and from where I was standing the horizon was only two miles away.

I lifted my eyes toward the peaks which no man had ever climbed, the peaks which, before the coming of terrestrial life, had watched the retreating oceans sink sullenly into their graves, taking with them the hope and the morning promise of a world. The sunlight was beating against those ramparts with a glare that hurt the eyes, yet only a little way above them the stars were shining steadily in a sky blacker than a winter midnight on Earth.

I was turning away when my eye caught a metallic glitter high on the ridge of a great promontory thrusting out into the sea thirty miles to the west. It was a dimensionless point of light, as if a star had been clawed from the sky by one of those cruel peaks, and I imagined that some smooth rock surface was catching the sunlight and heliographing it straight into my eyes. Such things were not uncommon. When the Moon is in her second quarter, observers on Earth can sometimes see the great ranges in the Oceanus Procellarum burning with a blue-white iridescence as the sunlight flashes from their slopes and leaps again from world to world. But I was curious to know what kind of rock could be shining so brightly up there, and I climbed into the observation turret and swung our four-inch telescope round to the west.

I could see just enough to tantalize me. Clear and sharp in the field of vision, the mountain peaks seemed only half a mile away, but whatever was catching the sunlight was still too small to be resolved. Yet it seemed to have an elusive symmetry, and the summit upon which it rested was curiously flat. I stared for a long time at that glittering enigma, straining my eyes into space, until presently a smell of burning from the galley told me that our breakfast sausages had made their quarter-million-mile journey in vain.

All that morning we argued our way across the Mare Crisium while the western mountains reared higher in the sky. Even when we were out prospecting in the space suits, the discussion would continue over the radio. It was absolutely certain, my companions argued, that there had never been any form of intelligent life on the Moon. The only living things that had ever existed there were a few primitive plants and their slightly less degenerate ancestors. I knew that as well as anyone, but there are times when a scientist must not be afraid to make a fool of himself.

"Listen," I said at last, "I'm going up there, if only for my own peace of mind. That mountain's less than twelve thousand feet high—that's only two thousand under Earth gravity —and I can make the trip in twenty hours at the outside. I've always wanted to go up into those hills, anyway, and this gives me an excellent excuse."

"If you don't break your neck," said Garnett, "you'll be the laughingstock of the expedition when we get back to Base. That mountain will probably be called Wilson's Folly from now on."

"I won't break my neck," I said firmly. "Who was the first man to climb Pico and Helicon?"

"But weren't you rather younger in those days?" asked Louis gently.

"That," I said with great dignity, "is as good a reason as any for going."

We went to bed early that night, after driving the tractor to within half a mile of the promontory. Garnett was coming with me in the morning; he was a good climber, and had often been with me on such exploits before. Our driver was only too glad to be left in charge of the machine.

At first sight, those cliffs seemed completely unscalable, but to anyone with a good head for heights, climbing is easy on a world where all weights are only a sixth of their normal value. The real danger in lunar mountaineering lies in overconfidence; a six-hundred-foot drop on the Moon can kill you just as thoroughly as a hundred-foot fall on Earth.

We made our first halt on a wide ledge about four thousand feet above the plain. Climbing had not been very difficult, but my limbs were stiff with the unaccustomed effort, and I was glad of the rest. We could still see the tractor as a tiny metal insect far down at the foot of the cliff, and we reported our progress to the driver before starting on the next ascent.

Inside our suits it was comfortably cool, for the refrigeration units were fighting the fierce sun and carrying away the body heat of our exertions. We seldom spoke to each other, except to pass climbing instructions and to discuss our best plan of ascent. I do not know what Garnett was thinking, probably that this was the craziest goose chase he had ever embarked upon. I more than half agreed with him, but the joy of climbing, the knowledge that no man had ever gone this way before and the exhilaration of the steadily widening landscape gave me all the reward I needed.

I don't think I was particularly excited when I saw in front of us the wall of rock I had first inspected through the telescope from thirty miles away. It would level off about fifty feet above our heads, and there on the plateau would be the thing that had lured me over these barren wastes. It was, almost certainly, nothing more than a boulder splintered ages ago by a falling meteor, and with its cleavage planes still fresh and bright in this incorruptible, unchanging silence.

There were no handholds on the rock face, and we had to use a grapnel. My tired arms seemed to gain new strength as I swung the three-pronged metal anchor round my head and sent it sailing up toward the stars. The first time it broke loose and came falling slowly back when we pulled the rope. On the third attempt, the prongs gripped firmly and our combined weights could not shift it.

Garnett looked at me anxiously. I could tell that he wanted to go first, but I smiled back at him through the glass of my helmet and shook my head. Slowly, taking my time, I began the final ascent.

Even with my space suit, I weighed only forty pounds here, so I pulled myself up hand over hand without bothering to use my feet. At the rim I paused and waved to my companion; then I scrambled over the edge and stood upright, staring ahead of me.

You must understand that until this very moment I had been almost completely convinced that there could be nothing strange or unusual for me to find here. Almost, but not quite; it was that haunting doubt that had driven me forward. Well, it was a doubt no longer, but the haunting had scarcely begun.

I was standing on a plateau perhaps a hundred feet across. It had once been smooth—too smooth to be natural—but falling meteors had pitted and scored its surface through immeasurable eons. It had been leveled to support a glittering, roughly pyramidal structure, twice as high as a man, that was set in the rock like a gigantic many-faceted jewel.

Probably no emotion at all filled my mind in those first few seconds. Then I felt a great lifting of my heart, and a strange, inexpressible joy. For I loved the Moon, and now I knew that the creeping moss of Aristarchus and Eratosthenes was not the only life she had brought forth in her youth. The old, discredited dream of the first explorers was true. There had, after all, been a lunar civilization—and I was the first to find it. That I had come perhaps a hundred million years too late did not distress me; it was enough to have come at all.

My mind was beginning to function normally, to analyze and to ask questions. Was this a building, a shrine—or something for which my language had no name? If a building, then why was it erected in so uniquely inaccessible a spot? I wondered if it might be a temple, and I could picture the adepts of some strange priesthood calling on their gods to preserve them as the life of the Moon ebbed with the dying oceans, and calling on their gods in vain.

I took a dozen steps forward to examine the thing more closely, but some sense of caution kept me from going too near. I knew a little of archaeology, and tried to guess the cultural level of the civilization that must have smoothed this mountain and raised the glittering mirror surfaces that still dazzled my eyes.

The Egyptians could have done it, I thought, if their workmen had possessed whatever strange materials these far more ancient architects had used. Because of the thing's smallness, it did not occur to me that I might be looking at the handiwork of a race more advanced than my own. The idea that the Moon had possessed intelligence at all was still almost too tremendous to grasp, and my pride would not let me take the final, humiliating plunge.

And then I noticed something that set the scalp crawling at the back of my neck—something so trivial and so innocent that many would never have noticed it at all. I have said that the plateau was scarred by meteors; it was also coated inches deep with the cosmic dust that is always filtering down upon the surface of any world where there are no winds to disturb it. Yet the dust and the meteor scratches ended quite abruptly in a wide circle enclosing the little pyramid, as though an invisible wall was protecting it from the ravages of time and the slow but ceaseless bombardment from space.

There was someone shouting in my earphones, and I realized that Garnett had been calling me for some time. I walked unsteadily to the edge of the cliff and signaled him to join me, not trusting myself to speak. Then I went back toward that circle in the dust. I picked up a fragment of splintered rock and tossed it gently toward the shining enigma. If the pebble had vanished at that invisible barrier I should not have been surprised, but it seemed to hit a smooth, hemispherical surface and slide gently to the ground.

I knew then that I was looking at nothing that could be matched in the antiquity of my own race. This was not a building, but a machine, protecting itself with forces that had challenged Eternity. Those forces, whatever they might be, were still operating, and perhaps I had already come too close. I thought of all the radiations man had trapped and tamed in the past century. For all I knew, I might be as irrevocably doomed as if I had stepped into the deadly, silent aura of an unshielded atomic pile.

I remember turning then toward Garnett, who had joined me and was now standing motionless at my side. He seemed quite oblivious to me, so I did not disturb him but walked to the edge of the cliff in an effort to marshal my thoughts. There below me lay the Mare Crisium—Sea of Crises, indeed —strange and weird to most men, but reassuringly familiar to me. I lifted my eyes toward the crescent Earth, lying in her cradle of stars, and I wondered what her clouds had covered when these unknown builders had finished their work. Was it the steaming jungle of the Carboniferous, the bleak shoreline over which the first amphibians must crawl to conquer the land—or, earlier still, the long loneliness before the coming of life?

Do not ask me why I did not guess the truth sooner—the truth that seems so obvious now. In the first excitement of my discovery, I had assumed without question that this crystalline apparition had been built by some race belonging to the Moon's remote past, but suddenly, and with overwhelming force, the belief came to me that it was as alien to the Moon as I myself.

In twenty years we had found no trace of life but a few degenerate plants. No lunar civilization, whatever its doom, could have left but a single token of its existence.

I looked at the shining pyramid again, and the more remote it seemed from anything that had to do with the Moon. And suddenly I felt myself shaking with a foolish, hysterical laughter, brought on by excitement and overexertion: for I had imagined that the little pyramid was speaking to me and was saying: "Sorry, I'm a stranger here myself."

It has taken us twenty years to crack that invisible shield and to reach the machine inside those crystal walls. What we could not understand, we broke at last with the savage might of atomic power and now I have seen the fragments of the lovely, glittering thing I found up there on the mountain.

They are meaningless. The mechanisms—if indeed they are mechanisms—of the pyramid belong to a technology that lies far beyond our horizon, perhaps to the technology of para-physical forces.

The mystery haunts us all the more now that the other planets have been reached and we know that only Earth has ever been the home of intelligent life in our Universe. Nor could any lost civilization of our own world have built that machine, for the thickness of the meteoric dust on the plateau has enabled us to measure its age. It was set there upon its mountain before life had emerged from the seas of Earth.

When our world was half its present age, *something* from the stars swept through the Solar System, left this token of its passage, and went again upon its way. Until we destroyed it, that machine was still fulfilling the purpose of its builders; and as to that purpose, here is my guess.

Nearly a hundred thousand million stars are turning in the circle of the Milky Way, and long ago other races on the worlds of other suns must have scaled and passed the heights that we have reached. Think of such civilizations, far back in time against the fading afterglow of Creation, masters of a Universe so young that life as yet had come only to a handful of worlds. Theirs would have been a loneliness we cannot imagine, the loneliness of gods looking out across infinity and finding none to share their thoughts.

They must have searched the star clusters as we have searched the planets. Everywhere there would be worlds, but they would be empty or peopled with crawling, mindless things. Such was our own Earth, the smoke of the great volcanoes still staining the skies, when that first ship of the peoples of the dawn came sliding in from the abyss beyond Pluto. It passed the frozen outer worlds, knowing that life could play no part in their destinies. It came to rest among the inner planets, warming themselves around the fire of the Sun and waiting for their stories to begin.

Those wanderers must have looked on Earth, circling safely in the narrow zone between fire and ice, and must have guessed that it was the favorite of the Sun's children. Here, in the distant future, would be intelligence; but there were countless stars before them still, and they might never come this way again.

So they left a sentinel, one of millions they have scattered throughout the Universe, watching over all worlds with the promise of life. It was a beacon that down the ages has been patiently signaling the fact that no one had discovered it.

Perhaps you understand now why that crystal pyramid was set upon the Moon instead of on the Earth. Its builders were not concerned with races still struggling up from savagery. They would be interested in our civilization only if we proved our fitness to survive—by crossing space and so escaping from the Earth, our cradle. That is the challenge that all intelligent races must meet, sooner or later. It is a double challenge, for it depends in turn upon the conquest of atomic energy and the last choice between life and death.

Once we had passed that crisis, it was only a matter of time before we found the pyramid and forced it open. Now its signals have ceased, and those whose duty it is will be turning their minds upon Earth. Perhaps they wish to help our infant civilization. But they must be very, very old, and the old are often insanely jealous of the young.

I can never look now at the Milky Way without wondering from which of those banked clouds of stars the emissaries are coming. If you will pardon so commonplace a simile, we have set off the fire alarm and have nothing to do but to wait.

I do not think we will have to wait for long.

London   *December 1948*

Transience

The forest, which came almost to the edge of the beach, climbed away into the distance up the flanks of the low, misty hills. Underfoot, the sand was coarse and mixed with myriads of broken shells. Here and there the retreating tide had left long streamers of weed trailed across the beach. The rain, which seldom ceased, had for the moment passed inland, but ever and again large, angry drops would beat tiny craters in the sand.

It was hot and sultry, for the war between sun and rain was never-ending. Sometimes the mists would lift for a while and the hills would stand out clearly above the land they guarded. These hills arced in a semicircle along the bay, following the line of the beach, and beyond them could sometimes be seen, at an immense distance, a wall of mountains lying beneath perpetual clouds. The trees grew everywhere, softening the contours of the land so that the hills blended smoothly into each other. Only in one place could the bare, uncovered rock be seen, where long ago some fault had weakened the foundations of the hills, so that for a mile or more the sky line fell sharply away, drooping down to the sea like a broken wing.

Moving with the cautious alertness of a wild animal, the child came through the stunted trees at the forest's edge. For a moment he hesitated; then, since there seemed to be no danger, walked slowly out onto the beach.

He was naked, heavily built, and had coarse black hair tangled over his shoulders. His face, brutish though it was, might almost have passed in human society, but the eyes would have betrayed him. They were not the eyes of an animal, for there was something in their depths that no animal had ever known. But it was no more than a promise. For this child, as for all his race, the light of reason had yet to dawn. Only a hairsbreadth still separated him from the beasts among whom he dwelt.

229

The tribe had not long since come into this land, and he was the first ever to set foot upon that lonely beach. What had lured him from the known dangers of the forest into the unknown and therefore more terrible dangers of this new element, he could not have told even had he possessed the power of speech. Slowly he walked out to the water's edge, always with backward glances at the forest behind him; and as he did so, for the first time in all history, the level sand bore upon its face the footprints it would one day know so well.

He had met water before, but it had always been bounded and confined by land. Now it stretched endlessly before him, and the sound of its laboring beat ceaselessly upon his ears.

With the timeless patience of the savage, he stood on the moist sand that the water had just relinquished, and as the tide line moved out he followed it slowly, pace by pace. When the waves reached toward his feet with a sudden access of energy, he would retreat a little way toward the land. But something held him here at the water's edge, while his shadow lengthened along the sands and the cold evening wind began to rise around him.

Perhaps into his mind had come something of the wonder of the sea, and a hint of all that it would one day mean to man. Though the first gods of his people still lay far in the future, he felt a dim sense of worship stir within him. He knew that he was now in the presence of something greater than all the powers and forces he had ever met.

The tide was turning. Far away in the forest, a wolf howled once and was suddenly silent. The noises of the night were rising around him, and it was time to go.

Under the low moon, the two lines of footprints interlaced across the sand. Swiftly the oncoming tide was smoothing them away. But they would return in their thousands and millions, in the centuries yet to be.

The child playing among the rock pools knew nothing of the forest that had once ruled all the land around him. It had left no trace of its existence. As ephemeral as the mists that had so often rolled down from the hills, it, too, had veiled them for a little while and now was gone. In its place had come a checkerboard of fields, the legacy of a thousand years of patient toil. And so the illusion of permanence remained, though everything had altered except the line of the hills against the sky. On the beach, the sand was finer now, and the land had lifted so that the old tide line was far beyond the reach of the questing waves.

Beyond the sea wall and the promenade, the little town was sleeping through the golden summer day. Here and there along the beach, people lay at rest, drowsy with heat and lulled by the murmur of the waves.

Out across the bay, white and gold against the water, a great ship was moving slowly to sea. The boy could hear, faint and far away, the beat of its screws and could still see the tiny figures moving upon its decks and superstructure. To the child —and not to him alone—it was a thing of wonder and beauty. He knew its name and the land to which it was steaming; but he did not know that the splendid ship was both the last and greatest of its kind. He scarcely noticed, almost lost against the glare of the sun, the thin white vapor trails that spelled the doom of the proud and lovely giant.

Soon the great liner was no more than a dark smudge on the horizon, and the boy turned again to his interrupted play, to the tireless building of his battlements of sand. In the west the sun was beginning its long decline, but the evening was still far away.

Yet it came at last, when the tide was returning to the land. At his mother's words, the child gathered up his playthings and, wearily contented, began to follow his parents back to the shore. He glanced once only at the sand castles he had built with such labor and would not see again. Without regret he left them to the advancing waves, for tomorrow he would return and the future stretched endlessly before him.

That tomorrow would not always come, either for himself or for the world, he was still too young to know.

And now even the hills had changed, worn away by the weight of years. Not all the change was the work of Nature, for one night in the long-forgotten past something had come sliding down from the stars, and the little town had vanished in a spinning tower of flame. But that was so long ago that it was beyond sorrow or regret. Like the fall of fabled Troy or the overwhelming of Pompeii, it was part of the irremediable past and could rouse no pity now.

On the broken sky line lay a long metal building supporting a maze of mirrors that turned and glittered in the sun. No one from an earlier age could have guessed its purpose. It was as meaningless as an observatory or a radio station would have been to ancient man. But it was neither of these things.

Since noon, Bran had been playing among the shallow pools left by the retreating tide. He was quite alone, though the machine that guarded him was watching unobtrusively from the shore. Only a few days ago, there had been other children playing beside the blue waters of this lovely bay. Bran sometimes wondered where they had vanished, but he was a solitary child and did not greatly care. Lost in his own dreams, he was content to be left alone.

In the last few hours he had linked the tiny pools with an intricate network of waterways. His thoughts were very far from Earth, both in space and time. Around him now were the dull, red sands of another world. He was Cardenis, prince of engineers, fighting to save his people from the encroaching deserts. For Bran had looked upon the ravaged face of Mars; he knew the story of its long tragedy and the help from Earth that had come too late.

Out to the horizon the sea was empty, untroubled by ships, as it had been for ages. For a little while, near the beginning of time, man had fought his brief war against the oceans of the world. Now it seemed that only a moment lay between the coming of the first canoes and the passing of the last great Megatheria of the seas.

Bran did not even glance at the sky when the monstrous shadow swept along the beach. For days past, those silver giants had been rising over the hills in an unending stream, and now he gave them little thought. All his life he had watched the great ships climbing through the skies of Earth on their way to distant worlds. Often he had seen them return from those long journeys, dropping down through the clouds with cargoes beyond imagination.

He wondered sometimes why they came no more, those returning voyagers. All the ships he saw now were outward bound; never one drove down from the skies to berth at the great port beyond the hills. Why this should be, no one would tell him. He had learned not to speak of it now, having seen the sadness that his questions brought.

Across the sands the robot was calling to him softly. "Bran," came the words, echoing the tones of his mother's voice, "Bran—it's time to go."

The child looked up, his face full of indignant denial. He could not believe it. The sun was still high and the tide was far away. Yet along the shore his mother and father were already coming toward him.

They walked swiftly, as though the time were short. Now

and again his father would glance for an instant at the sky, then turn his head quickly away as if he knew well that there was nothing he could hope to see. But a moment later he would look again.

Stubborn and angry, Bran stood at bay among his canals and lakes. His mother was strangely silent, but presently his father took him by the hand and said quietly, "You must come with us, Bran. It's time we went."

The child pointed sullenly at the beach. "But it's too early. I haven't finished."

His father's reply held no trace of anger, only a great sadness. "There are many things, Bran, that will not be finished now."

Still uncomprehending, the boy turned to his mother.

"Then can I come again tomorrow?"

With a sense of desolating wonder, Bran saw his mother's eyes fill with sudden tears. And he knew at last that never again would he lay upon the sands by the azure waters; never again would he feel the tug of the tiny waves about his feet. He had found the sea too late, and now must leave it forever. Out of the future, chilling his soul, came the first faint intimation of the long ages of exile that lay ahead.

He never looked back as they walked silently together across the clinging sand. This moment would be with him all his life, but he was still too stunned to do more than walk blindly into a future he could not understand.

The three figures dwindled into the distance and were gone. A long while later, a silver cloud seemed to lift above the hills and move slowly out to sea. In a shallow arc, as though reluctant to leave its world, the last of the great ships climbed toward the horizon and shrank to nothingness over the edge of the Earth.

The tide was returning with the dying day. As though its makers still walked within its walls, the low metal building upon the hills had begun to blaze with light. Near the zenith, one star had not waited for the sun to set, but already burned with a fierce white glare against the darkling sky. Soon its companions, no longer in the scant thousands that man had once known, began to fill the heavens. The Earth was now near the center of the Universe, and whole areas of the sky were an unbroken blaze of light.

But rising beyond the sea in two long curving arms, something black and monstrous eclipsed the stars and seemed to cast its shadow over all the world. The tentacles of the Dark

Nebula were already brushing against the frontiers of the Solar System. . . .

In the east, a great yellow moon was climbing through the waves. Though man had torn down its mountains and brought it air and water, its face was the one that had looked upon Earth since history began, and it was still the ruler of the tides. Across the sand the line of foam moved steadily onward, overwhelming the little canals and planing down the tangled footprints.

On the sky line, the lights in the strange metal building suddenly died, and the spinning mirrors ceased their moonlight glittering. From far inland came the blind flash of a great explosion, then another, and another fainter yet.

Presently the ground trembled a little, but no sound disturbed the solitude of the deserted shore.

Under the level light of the sagging moon, beneath the myriad stars, the beach lay waiting for the end. It was alone now, as it had been at the beginning. Only the waves would move, and but for a little while, upon its golden sands.

For man had come and gone.

London   *March 1947*

The Star

It is three thousand light-years to the Vatican. Once, I believed that space could have no power over faith, just as I believed that the heavens declared the glory of God's handiwork. Now I have seen that handiwork, and my faith is sorely troubled. I stare at the crucifix that hangs on the cabin wall above the Mark VI Computer, and for the first time in my life I wonder if it is no more than an empty symbol.

I have told no one yet, but the truth cannot be concealed. The facts are there for all to read, recorded on the countless miles of magnetic tape and the thousands of photographs we are carrying back to Earth. Other scientists can interpret them as easily as I can, and I am not one who would condone that tampering with the truth which often gave my order a bad name in the olden days.

The crew were already sufficiently depressed: I wonder how they will take this ultimate irony. Few of them have any religious faith, yet they will not relish using this final weapon in their campaign against me—that private, good-natured, but fundamentally serious war which lasted all the way from Earth. It amused them to have a Jesuit as chief astrophysicist: Dr. Chandler, for instance, could never get over it. (Why are medical men such notorious atheists?) Sometimes he would meet me on the observation deck, where the lights are always low so that the stars shine with undiminished glory. He would come up to me in the gloom and stand staring out of the great oval port, while the heavens crawled slowly around us as the ship turned end over end with the residual spin we had never bothered to correct.

"Well, Father," he would say at last, "it goes on forever and forever, and perhaps *Something* made it. But how you can believe that Something has a special interest in us and our miserable little world—that just beats me." Then the argument would start, while the stars and nebulae would swing around us in silent, endless arcs beyond the flawlessly clear plastic of the observation port.

It was, I think, the apparent incongruity of my position that caused most amusement to the crew. In vain I would point to my three papers in the *Astrophysical Journal*, my five in the *Monthly Notices of the Royal Astronomical Society*. I would remind them that my order has long been famous for its scientific works. We may be few now, but ever since the eighteenth century we have made contributions to astronomy and geophysics out of all proportion to our numbers. Will my report on the Phoenix Nebula end our thousand years of history? It will end, I fear, much more than that.

I do not know who gave the nebula its name, which seems to me a very bad one. If it contains a prophecy, it is one that cannot be verified for several billion years. Even the word "nebula" is misleading; this is a far smaller object than those stupendous clouds of mist—the stuff of unborn stars—that are scattered throughout the length of the Milky Way. On the cosmic scale, indeed, the Phoenix Nebula is a tiny thing—a tenuous shell of gas surrounding a single star.

Or what is left of a star . . .

The Rubens engraving of Loyola seems to mock me as it hangs there above the spectrophotometer tracings. What would *you*, Father, have made of this knowledge that has come into my keeping, so far from the little world that was all the Universe you knew? Would your faith have risen to the challenge, as mine has failed to do?

You gaze into the distance, Father, but I have traveled a distance beyond any that you could have imagined when you founded our order a thousand years ago. No other survey ship has been so far from Earth: we are at the very frontiers of the explored Universe. We set out to reach the Phoenix Nebula, we succeeded, and we are homeward bound with our burden of knowledge. I wish I could lift that burden from my shoulders, but I call to you in vain across the centuries and the light-years that lie between us.

On the book you are holding the words are plain to read. AD MAIOREM DEI GLORIAM, the message runs, but it is a message I can no longer believe. Would you still believe it, if you could see what we have found?

We knew, of course, what the Phoenix Nebula was. Every year, in our Galaxy alone, more than a hundred stars explode, blazing for a few hours or days with thousands of times their normal brilliance before they sink back into death and obscurity. Such are the ordinary novae—the commonplace disasters of the Universe. I have recorded the spectrograms and light curves of dozens since I started working at the Lunar Observatory.

But three or four times in every thousand years occurs something beside which even a nova pales into total insignificance.

When a star becomes a *supernova,* it may for a little while outshine all the massed suns of the Galaxy. The Chinese astronomers watched this happen in A.D. 1054, not knowing what it was they saw. Five centuries later, in 1572, a supernova blazed in Cassiopeia so brilliantly that it was visible in the daylight sky. There have been three more in the thousand years that have passed since then.

Our mission was to visit the remnants of such a catastrophe, to reconstruct the events that led up to it, and, if possible, to learn its cause. We came slowly in through the concentric shells of gas that had been blasted out six thousand years before, yet were expanding still. They were immensely hot, radiating even now with a fierce violet light, but were far too tenuous to do us any damage. When the star had exploded, its outer layers had been driven upward with such speed that they had escaped completely from its gravitational field. Now they formed a hollow shell large enough to engulf a thousand solar systems, and at its center burned the tiny, fantastic object which the star had now become—a White Dwarf, smaller than the Earth, yet weighing a million times as much.

The glowing gas shells were all around us, banishing the normal night of interstellar space. We were flying into the center of the cosmic bomb that had detonated millennia ago and whose incandescent fragments were still hurtling apart. The immense scale of the explosion, and the fact that the debris already covered a volume of space many billions of miles across, robbed the scene of any visible movement. It would take decades before the unaided eye could detect any motion in these tortured wisps and eddies of gas, yet the sense of turbulent expansion was overwhelming.

We had checked our primary drive hours before, and were drifting slowly toward the fierce little star ahead. Once it had been a sun like our own, but it had squandered in a few hours the energy that should have kept it shining for a million years. Now it was a shrunken miser, hoarding its resources as if trying to make amends for its prodigal youth.

No one seriously expected to find planets. If there had been any before the explosion, they would have been boiled into puffs of vapor, and their substance lost in the greater wreckage of the star itself. But we made the automatic search, as we always do when approaching an unknown sun, and presently we found a single small world circling the star at an immense distance. It must have been the Pluto of this vanished Solar System, orbiting on the frontiers of the night. Too far from the central sun ever to have known life, its remoteness had saved it from the fate of all its lost companions.

The passing fires had seared its rocks and burned away the mantle of frozen gas that must have covered it in the days before the disaster. We landed, and we found the Vault.

Its builders had made sure that we should. The monolithic marker that stood above the entrance was now a fused stump, but even the first long-range photographs told us that here was the work of intelligence. A little later we detected the continent-wide pattern of radioactivity that had been buried in the rock. Even if the pylon above the Vault had been destroyed, this would have remained, an immovable and all but eternal beacon calling to the stars. Our ship fell toward this gigantic bull's-eye like an arrow into its target.

The pylon must have been a mile high when it was built, but now it looked like a candle that had melted down into a puddle of wax. It took us a week to drill through the fused rock, since we did not have the proper tools for a task like this. We were astronomers, not archaeologists, but we could improvise. Our original purpose was forgotten: this lonely monument, reared with such labor at the greatest possible distance from the doomed sun, could have only one meaning. A civilization that knew it was about to die had made its last bid for immortality.

It will take us generations to examine all the treasures that were placed in the Vault. They had plenty of time to prepare, for their sun must have given its first warnings many years before the final detonation. Everything that they wished to preserve, all the fruits of their genius, they brought here to this distant world in the days before the end, hoping that some other race would find it and that they would not be utterly forgotten. Would we have done as well, or would we have been too lost in our own misery to give thought to a future we could never see or share?

If only they had had a little more time! They could travel freely enough between the planets of their own sun, but they had not yet learned to cross the interstellar gulfs, and the nearest Solar System was a hundred light-years away. Yet even had they possessed the secret of the Transfinite Drive, no more than a few millions could have been saved. Perhaps it was better thus.

Even if they had not been so disturbingly human as their sculpture shows, we could not have helped admiring them and grieving for their fate. They left thousands of visual records and the machines for projecting them, together with elaborate pictorial instructions from which it will not be difficult to learn their written language. We have examined many of these records, and brought to life for the first time in six thousand years the warmth and beauty of a civilization that in many ways must have been superior to our own. Perhaps they only showed us the best, and one can hardly blame them. But their worlds were very lovely, and their cities were built with a grace that matches anything of man's. We have watched them at work and play, and listened to their musical speech sounding across the centuries. One scene is still before my eyes—a group of children on a beach of strange blue sand, playing in the waves as children play on Earth. Curious whip-like trees line the shore, and some very large animal is wading in the shallows yet attracting no attention at all.

And sinking into the sea, still warm and friendly and life-giving, is the sun that will soon turn traitor and obliterate all this innocent happiness.

Perhaps if we had not been so far from home and so vulnerable to loneliness, we should not have been so deeply moved. Many of us had seen the ruins of ancient civilizations on other worlds, but they had never affected us so profoundly. This tragedy was unique. It is one thing for a race to fail and die, as nations and cultures have done on Earth. But to be destroyed so completely in the full flower of its achievement, leaving no survivors—how could that be reconciled with the mercy of God?

My colleagues have asked me that, and I have given what answers I can. Perhaps you could have done better, Father Loyola, but I have found nothing in the *Exercitia Spiritualia* that helps me here. They were not an evil people: I do not know what gods they worshiped, if indeed they worshiped any. But I have looked back at them across the centuries, and have watched while the loveliness they used their last strength to preserve was brought forth again into the light of their shrunken sun. They could have taught us much: why were they destroyed?

I know the answers that my colleagues will give when they get back to Earth. They will say that the Universe has no purpose and no plan, that since a hundred suns explode every year in our Galaxy, at this very moment some race is dying in the depths of space. Whether that race has done good or evil during its lifetime will make no difference in the end: there is no divine justice, for there is no God.

Yet, of course, what we have seen proves nothing of the sort. Anyone who argues thus is being swayed by emotion, not logic. God has no need to justify His actions to man. He who built the Universe can destroy it when He chooses. It is arrogance—it is perilously near blasphemy—for us to say what He may or may not do.

This I could have accepted, hard though it is to look upon whole worlds and peoples thrown into the furnace. But there comes a point when even the deepest faith must falter, and now, as I look at the calculations lying before me, I know I have reached that point at last.

We could not tell, before we reached the nebula, how long ago the explosion took place. Now, from the astronomical evidence and the record in the rocks of that one surviving planet, I have been able to date it very exactly. I know in what year the light of this colossal conflagration reached our Earth. I know how brilliantly the supernova whose corpse now dwindles behind our speeding ship once shone in terrestrial skies. I know how it must have blazed low in the east before sunrise, like a beacon in that oriental dawn.

There can be no reasonable doubt: the ancient mystery is solved at last. Yet, oh God, there were so many stars you could have used. What was the need to give these people to the fire, that the symbol of their passing might shine above Bethlehem?

London   October 1954